"Good." She could actually hear the ticking of the clock on the wall now. She never noticed it being that loud before.

Harris made a face. "Are you ready to pick up the conversation where we left off earlier?"

Man, he was not getting this situation at all. Could he really not read her mood? She was all but sitting in his lap.

For a second she worried she was the only one who felt this head-spinning buzz of attraction. It swamped her. He talked and she watched his mouth. He stared at her and her heartbeat sped to a gallop.

"Actually?" She slid off the armrest. One knee landed on the cushion next to his thigh. She kept going until she straddled his lap, facing him. Not the smoothest move, but it put her where she wanted to be. "No."

He frowned at her. "What are you doing?"

So much for subtlety.

She trailed her fingers up his chest to the base of his neck then over his shoulders. "I want to do something other than talk this evening."

By HelenKay Dimon

THE PRETENDER
THE ENFORCER
THE FIXER
UNDER THE WIRE
FACING FIRE
FALLING HARD
PLAYING DIRTY
RUNNING HOT (novella)

the
Pretender

Games People Play

HELENKAY DIMON

AVONBOOKS

An Imprint of HarperCollinsPublishers

THE PRETENDER. Copyright © 2018 by HelenKay Dimon. All rights reserved. Printed in the United States of America. No part of this book may be used or reproduced in any manner whatsoever without written permission except in the case of brief quotations embodied in critical articles and reviews. For information, address Harper-Collins Publishers, 195 Broadway, New York, NY 10007.

First Avon Books mass market printing: January 2018

Print Edition ISBN: 978-0-06-269221-4
Digital Edition ISBN: 978-0-06-269219-1

Cover photograph by Yasmeen Anderson Photography

Avon, Avon & logo, and Avon Books & logo are registered trademarks of HarperCollins Publishers in the United States of America and other countries.

HarperCollins is a registered trademark of HarperCollins Publishers in the United States of America and other countries.

FIRST EDITION

17 18 19 20 21   QGM   10 9 8 7 6 5 4 3 2 1

For my husband, James, who immediately handled the crisis when my computer imploded during the editing of this book, saving me hours of turmoil and proving once again that not all heroes wear capes.

CHAPTER 1

Harrison Tate didn't believe in luck. He believed in planning. Right now, he needed the luck.

He blinked a few times, hoping the scene in front of him would change. No body, no blood . . . nope, it was all still there.

A woman—*the* woman—the one who stuck to a schedule and rarely ventured outside a three-mile area. She should have been reading at the dock, as she did every nonrainy day at this time for the last three weeks. Sitting there, watching the waves lap up on the stone retaining wall that separated the Chesapeake Bay from Tabitha Island. Her private island.

He'd staked out the isolated land, this house and this woman for more than a month. Watched from a boat at one point and from the small uninhabited island a short distance away at another. He'd been able to hack into the camera on her laptop. He knew when she was working on it, which was almost always.

He'd tracked her movements, knew her schedule. But on the ride over here he'd missed seeing someone else go into her house. Someone who wanted more from her than a painting.

The longer he stood there, looming over her still body, the more he became locked in a confining shell he could not break. Less than thirty seconds had passed since he walked into the old-school library with its dark floor-to-ceiling bookshelves and massive desk positioned in front of the french doors to the small patio outside. He'd found her there, sprawled on the floor with her eyes closed and her chest not moving. Blood pooled around her and seeped into the muted gray carpet beneath her.

Just as his brain signaled to his hand to grab his cell and call for help, her eyes popped open. Stunning green. That fact registered in his mind. Next came her fear. It bounced off the walls and pummeled him. Her body shook with it.

She reached out and her fingertips brushed his pants right near his calf. She likely thought she grabbed him and pulled hard, but he barely felt the touch. Whatever energy she possessed had been spent during the furious battle that waged in the room before he got there. Glass shattered on the floor, an overturned table. Books and papers scattered everywhere.

He dropped down, balancing on the balls of his feet, and reached for her hand. He still wore his gloves, but she didn't seem to notice. She kept mouthing something. A soundless word he couldn't make out. He leaned in with his ear right over her mouth, trying to pick up a thread or any noise but that didn't work either.

He pulled back and looked into her eyes. They were clouded now and unfocused. "Tabitha?"

He knew her name because he made it his business to know the people from whom he planned to liberate any number of items. In her case, a specific painting that usually hung over the fireplace in this room. It balanced there now, ripped from the wall with one edge hanging over the mantel. Teetering, ready to fall. All eleven million dollars of it.

"Help me." The words came out of her on a strangled cry. Her chest heaved as she fought for breath.

He could see her wince as she inhaled. Her hand slipped out of his as all the tension drained out of her. Her eyes rolled back then closed.

"No, no, no." This time he started mouth-to-mouth. He blew and counted, trying to remember the precise sequence from every television show where he'd seen it performed and from a class he'd taken more than a decade ago.

Nothing worked.

He moved, thinking to press down on her chest, but the wound was right there. A slashing cut that left a gaping seam close to her sternum. Another slice into her abdomen. There was no question her attacker had unleashed a wild frenzy on her. Someone wanted her dead. He didn't, but he had no idea where to push to save her or how to get her heart beating again either.

A crackling energy raced through him right behind an uncharacteristic panic. He prided himself on his ability to stay calm and handle nearly anything. He'd been trained to maneuver through any situation. Use charm, strength or pure nerve to battle his way out. Right now, every cell was alive and on fire and desperate to do something.

He clamped down on his fight-or-flight instincts and reached for the burner cell tucked in his back pocket. He had no idea how long it would take for reinforcements to arrive, but he'd stay as long as possible. Try to keep her breathing but leave enough lead time to escape.

One thing was true. He could not be caught here . . . or anywhere.

He'd just hit the first button to make the call as he heard the sound. A gurgling in her throat, as if she was drowning in her own body. An openmouthed, labored breath . . . then a shocking stillness. Saliva dribbled out of the corner of her mouth as her head dropped to one side.

The death rattle. Had to be. He'd never heard it before and never wanted to hear it again.

He slid off his gloves and checked for a pulse. Nothing. She was gone.

With his brain in free fall, he lost his balance and tipped forward. Landed hard on his knees as every part of him shut down. For a few seconds he couldn't think. Couldn't get a single muscle to move. He stared at her, willing her to jump up or reach for him again. Anything.

The stillness in the room mirrored her unmoving body. He now knew silence could thump and beat just like a sound. The second later reality pounded him. Smells came rushing back to him. An unexpected scent he couldn't place.

A door thudded. He pegged it as a screen, which likely meant the front door.

"Tabitha?" A woman's voice floated through the oversized rooms. "I thought we were going to meet at the dock twenty minutes ago."

The sister.

She'd been a surprise. Intriguing . . . a mystery. People whispered about her. They jumped to conclusions based on rumors. He had and now regretted it. Under different circumstances he'd take the time to meet her and see how deep her secrets ran.

All the stories about the sisters' estrangement turned out to be untrue. All the talk about her being disowned. None of that mattered now because she was there, in the house. She was about to stumble into a horror and Harris couldn't protect her from it. She'd be plunged into a hell worse than his.

He scrambled to his feet. Right as he turned to run back through the doors to the outside a thought hit him. His mind rebelled at the thought of what he needed to do. The pure sickness of it. His gaze zipped to the doorway before he bent down and used his glove to wipe Tabitha's mouth. To erase any signs that he'd tried to save her.

When he stood back up a sensation hit him. Self-loathing. Maybe he was a fucking asshole just as his father claimed.

Footsteps sounded on the hardwood in the hallway. "Tabitha? Enough with the online sleuthing for today. It's beautiful outside."

Harris couldn't wait another second. In a soundless jog, he stepped around the body. He'd already kneeled and walked through the scene, likely made it impossible for a forensic team to discover anything of value. His only goal now was not to track blood in a path directly to him.

The handle slipped in his hand, but he finally got the door open. He'd made it outside and into the sunshine when he heard the sister's voice again.

"Hey, who are—"

He didn't stop or look around. Didn't wait to explain or comfort her. He pulled off the coverings on his shoes and started running.

And then the screaming started. A high-pitched wailing that tore through him. A mix of shock and pain so raw it ripped away his defenses and slammed his body to a halt. Right there on the perfect lawn with the blue water shining all around the island, he froze. Not for long, but long enough to hear the sister's gulping cries.

He shook his head and took off again. Ignoring the boat dock and the small beach there, he ran in the opposite direction to the rocky shoreline. To his small boat and backpack filled with supplies. He climbed over a rock ledge and down to the water's edge.

Waves crashed in a soothing beat that clashed with the images rewinding in his mind. They would haunt him. All of this would. Tabitha. Her sister. The blood.

He skipped the boat and went right for the water. Nothing in the stolen craft would trace back to him. He'd worn gloves most of the time and wiped off everywhere he touched when he didn't, so no fingerprints to be found. The neoprene dive suit he wore under his clothes should keep him warm enough to stand the cold temperature of the water. As he plunged into the water, splashes of red mixed with the blue. He looked down and realized blood coated his pants. Now it mixed with the Bay and slipped farther away from him with each new wave.

Trying to call up every ounce of training, he mentally walked through his steps into the main house. It took only seconds but felt like a full-length movie unspooled in his brain. Satisfied he'd covered his tracks, he turned the boat over and pushed it down until water bubbled up inside. He didn't need to sink it, just be sure any unexpected traces and fibers disappeared.

He heard yelling. A man's voice. It grew more faint as Harris saw a figure running for the front porch of the house from the far edge of the island. Away from Harris, not toward him. Likely the island caretaker responding to the sister's screams.

That was all the incentive Harris needed. People were moving. Law enforcement would appear. The press—everyone. The Wright family had money. Stupid money. They would not stop until they caught the killer, and he refused to be tagged as that.

He needed to swim. To get to the smaller island nearby. From there he could call his reinforcements.

The way he got to the main island, by rowing, was too dangerous now. People would remember everything they saw the day Tabitha Wright was stabbed to death. A man rowing at breakneck speed dressed all in black and wearing gloves would stick out. No, he had to bide his time. Hide among the overgrown trees on the island two hundred feet away and let the people he trusted figure out how to extract him.

But he had to get there first, so he started swimming with his backpack. A few strokes then he dove under. The tide crashed on him, stealing his breath. He didn't care. This was life or death. First, hers. Now his.

Even being in good shape and with the protection of the narrow strait between the two islands minimizing the waves, the tide spun him around. For every two strokes he seemed to fall back one. He forced his mind to focus and his body to pump even harder. Water filled his mouth, not as salty as the ocean but the taste lingered. His ears clogged. The advance took an eternity and his lungs burned from the effort.

Just as his arms gave out, his knee brushed against the rocky coast of the smaller island. A thwapping sounded above him. He recognized it. Helicopters.

Keeping low, he crawled up into the brush. A jagged edge shredded his pants and slit his skin but he barely felt the cut. The sound of his heavy breathing echoed around him. Branches and some plant with sharp needles jabbed into him, but he kept going.

He shimmied on his knees and elbows until he landed in the protected cover of the overhanging trees.

Turning over, he stared up into the canopy of green. Patches of blue sky poked through the trees and fluffy white clouds blew by.

On any other day, under any other circumstances he would declare it a perfect day to be outside. But today was his nightmare. A job gone deadly wrong.

He closed his eyes and the haunting sound of the sister's cries came rushing back to him. He feared the noise would always fill his brain, as would the guilt of not being able to do enough for Tabitha, a woman he didn't actually know.

Exhaustion tugged at him. He could feel his muscles crying out for rest. For a bed. For quiet. For any place that was not here.

He turned onto his side and forced his body up on one elbow. His joints groaned in protest. At thirty-four that never happened, but he didn't have any energy left. The adrenaline surge that got him across that water had all but vanished. Now he lay there in the shade, wet and with cooling skin.

He pushed up to his knee and his body buckled. He couldn't put any weight on his left side. Even through the dark, soaked clothes he saw a fresh spurt of blood. It stained the ground where he'd just kneeled. He used his gloved palm to cover the red blotch with dirt.

Pushing the whole way up, he hobbled on one leg. Half bounced and half dragged his body over to the nearest tree trunk and tried to get his bearings. He'd staked out Tabitha Island from here and left backup supplies. His Plan B. Random items without any identifying marks. The most important being a satellite phone. The ultimate emergency safeguard that he had planned to double back and pick up when he finished the job.

So much for thinking today's work would be fast and easy.

It took another five minutes to get to his hiding place. A helicopter had landed on the island and boats were circling, some filled with tourists looking to see what was happening and others in transit to likely lock the place down.

He reached for the duffle bag and ripped the zipper open. He still wore the gloves. They were molded to his hands now and stiff. He dialed one of the few numbers he ever called. If the sat phone was the backup plan, this phone number qualified as the end-of-the-world measure he never wanted to invoke.

The line rang once then a deep voice came on the line. "Yes?"

That was it. No greeting or introduction. Just a stern, half-angry bark. For the first time in an hour Harris felt relief. Like he might actually survive today.

"It's Harris." He blew out a long breath and said the words he'd vowed *never* to say again. "I need you."

CHAPTER 2

Fourteen months later

Judgment Day.

She'd left Tabitha Island more than a year ago on a bright sunny day and never returned. Until now.

The private island measured about three miles. It sat off the western shore of the Chesapeake Bay in Maryland and could only be accessed by boat or helicopter. She used a private boat charter for her visit today. The boat's captain, a guy named Ed, wasn't her usual ride but she was trying to slip in unnoticed. The guy was chatty but grew more solemn the closer he got to the island. He'd circle back in exactly one hour, which was about fifty minutes longer than she wanted to stay.

Walking down the dock, she looked at the buildings scattered around the kidney-shaped piece of land. The beauty of the property always stole her breath. An impressive three-story Tudor house sat on the far edge, surrounded by a manicured lawn and mature trees. It had been built around 1900, along with the guesthouse and caretaker cottage on the opposite edge of the island and connected by a wandering rock path.

This was the much-talked-about jewel in what was once the Wright family property portfolio. It had been photographed, mostly from the outside, for decades. The property passed from one generation to the next, never daring to hint at neglect. The last generation refurbished it to use as a summer retreat. A place for parties and charity events.

But for fourteen months it had been reduced to a crime scene and endless source of gossip and speculation. A monument to family dysfunction and aching loneliness. There was no sign of that changing anytime soon.

There were whispers that books were being written about the tragedy that happened here. But the bigger news was the court's recent decision to move forward with the estate distribution. The police investigation hadn't resulted in any arrests. The judge insisted that absent additional evidence he didn't have a choice but to finalize the finances and set a date thirty days from now for a new hearing to move forward with the distribution of assets.

The decision resulted in a new surge of interest in the case. Complex theories and a lot of finger-pointing. Amateur detectives itched to swarm the private property in search of clues. Some true crime fans snuck on only to be removed by the island's caretaker, who still stood watch.

With the renewed attention came talk of upgraded

alarms, complete with motion sensors, more cameras and private security. The judge approved those expenses and all would be added starting early next week. That meant she had to move fast.

She wrapped her arms around her to ward off the chill coming off the water. The sun was warm for early March but the burst of purple color on the trees and the cool wind hinted that spring would soon give way to an early summer.

She followed the winding path through the budding blooms of the season's first flowers. The estate might be empty, but the caretaker made sure it didn't look that way. The upkeep continued at a furious pace.

The path branched into a Y with one section shifting off toward the guesthouse. She hesitated there. *Turn right.* That message kept flashing in her brain. She needed to go right, do what she came here to do and then get out. Not be seen.

One glance at the big house on top of the slight hill to her left and her plans derailed. Ignoring the job she came to do, she stayed on the larger section of path and continued past the fifty-foot gunite pool toward the main house. She wouldn't go inside. Couldn't. But something about the structure with its massive wrap-around front porch made of stacked stones called to her to come closer.

Her footsteps halted at the base of the porch as if some unseen barrier slammed down in front of her. An internal wall that lowered, shoved her back and kept her there.

She didn't carry much with her on this unwanted journey, just the cell in her back pocket and the small gardening shovel in her hand. Craig hadn't noticed on the boat because she'd kept the sweater off and the tool wrapped up in it. The cool early-spring wind had bitten into her arms as they crossed the waterway to the island with the jumbled ball of cotton and stainless steel secure on her lap.

Now she kept the shovel handy. She needed it for her job here. The job that had to happen now . . . before it was too late.

The excuses ran through her head, bounced around and echoed through her. She'd waited until now because she had no choice. The entire island had been a crime scene. Technically, still was.

That thought got her moving. She turned, determined to head back to the guesthouse and finish this. After two steps, she stopped. Her heartbeat ticked up until it thumped in her ears. She didn't see anything or hear anything, but she knew. She didn't need a shadow to fall across the path or anyone to appear in front of her or shout.

She was not alone.

"I knew you'd come back now."

That deep scolding voice. She'd heard it a thousand times over the years. It haunted her now as an adult. All the threats and promises of catching her. The determination to destroy her.

She turned around to face the porch again. There

he was. Stephen Wright. Businessman, millionaire and heir. Uncle to his famously slain niece.

He was pushing sixty and could easily pass for forty-five. Tall and lean, handsome with graying hair and a firm chin. He'd fit in at any yacht club or country club on the East Coast. More than likely with his overstuffed bank account he'd be welcomed at any of them without question.

His father had been a financial genius. His grandfather a bootlegger. Both filled the family coffers and supplied the money to build this estate and fuel his lifestyle.

His gaze slipped to the shovel in her hand. "Looks like I came outside too early."

She glanced past him to the screen door. The mesh hid the rooms inside but she saw enough for the rumbling sensation to start deep inside her. That familiar rush of bile worked its way up her throat. The desperate need to drop to her knees and cry or throw up until she lost the strength to do either hit her out of nowhere.

"Well?" That was all he said as hatred spewed out of every cell.

The hate was the part she noticed. The tremor of fury in his voice. His mouth screwed up in a grimace as if he'd just tasted something sour.

"I didn't know you were here." It was a stupid thing for her to say but it was honest.

"Obviously." He took out his cell and started dialing.

Anxiety welled up inside her. It churned in her stomach and started a banging in her head. "What are you doing?"

"Calling the police."

The urge to grab the phone and smash it nearly overwhelmed her. It took all of her energy to stand still, to not fidget. To not lunge for him.

He held the cell to his ear. "It's over, Gabrielle. I finally caught you."

Gabrielle. He always used her full name. He never called her Gabby, no matter how many times she asked. Since the murder he hadn't talked to her at all. He referred to her in interviews as Gabrielle Elizabeth Wright, as if stating her full name somehow separated her from him. Made her less human.

"I'm just standing here." She needed to bolt. Swim, if she had to. Maybe the numb shell that surrounded her would protect her from the icy cold of the Bay.

He glared at the shovel. "Whatever you've been hiding . . . we're going to find it this time."

"What are you—"

"Save it." He shook his head. "I specifically told my attorney not to fight the newest estate decision because I knew it would bring you out of hiding. That you wouldn't be able to ignore all that money and the prospect of experts coming here to assess the value of the personal items and furniture. Going through everything, pulling things apart. Possibly finding whatever you hid here that day."

"I've never cared about the money or the stuff." She

didn't then. She didn't now. But no one would ever believe that. Not with her past.

"You buried evidence right here on the island, didn't you? The shovel proves that." He swore under his breath. "Were you not even smart enough to throw the knife in the water after you killed her?"

Gabby's mind flashed back to that day. To the blood. The thudding footsteps. Tabitha's outstretched arm. How she shouted and begged people to believe her about the intruder but no one would listen. Every piece of the nightmare washed through her.

The gagging sensation had her chest heaving. It took another second before she could say anything. "There is no evidence to find. You're wrong about me."

How many times had she said that over the years? Too many to count.

"You're responsible for all of this," he said.

"I'm not. There was someone else on the island that day. A man and he ran." But maybe she did own some responsibility for what happened. If she had gotten to the house sooner. Suggested they go out to the dock earlier. There were so many ifs and maybes. Every single one dragged her down, refused to be tucked away in the back of her mind. The guilt was always right there, kicking to the surface.

"You're disgusting." He practically spit at her.

The words punched into her gut, but she refused to let him know he hurt her. Again. "I loved my sister."

He shook his head. "You've never loved anything but the money. And I'll prove it."

HARRIS CLIMBED THE last few feet to the second-floor window of the redbrick four-story town house. Breaking in had been no easy feat. The property sat on a stretch of Massachusetts Avenue in Washington, DC, known as Millionaires' Row. The street was home to embassies and billionaires. Private security roamed the neighborhood, protecting the international power-brokers and diplomats.

It was *the* perfect target, seemingly impenetrable between the guards and alarms and high walls with locked gates. Naturally, he couldn't resist.

He knew from experience the back of the property provided the most cover. Scaling the side gate to get there had been the only answer thanks to the fancy new lock and corresponding keypad that would take too long to crack, especially with it being nighttime and roving patrols moving around. The uneven spikes at the top of the gate added some excitement, but he'd long ago figured out how to maneuver around those and jump to safety.

A light clicked on the minute his feet touched the back patio. He didn't make that mistake twice. He pressed his back against the wall and slid the rest of the way. The back double doors were locked and protected with computer alarm pads. He could see the motion sensors in the upper and lower corners of each door, plus the deadbolt lock into the floor. The home security was no joke. He could break it, but he'd need time, planning and equipment.

That left one direction to go—up. He preferred to

start a few houses away, jump roofs then rappel down, but this way also worked. The added flair of entering through the second story would make the climb worth it.

With a throw, he hooked the metal end of his gear to the edge of the roof ledge and set off. The rope dug into his palms through the gloves, but he kept climbing. Once he reached the right height he debated shattering the glass as he dangled outside the floor-to-ceiling dining room windows. A part of him expected to be caught, so why prolong the journey trying to figure out how to get around the window sensor? But the challenge of getting away with it had excitement spiking inside him.

Adrenaline pulsed through every vein as he used the thin blade in his slim black toolkit to cut a hole in the glass. Despite working with some speed, he was careful not to rattle the window. Then came the slow ease of the piece of metal he held in front of the sensor at just the right speed, just the right time, to trick it into thinking the seal hadn't been broken.

It was tedious work, especially as he balanced twenty-five feet in the air with neighboring backyards facing him. He could be seen at any time, but that only added to the thrill.

With the sensor covered, he reached up through the window and unlocked it. Sliding it high enough to fit through the open space, he slipped inside the impressive house.

His feet touched the hardwood floor with only the

barest tap. He untied the safety rope from his waist and headed for the bar set up at the far end of the room. The glass jangled as he picked up the decanter and lifted the topper for a quick sniff. Whiskey, just as he expected.

After pouring a glass, he walked over and sat down at the dining room table. He removed his gloves and set them down next to a stretch of rope he'd used to anchor his weight on the climb.

And then he waited.

Less than a minute later the light at the top of the curving stairway flipped on. He didn't see or hear anyone. Another light under the oven hood cast a soft glow on the nearby kitchen and bounced off the expansive marble countertops, highlighting the fact he was alone.

He leaned back in the chair, wincing when the wood groaned under him. The sharp noise filled the otherwise silent floor, but still no one ran downstairs. The alarm didn't whirl to life. Not that he thought he'd hear it anyway. This place definitely would have a silent alarm.

"Tick tock." He whispered the words as he swirled the liquor around in the heavy crystal glass. He had no intention of drinking it, but holding it fit the mood.

He had barely counted to three when a face peeked around the corner of the wall. The light from upstairs cast her part in shadow and part not. He could make out the shoulder-length brown hair. Definitely a she, a very pretty *she* with big eyes and a round face.

Her eyes widened then she popped back out of sight. Didn't make a sound but the phone started ringing.

"What the hell?" Racing footsteps followed the male voice. He came down and rounded the corner holding a gun. Stopped as if he'd been hit with a brick.

Yeah, Levi Wren was home and very much awake.

Well, he was now.

Harris waved. "Hello."

"Damn it, Harris." Wren lowered the gun. He marched over to the alarm panel and typed in a series of numbers. Then he lifted his cell and mumbled a word that didn't make much sense before turning on Harris again. "You've got to be kidding with that entrance."

"What's going on?" The woman came into view again.

Wren looked at her this time. "Next time, wake me up. Don't just run downstairs to check out a burglar."

Not wanting to start a household dispute, Harris jumped in. "Technically, I don't intend to take anything."

"Shut up." Wren responded to Harris without breaking eye contact with her.

"I set off the alarm as soon as I saw him." She shrugged. "And I only came down in the first place because I figured it was Garrett."

They both stood on the bottom step talking about Wren's right-hand man in his business, Garrett McGrath. Wren had tucked the woman slightly behind his shoulder. They looked at each other and at Harris. There was a lot of gawking and frowning.

She wore a man's white cotton shirt, which dropped

to her upper thighs but not much farther. Wren wore boxer briefs, a gray T-shirt and a scowl that could melt steel.

Harris was enjoying every second of his surprise visit so far.

"This is Harrison Tate." Wren made the introduction as he ushered the woman into the room. "You can call him Harris or dumbass. Both fit."

"You actually know the guy breaking into the house?" Before anyone could answer, she rolled her eyes. "Forget that. Of course you do."

It was a typical Wren response. Harris couldn't help but smile when he heard it come from her.

Harris and Wren had been friends for years, long enough for Harris to know Wren's real name, which was not Levi Wren and not something most people knew. He was a professional fixer. He negotiated deals and made problems disappear. Most people considered him *the fixer*, the only person the wealthy and connected contacted when a life-threatening event occurred.

He went by an alias. The guy had a birth name and an alias and a fake name he'd chosen for himself. It was all pretty convoluted, but Harris played along. The few who did know about the fixer job and his life referred to him by the last name he'd taken long ago— Wren. But a handful of people, most of them now men around the same age who all met in their late teens and early twenties, knew his first name as Levi but still called him Wren.

They'd lived together, ran together, fought together, all under the careful watch of their mentor, a man named Quint who'd taken them all in and saved them from an inevitable life choice of death or prison. Back then there were five of them. Quint taught them about privacy and subterfuge. He gave them purpose and tried to redirect their criminal tendencies. That worked to varying degrees, depending on which member of the group you talked to.

Harris considered Wren family, more so than the one he was born into. They'd survived rough upbringings and formed a bond. And one day fourteen months ago, Wren saved his life.

"For what it's worth, I prefer Harris to dumbass." He looked from Wren to the woman. Harris knew who she was without hearing her name. Emery Finn, the woman who changed everything. She walked into Wren's life and turned it upside down. They were in love and living together, and if the whispers among their circle of friends were right, not far from a walk down the aisle. Once Wren got around to buying a ring and actually asking her.

"Harris is one of the Quint Five." Wren exhaled. "The annoying one."

Interesting. Wren wasn't the type to cough up information. Harris knew that meant Wren had likely told her everything. She might even know about *his* past, which was the kind of thing guaranteed to keep Harris up at night.

"Blame yourself for the intrusion. I'm here because

you called me and said we needed to talk." Harris had specifically stayed far away from the DC metro area and Chesapeake Bay for more than a year. He had no interest in this part of the country and chose jobs carefully to only be in town when he had to, and even then only for a short period.

He'd come back this time at Wren's request because Wren never asked anything of anyone.

"I didn't actually invite you to break into my house," Wren said.

Emery stepped away from Wren then and moved closer to the dining room table. "Wait, how did you get in here?"

"The window." Harris pointed at the one opened behind him.

Wren focused on the glass. "Is that a hole? You actually cut a hole in my window?" He dropped his cell on the table. "You're paying for that."

Emery walked over to the windows and leaned out. Looked up and down the outside wall. "That's amazing."

"No," Wren said. "Please don't encourage him."

She snorted. "You can be grumpy if you want, but it kind of is awesome. That's a big drop."

Harris watched her because it was hard not to. The long legs. The sexy sway of her hips. The charm. The way Wren stared at her with that ridiculous look on his face.

"I'm guessing you're Emery, the woman who won over one of my oldest and most difficult friends." At the mention of her name she faced Harris and smiled.

He could see why Wren had fallen hard. There was something about her. In their closed-off, sometimes dark and insular worlds, she struck Harris as a clear beam of light.

Wren grabbed Harris's full glass and drank it down. "You think I'm the difficult one?"

Emery reached over and snapped up the empty glass before either of the men could refill and try for a second round. It was a slick move. One sweep and all of the attention shifted back to her.

"Is there a reason you broke in? I mean, it's pretty cool and all . . ." When Wren made a strangled noise, she shot him an oh-come-on glance. "It is. Get over it."

"I like her." Harris did. From all he'd heard from their friends who'd met her and the interaction he saw in front of him, complete with the blazing attraction arcing between the two of them, Harris liked Wren and Emery together. He knew her background wasn't easy. Maybe that was why the two of them matched up so well because Wren's personal history was the stuff of nightmares. Harris just cared that they fit. "And I like to make an entrance."

Wren leaned against the wall. If he cared that he was almost undressed, he didn't show it. "He's also a thief."

Harris held up a hand. "The correct term is former thief."

Technically he was retired. He did the odd job now and then. He'd liberate an item to balance the scales, but the days of stealing to steal or to get money or to finish a job were behind him. His legitimate career provided a cover that let him sneak around and target houses without putting him in law enforcement's crosshairs.

She nodded at the rope sitting on the edge of the table. "You seem to still have the equipment."

"She's got you there."

Harris ignored the amusement in Wren's voice and answered the question Emery sort-of asked. "I am paid by insurance companies and very wealthy patrons to find lost works of art and return them to their rightful owners."

"It's the way he says it." She smiled as she looked at Wren. "Can you hear the dodging-the-truth thing when he does it?"

Wren made a humming sound. "He is an expert at evasion."

"You two are adorable," Harris said, hoping to turn the conversation to a new topic. "I'd heard you were living together, but for some reason my invitation to come over for a visit got lost in the mail."

She pointed at Harris. "There it is again. The attempted change in direction."

"Huh. I see what you mean." Wren nodded. "It is annoying."

Harris wasn't exactly sure what they were talking about, so he jumped topics again. "Back to the reason for my visit. You left a message. I'm here, Wren. Talk."

"For the record, you're welcome in our home anytime, but for the next visit use the front door or I'll shoot you." Wren yawned as he took a seat across from Harris.

"A totally boring way to enter, but fine." Harris appreciated the offer because he knew Wren meant it. He didn't throw out words to be nice. There was a pledge behind every sentence.

Wren rolled his eyes. "You have a serious problem."

Harris decided to stand. He felt more in control with his hands balanced on the back of the chair. Watching and waiting. "So you've been saying for years."

"Gabby Wright." Wren leaned back in the chair but didn't say anything else.

He didn't have to. The name vibrated through Harris. He could feel it spin inside him, crashing through every defense he'd built up over the months. Through every ounce of fake casual indifference he tried to wear as he moved through the day.

"What about her?" Harris asked, struggling to keep his voice even.

Emery pulled out the chair next to Wren. "Wait, you're talking about the woman who killed her sister?"

"She didn't." Harris didn't know what happened that day, but he knew that much was true.

Emery sat down hard. "I almost hate to ask how you're so sure."

"He knows because he was there," Wren said.

"Damn it, Wren."

"Get used to her knowing stuff." Wren shrugged. "You can trust her."

Easy for him to say. "Not that you're giving me a choice."

For a second Wren didn't respond. He glanced down to where his hands rested on top of the table. When he finally looked up again, all amusement had disappeared from his face. A clear and determined intensity radiated off him. "I called because there's movement in Gabby's case. The uncle is on a rampage. He wants her arrested before the next estate hearing a month from now and is hiring experts to make it happen."

Harris felt the life drain out of him and struggled to keep his voice even. "Shit."

He'd spent so much time thinking about Gabby. So many hours planning what he would do if anyone tried to put her in jail. He'd watched over her from a distance, ready to step in and hoping he'd never need to. He'd called on Wren to divert attention away from her more than once over the last fourteen months when the rumors turned wild. It was Harris's way of protecting her from afar—not good enough but it was something.

"She's in real trouble, Harris. Her uncle isn't backing down and he has the resources to make her life miserable in a way even I can't stop."

That serious tone. Wren brought that out more than once during their discussions over the years. The last time was when he told Harris to get his head out of his ass and find a legitimate job. Harris had the same answer this time. "I get it."

"Lucky for you, I created a reason for you to be on the island. A legitimate and legal one."

Harris was pretty sure he'd missed a jump in the conversation. "Wait, what?"

"You need to step in. Get to that house and control the uncle while you still can."

The day had arrived but Harris wasn't ready. He started shaking his head before Wren finished his sentence. "I'm not going back to that island."

He already spent too much time on the island in his head. Sometimes he'd hear Gabby's voice. That pained and desperate screaming as she begged Tabitha to wake up.

Fucking hell. He'd do almost anything to protect Gabby from being charged with a crime she didn't commit, but he could not willingly step back into that nightmare. Not when he hadn't recovered from the last round.

Wren exhaled. "You'll have help there with you."

"Garrett?" He and Wren were almost inseparable. Garrett basically had been adopted by the Quint group. He was also on the verge of getting married thanks to a quick dating-to-engagement move on his part around Christmas.

"No." Wren didn't offer anything else.

Leave it to Wren to pick that moment to become even more secretive than usual. Harris looked at Emery but she didn't say anything. She just sat there with a mix of concern and frustration showing in her frown. She clearly didn't know the background of this discussion, but Harris knew she would before she went back to sleep tonight.

"Did you weasel your way in and put your people in place of the ones the uncle intended to hire?" Emery asked.

"I *fix* things. It's what I do," Wren explained to her before looking at Harris again. "And I'm trying to help you fix this."

"If only you could help me forget it." But Harris knew it wasn't that simple. A woman was dead and he'd been the one to make it harder to find her killer. Not on purpose, but his intent didn't matter.

"Gabby could go to prison, Harris." Wren's voice was louder and more urgent this time.

"You don't think I know that?" He thought about little else.

The nightmare played in his head all the time. He tried to push the worries out and convinced himself she was fine. Beaten down but not out. Emotionally battered because of him but a survivor. None of it worked. Every night the doubts and guilt would seep back in. He'd think about her, remember the heart-breaking grief on her face in those photos in the news. Her screams of horror from that night never left him.

Wren continued to stare at Harris. "So?"

As much as Harris fought it, he knew he'd have to return to Tabitha Island one day. For Gabby. Apparently that day had arrived.

"When do I leave?"

CHAPTER 3

Two days after the showdown with her uncle, Gabby sat on the porch of the main house on Tabitha Island. She'd just arrived with little more than a small duffle bag and a load of panic bouncing around inside her. A month ago her uncle restarted his very public campaign against her, one that caused her to lose the receptionist job she'd managed to land. Now she was back to being unemployed and worrying every two seconds about being arrested.

With the press closing in and the daily barrage of new threats against her, her life unraveled. She traveled to the one place she hated, Tabitha's special island, because she didn't have any other option. Control had slipped away and she was desperate to get it back.

Her uncle didn't want her there, which was a bonus. Ticking him off was her only revenge for how he'd upended her life. But being on the island also provided her with the chance to complete the one task she needed to finish. With a new investigator headed to the island and an appraiser who would be wandering around, she had to be efficient and fast. Not give her movements away.

She'd spent so much of the last fourteen months running and trying to figure out who would want her sweet sister dead that she'd skipped the grieving stage. It swamped her here. She couldn't go into the guesthouse because her uncle had locked it down. That meant sleeping in Tabitha's house, and since it had taken her two hours to work up the nerve just to sit on the front porch, Gabby didn't know how she'd ever get through the front door.

Sitting there, memories floated back to her of Tabitha hanging out on the porch while reading. As a kid, Tabitha would race across the lawn to get to the oversized rocking chair first then wouldn't move from it for hours. Back then she was five or six, seven years younger than Gabby. As the youngest, Tabitha won most arguments and she'd always loved the island. It made sense since their parents named it after her. She was the "surprise" baby. The one their parents coddled and overprotected from birth.

"Gabrielle."

At the sound of her uncle's disappointed tone she looked up. He stood there in his usual expensive suit, this one gray. He wasn't alone. Another man stood next to him. He lacked Uncle Stephen's stern expression and stiff stance. No, this guy wore a hint of a smile. She noticed because he was a hard man not to notice. She wouldn't call him pretty, but he was damn close.

He had a face people would remember. Firm chin with a sexy little bit of scruff around his mouth and over his cheeks. Hazel eyes in this incredible hazy green-brown shade. The muscular frame, yet not bulky. From the brown hair to the broad shoulders, he stood out. Even his clothing, stylish but not too much so.

He checked every single box. It was almost as if someone built him from a list of Tall, Dark and Hot characteristics. And since he was with her uncle, she disliked him immediately. Any friend of her uncle was likely to be an enemy of hers.

"Uncle Stephen." She nodded to him then turned to the unexpected guest. "I prefer to be called Gabby."

"You still insist on using that ridiculous nickname?" Stephen made a dismissive sound. He balanced his foot against the bottom step to the porch and glanced at the front door. "We might be more comfortable inside."

Not going to happen. Her first trip inside would not be with a man who would rather chuck her into the water than sit down to have a meal with her. "I'm fine here."

The wind whipped around the island but the early-spring sun had grown warm. Gabby had always loved this time of year on Tabitha Island. The tourists hadn't arrived in the area yet. It was the intake of breath before the wild stage started. All the pleasure boaters and partygoers would show up soon enough.

She looked out at the water, seeing boats. Every now and then a helicopter circled. The press had found her. She wouldn't be surprised if Uncle Stephen tipped them off.

Stephen shook his head before gesturing at the man next to him. "This is Harrison Tate."

The introduction pulled her gaze back to the quiet cutie. "Okay."

"He'll be appraising the personal property. Doing an inventory." Stephen's foot slipped off the step with a thud. "He may have questions for you."

Right, because that sounded like something an appraiser would do. Her skepticism level rose along with her anxiety. Much more of this crazy bouncing around in her stomach and she'd never be able to eat again. "I don't know anything about the furniture."

The guy's faint smile broke wide. "I'll mostly be handling the antiques and artwork."

Yeah, no way was she being lured in by that look. She'd learned long ago that a guy with a pretty face could be just as dangerous as the bossy, controlling-guy type. "I know even less about those things."

He grew more serious. "I'm very sorry to hear about your sister's death."

He'd just committed an almost unpardonable sin in her book. "Murder."

His eyes widened. "Excuse me?"

"She was murdered." Gabby's fingers curled and tightened around the ends of the armrests. "She didn't fall out a window or drown in the pool. Someone killed her."

He opened his mouth as if he was about to respond,

but her uncle jumped in. "We're all well aware of how she died, Gabrielle. I, for one, have studied the reports."

Of course he had, and he blamed her. Gabby didn't need to hear the words. They were right there in every sentence, in every look. He'd come to his conclusions the day after the murder and told the investigator. As soon as he knew she'd been on the island, visiting Tabitha, he shut down on her. Any emotion, any genuine feelings he had for her died that day. He'd never said another kind word or offered one second of affection or comfort.

He even tried to have her barred from Tabitha's funeral, but that didn't work. Gabby had been prepared to make a scene. The minister had stepped in and soothed the rising tensions.

"I'm not going to agree to finalize anything and distribute assets while questions remain," Stephen said.

As if she cared about any of that. He could have it all if he'd stop hating her for ten minutes and work with her to find Tabitha's killer. "About me, you mean."

The Harrison guy scoffed. "He doesn't mean—"

"He does." It was sweet but hugely naïve for the guy to think her uncle didn't choose each word for maximum damage. The object of this game, of being on the island together, was emotional torture. He wanted her to suffer and was willing to go sentence by sentence to do it.

"The police have failed to find your sister's killer." Stephen folded his arms over his chest and glanced around the property.

"I'm aware of that, yes."

His gaze whipped back to her. "The case is open, but the police have limited resources."

Oh, she got the message. "But you don't."

"Mine are better." For the first time in months, Stephen smiled. This topic clearly made him happy when nothing else could. "As such, I have hired an investigator to conduct a complete review of the evidence and facts. You may have been told that he would be here tomorrow."

"Okay." She forced her voice to stay calm even as her insides jumped. Her mind took off on a frenzy of planning. The things she wanted to check and do. Her movements would be restricted, if not impossible, as more people—people paid by Uncle Stephen—descended on the island. She glanced at the guy who stood there, acting as if this wasn't the most awkward family conversation ever. "That still doesn't explain why you need to be here right now."

"Please call me Harris." He smiled again, this time less bright and more with a touch of something that looked almost like empathy. "The court has imposed a rather tight timeline for valuation. I need to be here, on the grounds, until every item is catalogued and inspected."

"And you will stay out of his way," her uncle ordered.

She didn't bother looking at her uncle. Not when he talked to her like she was five.

Her attention settled on Harris. She stared at him

and he stared back. "I figured you were here to baby-sit me."

Harris winced. "That's not really in my job description."

The longer she watched, the more unsure she became. A sensation Gabby couldn't really name or pinpoint hit her. She didn't buy for a second that his work on the island was about tables and lamps. But she didn't get the sense he was a mouthpiece for her uncle either. If anything, he seemed unimpressed with Uncle Stephen's bluster. More than once, Uncle Stephen spoke and Harris looked ready to roll his eyes.

"The investigator is your bigger concern. He will need to speak with you at length." Stephen shoved his hands in the pockets of his dress pants. "He will also have access to family information, including any history that may be relevant."

The jab wasn't subtle. Gabby got the point. Every accusation from over the years would be dug up and thrown at her again, including the one that changed everything. "I do have a phone. Your guy can call me."

"No more running, Gabrielle. It's time this family faces the truth."

She dug her nails deeper into the wood of the chair. "I'm ready if you are."

Without another word, Stephen turned around and stormed off. He walked down the paved path and kept going. Halfway across the lawn he pulled his cell out of his jacket pocket and put it to his ear. Between the distance and crash of the waves, she couldn't hear a word.

She watched his outline and that familiar bounce to his step. He always carried his body with a could-take-on-anyone confidence. Today was no different. Fury had surged through him until there was almost nothing left inside him. She's heard rumors about his marriage being in trouble. That his quest for vengeance had overcome everything else.

Under all the hurt Gabby had to admit Stephen was just one more victim in a series of family tragedies. One more Wright who got buried under all the pain and despair. Still, it was hard for her to feel anything but frustration because he chose his current lonely course. He refused to listen to her.

Harris cleared his throat. "You two seem close."

"That business he has to rush off to likely involves having me arrested." She said it as a joke but she feared it might not be.

"For talking back to him?" Harris sat down on the stone porch railing right across from her.

"At this point I think he's actually convinced I'm guilty of multiple murders."

Harris frowned. "That's a pretty extreme level of family dysfunction."

His voice sounded so genuine. The comment even carried a note of question, as if he were wondering out loud what could possibly lead an uncle to making those sort of comments to his own niece.

It was garbage. Oh, Harris had a good act. All concerned and acting as if he was just dropped there and doing his job. She didn't buy it at all. "Let's not do this."

"What?"

"You don't need to pretend you don't know."

He shook his head. "You lost me."

"I assume someone filled you in on my family. If not Uncle Stephen, you've at least seen the news or heard rumors." Pundits and so-called experts had spent hours of television time dissecting every move and every Wright holiday for years. "The only thing I ask is that you give me the courtesy of not pretending to be surprised when you're not."

To his credit, he nodded. She'd expected more denial and maybe a ratcheting up of the I'm-just-sitting-here act he had going, but he abandoned it all.

"Fair enough." He tapped his fingertips together as his gaze searched her face.

"I'm guessing you have a hundred questions." Not that she intended to answer any of them.

"There are whispers you killed your sister."

Gabby tucked one of her legs beneath her and rocked the chair with her other foot. "They're more than whispers. I've been questioned by the police multiple times."

"There are those who believe you killed your parents before you killed your sister."

The allegation sliced through her until an ache settled deep in her bones. "Their plane crashed. But yes, there are those who think I picked up a mechanical engineering degree—in secret, I guess—and then used that knowledge to kill them. Really, people will make up any fact to fit with their theories about my supposed guilt."

He shot her a sad smile. "You've been busy."

"And a sociopath, apparently." She couldn't imagine the kind of person she'd have to be to cut a swath through her family the way people claimed.

"The only other piece of information I know is that you've been disinherited."

"You forgot the part where I faked my own kidnapping when I was nineteen." Everything started there with the allegations she had set it all up to get her parents' money. Once people believed that, they would believe any horror story about her.

She could still hear the claims. The spoiled college kid and her friends trying to rob the poor, innocent rich couple. That was the spin the magazines and newspapers put on the story. Never mind the truth.

He shrugged. "I just hadn't gotten to that one yet."

His light tone kept her anxiety from spiking. She never talked about family. Certainly didn't discuss rumors with strangers. But sitting there with the cool breeze hitting her face, rocking back and forth with her head resting against the chair, the rest of the world fell away.

His voice, so soothing, almost inviting, had the tension unspooling inside her. If he was judging her, he hid it well. If this was an interrogation, he wouldn't get anything out of her anyway. The truth was the truth.

"My list of supposed sins is pretty long," she said.

He nodded. "You do have quite the colorful history."

"I actually don't. That's the point."

He leaned forward with his elbows balanced on his thighs. "Every family has secrets, Gabby."

"You say that as if you think all family secrets are the same." She almost laughed at the thought. "My great-aunt Barbara married her brother-in-law, but that's not what we're talking about here, are we?"

"Naughty Aunt Barbara."

The back-and-forth, the verbal sparring, felt oddly good. Gabby couldn't remember the last time she joked with anyone. "Did I mention she was still married to Uncle Thaddeus at the time she took on his brother, too?"

"I hope there wasn't a third sibling. The poor woman would have been exhausted." Harris looked up at the porch ceiling. "For the record, would that be trigamy?"

Laughter escaped her and she almost didn't recognize the sound. "Probably. Try to top that."

"I'm not trying to get into a competition with you." He took a deep breath. "I'm just saying circumstances can stack up and sometimes people mistake a pile of innuendo and happenstance for facts."

She lowered both feet, stopping the chair midrock. "But you don't?"

"I make my own decisions about people."

No, too easy. The camaraderie, the gentle back and forth. She didn't have to work at talking with him or weigh her words. They'd known each other for all of an hour, probably less, and her usual defenses crumbled. She didn't feel the rushing panic to shut down the conversation before she said too much. That scared the hell out of her.

She mentally slammed on the brakes and retreated to that place where she questioned every nice gesture and doubted every intention. "Well, I hope you're being paid well for your time, Harris."

The snap returned to her tone. He must have heard it or sensed a change because for a few seconds he sat there not talking. His gaze roamed over her face, as if he were assessing her.

"My services aren't free." He sat up straight again. "But your uncle is not paying me. I'm independent."

That didn't even sound real. "Sure you are."

Harris shook his head. "You sound so skeptical."

It was possible Harris didn't fully understand his role, but she doubted it. He struck her as a smart guy. He knew what to say and when to pour on the charm. It was hard to imagine him being caught up in her uncle's scheme without knowing it. "Uncle Stephen is going to try to use you for intel. He's determined to gather enough information to have me arrested."

"Is there intel to gather?"

Now, that sounded like a guy on her uncle's payroll. "As you pointed out, we all have secrets."

"I'm here to do a job." He held up a finger. "One job. Following you and reporting back on how many hours you sit on the porch isn't part of it."

Possibly, but she still intended to be wary. "The investigator is coming. We have a caretaker and his son here, working to keep the property in order. A boat comes back and forth."

"Meaning?"

"There are about to be a lot of people in and around this piece of land."

"Good thing there are plenty of beds."

The comment spun around in her head. "You're staying here?"

Harris groaned. "Your uncle didn't tell you?"

"Believe it or not, we don't share a lot of information."

"Yeah, I can't exactly imagine the two of you having brunch."

"Depends. Do people scream at each other at brunch?" She'd survived a decade of yelling. It had been exhausting. Now that only silence surrounded her, she missed the yelling.

"They did in my family."

She wanted to ask, to know more about him and what that meant. She clamped down on that instinct, too.

"My parents were big fans of the quiet condemnation." She shook her finger in the air. *"We're disappointed in you, Gabrielle."*

He whistled. "Ouch."

"Right?" She crossed her legs then uncrossed them. When she realized she'd started shifting around in her chair, she forced her body to still. "Are your bags already inside the house?"

"I was told to take the guesthouse." He leaned to

the side and pulled a set of keys out of his front pants pocket. They jangled in his hand.

"That's usually where I stay." A lump gathered in her throat and she had to choke it back.

One of his eyebrows lifted. "You're welcome to join me."

"Tempting, but no." She stood up then because the energy pinging around inside her had her ready to break into a run. "Enjoy your appraising."

This time his gaze dipped past her face. Lower, down her body to her legs and back up again. "Oh, I intend to."

CHAPTER 4

A few hours later the sun dove behind a bank of clouds and Harris slipped inside the double doors of the boathouse. He tried to ignore the fact it matched the Tudor style of the main house. Like a little replica. One of those rich-people things, he guessed.

The smell of salt and fish smacked into him as he surveyed the inside of the two-story structure. Not much to see on this floor but the water lapping into the empty boat slip. Kayaks and paddles hung in rows on the wall. He couldn't imagine a recluse out riding on the water but then a lot about the Wright family didn't make sense to him.

Gabby continued to be the biggest surprise. After Tabitha's murder, in a haze of guilt while he'd been desperate to learn everything about her, he'd seen photos. As the months flowed one into the other he studied more about her life, looked through more images, but those didn't come close to capturing the punch of the live version. He'd never had a preference for brunettes or any other hair color . . . until now. Her dark hair turned deep auburn when the light hit it. She stood maybe five-seven and every inch of that proved to be a formidable verbal sparring companion.

And that body. *Fucking hell*. Those faded jeans hugged every curve of her long legs and fine ass. She wore a bright blue sweater that matched her eyes. It was cotton and bulky but when she moved just right or crossed her arms in front of her, the outline of her impressive breasts came into view.

Pretty was the wrong word. She had this sexy mix of wise worldliness and girl-next-door cuteness. The big eyes and smooth skin. That underlying hint of intelligence that laced through every word.

Smoking hot. Yeah, those were the right words.

Pushing her sexy voice and sharp comebacks out of his head, he climbed the fixed ladder to the second floor. Boxes lined the walls up here. Light streamed in through the windows and through the doors to the balcony on the water's edge, highlighting the layer of dust on the hardwood floor. He strained, looking for signs of footsteps but saw only a room used for storage.

Back downstairs, he maneuvered around the water's edge to the doors. He stepped outside and into the grass. After fastening the door, he turned around and stopped just inches before slamming into a man.

"Holy shit." That was only a fraction of the profane words running through Harris's head as the adrenaline kick nailed him.

The guy's age was tough to pin down. His skin was tan but smooth. He looked like he could be anywhere from fifty to seventy. The baggy blue utility pants didn't help narrow the gap. Neither did the graying hair tucked into the fraying baseball cap.

He held a rake and stabbed it into the ground before leaning on it. "You need something?"

A little less drama would be nice. "I'm just getting to know the island."

Harris had studied the file Wren compiled *because of course Wren had a file on the Wright family*. Wren probably had a file on anyone who had ever been in the news and a few who hadn't. Harris could guess who stood in front of him. The island's caretaker. Had to be.

The guy took off his hat only long enough to scratch his head then pulled it back on again. "It's not that big a piece of land, so it shouldn't take you long."

"Harris Tate." He lifted his hand in greeting.

The man stared down at the offer but didn't shake. "Kramer."

So much for getting on the guy's good side. Harris wasn't convinced he had any side other than the crotchety-old-dude side. "Is that a first or last name?"

Kramer shrugged. "Does it matter?"

"I guess not." Harris knew the answer anyway—last name. The full name was Burton Kramer but he only ever went by Kramer.

Harris admired the older man's grumpiness. Kramer didn't try to impress, which meant he should speak his mind if asked the right question. Since Harris would bet most of the cash he had on him that most of his talks with Gabby would follow the same pattern as the one from earlier today—all circular and analyzing with brief breaks of amusement—it would be a welcome change to have someone on the island just say what they meant.

Harris decided to lay some groundwork for his continued snooping. "I'm here to—"

"I know who you are. Stephen Wright filled me in." Kramer picked up the rake then plunged it into the grass again.

"The uncle." Sounded like good ol' Uncle Stephen had been busy.

"And your boss."

Harris had been on the island less than a day and Kramer was the second person to raise the issue of Stephen's payroll. Apparently the Wright family threw money at problems and people. Harris admitted he possessed many character defects but he didn't get lured in by people who flashed money. If anything, that kind of entitled behavior made him more likely to liberate an item from a person's home without them knowing. Taking art or an antique meant he never owed anyone a favor. He held the power.

"No, I was hired by the insurance company," Harris said.

"Waste of time."

Not the answer he expected. "Excuse me?"

Kramer threw out his free arm. "The island, the house, all the stuff here, belongs to Gabby. Why appraise anything? Just hand it over to her and be done."

Interesting. Gabby might think no one believed in

her innocence but Kramer sounded like a one-person cheerleading squad. Unlike Stephen, who managed to drop ten negative comments about Gabby in the ten minutes Harris spent alone with him, Kramer immediately rushed to her defense. If he thought she killed Tabitha or deserved to be punished, he sure hid it well.

Grumpy or not, the actions made Harris like the older man. "There are legal issues. There's also the part about Gabby being disinherited."

Kramer made a tsk-tsking sound. "Looks like you don't know as much as you think you do."

"I know about art."

"Then you should stick to that."

Yeah, Harris appreciated the other man's style. Working around him was not going to be easy. "Is that a warning?"

"An observation." Kramer lifted the rake's spokes out of the grass. "But you'd be wise to follow it."

"I'll keep that in mind."

But Kramer was already walking away. He gave a wave over his shoulder. "You do that."

GABBY DEBATED VENTURING into a second discussion with Harris. The first one had her off balance. She'd gotten so good at ducking topics and engaging in subterfuge that when those go-to moves abandoned her, she got twitchy.

But the house wasn't an option tonight and the guesthouse was off-limits, which left her with few refuges now that the sun had gone down. And he'd started a fire. She had almost no defenses against the famous Wright fire pit with its stone rock wall and submerged circle in the center of a special patio area built by the water's edge.

Wishing she'd reached for a jacket, she wrapped her sweater tighter around her body and walked across the grass to the pit area. She didn't have to announce her arrival because he watched every step.

The fire roared with life. He wore a zip-front sweater that molded to his arms, showing off every line. She'd never actually seen a muscle strain through clothing before but now she knew it was possible.

No way this guy sat at a desk valuing artwork all day.

The closer she got the more she could see. He had a bag of something on the bench next to him. The stick . . . and was that a marshmallow?

Ignoring seating protocol strangers usually followed and leaving a space, she sat down right next to him. The idea of yelling at him over a fire didn't hold much appeal. "I've been watching you for the last few hours."

He continued to twirl the stick as the edge of his marshmallow turned brown over the fire. "That sounds like a pretty boring day."

"You have walked around the island and lingered around the outside of the main house. I've seen you by the water and at the boathouse." Peeking in on him was no hardship. He moved with purpose. Long, sure steps that gobbled up the ground beneath him. Perfect posture and legs that went on forever.

She loved the way his pants balanced low on his

hips, showing off his long torso. She didn't know if he swam or rowed or played basketball, but whatever he did to earn a lean, muscular body like that, he should keep doing it because *damn*.

He looked at her and smiled. "You could have said hello."

Uh-huh. He was missing her point. She guessed that was on purpose. "You didn't go inside the house, Harris."

"And . . . ?" He went back to staring at his stick and toasting the marshmallow.

"Your job is to appraise antiques and artwork. We keep that sort of thing indoors."

"Ah." He nodded as he reached into the bag and took out two graham crackers and set them on his lap.

His movements pulled her mind away from the conversation. She was trying to catch him in a lie and make him admit he was there to watch over her, not to value things. Instead, he mesmerized her with those long fingers and strong hands.

With a small shake of her head she forced her brain back to the topic. "You see my confusion."

"I do." With one hand he opened the paper on a chocolate bar . . . or tried to. "I'm actually waiting for the investigator."

"What?"

All that fumbling had her reaching over to help. She took the chocolate bar out of his hand and ripped the paper back. Broke off two chunks then handed them to him.

"Thank you." He trapped one end of the stick between his knees. The marshmallow dipped down closer to the fire. "The items we were talking about are likely worth a lot of money. Poking around before the investigator gets here struck me as a way to get blamed for something I didn't do."

The marshmallow was on fire now. She had trouble concentrating on anything else. "You think someone will accuse you of stealing?"

"Your uncle seemed to have the blame gene."

"Definitely." *For God's sake*. She grabbed the stick. A quick blow on the end and she saved the marshmallow from a fiery death. "So, your plan is to sleep outside all night?"

"I'll venture into the guesthouse eventually. But this setup looked pretty inviting."

"My parents added this when I was about sixteen. Tabitha had just turned nine and she loved s'mores."

He put his chocolate cracker concoction together and handed it to her. "Of course. Who doesn't?"

She waved him off. "Me."

"What?" His eyes widened as his hand dropped to his lap. "That's an outrage."

Fake or not, the horror in his voice made her laugh. "Tabitha thought so, too. I think begging for the fire pit was her way of trying to cure me of my misguided ways."

For a second he stared at the dessert in his hand. When he looked at her again concern shined in his eyes. "I really am sorry about what happened to her."

Sensing he meant it, she skipped her usual smart-ass responses and dodging. "Thanks."

"Being here has to be—"

"Impossible." Gabby reached over and took a piece of the graham cracker that hadn't been ruined by marshmallow. "It's every nightmare, every dark and horrible thought rolled into one."

"Sounds like I might not be the only one toying with the idea of sleeping outside."

She nodded toward the house. "I'm not going in there."

"You mean, ever?" He took a bite of the s'more.

"Not yet." She reached across his thighs to the bag and took a full graham cracker this time. "How did you think I was able to spy on you all day? I was lingering outside as well."

"Impressive skills, by the way."

"I've gotten used to looking over my shoulder." She popped the cracker in her mouth but she really couldn't taste it.

"Is this the part where I'm not allowed to pretend ignorance?"

She was impressed he'd actually listened this afternoon. That was more than most people did. But it didn't mean that she wanted to revisit any part of that topic.

With a hard swallow, she got the cracker down then dumped the rest on the bench between them. "How exactly does one become an art appraiser?"

That sexy smile of his came roaring back. "We're changing the subject?"

She nodded. "Without even an ounce of subtlety."

The rich sound of his laugh floated through the dark night. "Then the answer is easy—misspent youth."

"What are you talking about? Art appraising sounds like something wealthy people would be into. Like, I'm looking at you and thinking private-school boy." She studied his face and hummed as she tried to pin him down, figure out his untold story. "Maybe even a boarding school."

He snorted. "Your people-reading skills are way off tonight."

That answer . . . it had her wanting to know more. She beat back the urge to pepper him with questions. If she took a turn, he would want one. No way.

She pointed at the gooey s'more oozing between his fingers. "Blame the marshmallow."

"They're growing on you."

"Not really." She'd never been a fan. "The sticky thing . . . it's annoying."

He held up a hand and wore a look of fake outrage. "Honestly, you keep talking like that and I'll have to leave the island."

"I wish I had that option." She hadn't meant to say that, but the words were out there now.

His head snapped back as he looked at her. "Do you really have to be here?"

"I owe it to Tabitha." And it was a debt Gabby took seriously. Her sweet, loving sister deserved so much more than the end she got. The idea of her dying alone and afraid twisted Gabby's insides into knots. She had faint memories of a man and footsteps that horrible afternoon, but Tabitha was gone by the time Gabby reached her. "Someone needs to care about what really happened to her."

"No theories?"

"Too many, actually." Someone looking for cash. Some jerk hoping to find a woman alone. Every option centered on the hazy figure she saw leaving the house. The one she'd almost convinced herself she'd dreamed up.

"Are you really not going to sleep inside tonight?" he asked.

"I might sleep on the porch." That was the plan. There or the boathouse, where there'd be some protection from the wind.

She'd thought about knocking on Kramer's door, but his son was on the island, trying to catch up on maintenance that had been limited when the police shut down the island to everyone to conduct an investigation. Poor Kramer got displaced for a few months. Once he came back the police limited the work he could do. So did the wrangling over the estate because Tabitha's trust fund had been frozen. But now that Kramer was back, he was behind on all but the most routine work. She knew because he'd grumbled about that while they shared breakfast at his house this morning.

"It's freezing out here." Harris rubbed his hands together in front of the fire as if to prove his point.

"I'll be fine." When he started to say something,

she talked over him. "I'm serious, Harris. I can't be in the house. Not yet. Tomorrow, maybe. In the light."

"Have you been in there since . . ."

He didn't need to finish the sentence because she knew where he was going. "Since I found her body? No."

He let out a long, loud breath as he wrapped up the chocolate bar again. "Take the guesthouse."

The idea sounded so much better than any other option. She'd stayed there on and off with Tabitha since their parents died. Her sister loved the solitude of the island but Gabby always worried the lack of companionship would prove to be too much. She stopped in. She swung through. She came up with excuses to be there for days at a time with her sister before jumping off again.

"Where would you sleep?" A not entirely unwelcome idea formed in her brain. "Or was that a really sloppy pass?"

"Sloppy?" He shook his head. "Woman, come on. It takes skill to look debonair while having your fingers stuck together with marshmallow."

He held up his fingers to show her.

"You're right," she said, ignoring the fact he pulled off the look just fine.

He picked up the chocolate bar then dropped it again. "Melting chocolate. I mean, I'm balancing a lot over here."

He really was adorable. Sexy and hot in a want-to-climb-him way, but kind of sweet, too.

Too bad she thought it was all a very calculated act.

"You're very impressive," she said in the most condescending voice she could muster.

"Thanks for noticing." He wiped his hands on a paper towel and put the rest of the s'mores ingredients away. "But the offer still stands. The guesthouse has a couch and a floor. I can sleep on one of those."

So tempting.

"No." The offer should have been easy to resist but she had to force the denial out. She stood up, thinking leaving might be the only way she could win this round. "I'll be fine."

He glanced up at her. "I get the impression you're always fine, Gabby."

"Then you're not looking very closely."

CHAPTER 5

Harris stood there for a second, watching Gabby sleep. An unwanted mix of guilt and interest slammed into him. He needed to ignore his attraction and focus on fixing the mess his ill-timed visit to this island fourteen months ago cost her. If he hadn't corrupted the crime scene, Gabby might have her answers about Tabitha. Gabby might have been able to move on instead of hovering in this holding pattern and sleeping outside.

It was a little past midnight. At some point she'd curled up on the porch swing around the corner from the front door of the main house and drifted off. He could see her thanks to the recessed lights in the porch ceiling.

During the day the seat had a perfect view of the inground pool and open water of the Bay beyond. Not that she'd notice that now since she lay on her side with her eyes closed. The edge of a paperback peeked out from under her elbow and a jacket fell over her as if she'd tugged it on as a blanket then it slipped as she moved around.

Haunting memories or not, the temperature had dipped low. There was no way she should be out here.

He walked up two steps, thinking to wake her but then stopped. Something about her, about all she'd endured and survived, pulled at him. He appreciated strong women. The stamina and the smarts. In some ways Gabby reminded him of his mother . . . maybe too much. His mother had pushed through life and overcome the unimaginable. She also wallowed in secrets until they almost drowned her.

That was how he saw Gabby. So many doubts swirled around her. He knew it was all nonsense. He didn't buy the theories about her parents and he was eyewitness to the fact she didn't kill her sister. When she spoke of her sister a wistful, pained tone moved into her voice as if it was hard for her to breathe through it. Maybe Stephen saw that as an admission of guilt. Harris saw genuine emotion.

But that didn't absolve her of every crime. He'd read over the police reports from around the time of the kidnapping more than a decade ago. Gabby gave partial answers and her story bounced around from interview to interview. The two classmates implicated in the kidnapping insisted it was all a joke gone wrong and received probation. Gabby's parents put her in a protective bubble and insisted in public that she was innocent, only to disinherit her and move her out of the house less than a year later.

Then there was the shovel. Stephen had made a

big deal about her "sneaking" onto the island with a shovel in hand just a few days ago. Even Harris had to admit that was an odd tool to carry around with her. He wanted an explanation but he couldn't exactly ask for one. Not in his role as appraiser.

She shifted her arm and the book fell to the porch. It landed with a soft thud but she didn't wake up.

"Gabby," he whispered as he moved closer.

That was all it took. The soft call of her name and she jumped up. Her legs whipped over the side of the swing and her jacket drifted down on top of her book.

She looked around, eyes wide in panic. "What's wrong?"

"Whoa." He put up his hands but shouldn't have bothered because she wasn't looking at him. He didn't think her eyes had even focused. "You're literally asleep on the porch."

She gulped in deep breaths. Her chest rose and fell as her fingers wrapped around the edge of the chair in a white-knuckle grip. "I was reading and—"

"I thought we had an agreement." He walked the final few steps and stopped in front of her.

She glanced up at him and her eyes cleared. "What do you mean?"

"About not playing lying games. So, can we skip over the part where you make up excuses?" When she didn't say anything, he closed the rest of the distance between them and sat down next to her. Scooped her jacket off the floor and balanced it over her shoulders, letting his fingers linger just long enough to feel the brush of her soft hair against the back of his hand.

Attraction kicked him in the nuts. He couldn't remember wanting a woman this hard and this fast. He didn't go in for commitment or even dating, really. He was too involved with his legitimate job and the one he did on the side, moving art back to its rightful owners whether the people holding it agreed or not.

But none of that mattered right now. She did, so he continued to stay quiet. There was no reason to rush this conversation. She'd talk if she wanted to. If not, they could sit here, gently swaying on the swing.

"Every time I try to walk through that door I see her." Her voice sounded flat, almost monotone, as she stared off in the distance.

"I can imagine."

"You really can't." She exhaled as she turned to face him. "I'm not trying to be a jerk, but nothing . . . There are no words to describe it."

She looked small huddled there in her coat. She'd kicked her shoes off and wore only socks. Now she curled her toes and raised her feet off the porch floor, likely to evade the cold wood.

Maybe to provide comfort or to stop his memories from that day from squeaking through, he reached down and lifted her legs. Balanced them on his lap and propped her calves up on his knees. She didn't squirm or shift. She settled in, leaning her body against his.

He rested his hand on her legs. Not really holding

them there, more like hoping she'd find the gesture soothing. That wouldn't ease his guilt but it might ease her suffering. "Tell me."

"I don't even know you." But she sounded resigned not angry.

"I'm thinking that might make it easier." He gave in to the urge to really touch her then. His fingers slipped through her hair and skimmed her cool cheek.

It took another full minute before she spoke. In the silence, he used his foot to send the swing into a gentle back and forth. Ignored the cold slicing through him.

"She was my baby sister. This beautiful, amazing, sweet person with an air of innocence. My parents coddled her, in general, then went into hyperspeed after what happened with me. The behavior stuck Tabitha in this odd state of arrested social development."

That was the part people whispered about, but no one seemed to know the extent of her issues. Now he had an idea. "Was she afraid of people?"

"That's just it, no. But they had to be here, on her turf. She got nervous in crowds and hated gossip. Her way of dealing was to hide from it. She craved this insular life on the island, attached to her laptop doing true crime research."

He'd never heard that fact before. "Wait, what kind of—"

"Losing her . . ." Gabby's face crumpled but she quickly got it under control before any tears fell. "At first I felt this screaming pain. It echoed in my head all the time, dragged me down, swamped me in migraines and made it impossible to get out of bed." She shook her head. "Now I don't feel anything. Literally, there is nothing left inside. It's this blank space. Dark and thick and suffocating in its stillness."

He'd never battled depression but he'd fought off nothingness. Years ago, watching his mother go and listening to his father's rampage. His loss didn't compare to Gabby's. He actually had no idea how she managed at all. He could barely handle what he'd seen that day on the island and he'd been emotionally detached. But she lived it, every second of it, alone.

He had Wren and the other guys. Those few friends scattered here and there. She had this trail behind her and in front of her, and neither seemed to lead anywhere.

"You need time." It was an empty platitude, but Harris thought it held a ring of truth. Time didn't heal but distance did make some things tolerable. Maybe that was as good as it got for some people.

"To what?"

It was a damn good question. One he didn't really know how to answer, but he tried anyway. "Deal with it? Grieve? Figure out how to move forward even though your brain screams for you to stop? I'm not even sure, but it seems to me not that many months have passed. What little time you've had has been bound up with accusations and fighting your uncle and the press."

She balanced her head against the back of the swing. "Why can I talk with you about this when I can't talk to my friends . . . the few I have left?"

"We're not trying to impress each other or look the best we can." Which was weird. He was wildly attracted to her, felt this odd sense of protectiveness whenever he saw her. At least one of those usually led him to turn on the charm. It was second nature to him. But with her, he wanted to throw off the costume and just be. "I'm guessing you don't care what I think of you."

"It's part of the numbness. I no longer see the stares or hear the whispers. I walk through life and everything around me blends into white noise." She skimmed the back of her hand down his arm.

"Sounds like a solid mental health self-defense strategy."

Her hand dropped to the bench between them. "I assume most people think I'm a killer."

Almost everyone he knew fell into that category. People who'd never met her and relied only on news reports. People who didn't hear her scream that night months ago. "I don't."

She stared at him, unblinking. "You don't believe the hype?"

He toyed with underplaying his response. But this close he could smell the scent of flowers in her hair and on her skin. Hear the small tremor in her voice as she talked about who she was now and the beloved sister she'd lost.

The truth. She deserved the truth, at least about this. "I don't think someone who is this paralyzed with pain could be a killer."

This time when she lowered her head she rested it

on his shoulder. "My uncle thinks I'm struggling with guilt."

"Your uncle's kind of an ass."

"Oh, he's definitely that. Always was."

"You didn't get along with him before?" This part intrigued Harris. He'd been raised in a modest house with very little in the way of possessions. His parents fought and when the police came for his mother the world exploded.

Even though he pretended to run in their circles and had amassed a fortune of his own, Harris really had no idea how rich people were supposed to act. His friends had accumulated wealth but none of them acted like it, outside of living in alarm-controlled houses.

"He thought Tabitha and I were spoiled. He and his wife couldn't have kids, so he spent a lot of time telling my parents how to raise us." She sighed. "He was the elder brother, so my dad listened. Listened then ignored."

"Sounds like a good call." Harris planned to ignore most of what Stephen said, too.

"Then the kidnapping happened and my uncle never looked back. He tagged me as a threat to the family. He watched me as if he was waiting for me to rip the family apart."

Questions bombarded Harris. That piece of the puzzle didn't fit with the woman in front of him now. Faking her own kidnapping for cash? It was so mercenary. So desperate when nothing about the way she lived from the small studio apartment to the entry-level job suggested she insisted on an entitlement to a lush lifestyle.

He went with the safest question. "Wasn't that a decade ago?"

"More than that. I was nineteen. I'm thirty now."

That was it. She didn't offer up another fact. Didn't provide any glimpse into what happened then or why.

He weighed his options and decided knowing more about what really happened back then could wait. Building the bond with her about Tabitha's death and her uncle's revenge was the better call. "The man can hold a grudge."

"Don't make me into a martyr, Harris. My uncle was right about some of it. I wasn't the perfect child."

"Something else we have in common." Since she sounded so beaten down, he tried for a little humor. "Clearly we should sleep together."

The comment sat there. Neither of them laughed. The idea suddenly didn't strike him as funny.

She slowly lifted her head. "I think you're skipping a few steps in getting to know each other."

She didn't say no.

Sweet Jesus, he needed her to say no.

"You in the bed. Me on the floor." He forced out the last part. "No touching."

She sat up and the color returned to her cheeks. Not a blush, but the deathly paleness disappeared. "You don't mix business with pleasure?"

Every word she said tempted him. That high road

was starting to get pretty damn steep. No wonder he usually didn't take it.

"Are you familiar with the concept of mixed messages?" he asked.

"Sorry." She smiled as she shook her head. "I'm tired and emotionally wrung out."

There, now she'd said the phrase guaranteed to stop any action tonight. He might act like an ass sometimes but he was not taking advantage of her. Not like this.

He shifted her legs off his lap and stood up. With his hand extended down to her, he closed this out for the night. "Then let's go to bed."

Her gaze shifted from his hand to his face. It traveled to his mouth and hesitated there before she nodded and took his hand. "You wore me down."

"That's what I like to hear."

She slipped her fingers through his and stood up next to him. "Be warned. If you try to crawl in with me, I'll kick you."

"You'd be surprised how often I hear that."

"That's sort of the point, Harris." She squeezed his fingers before letting go of his hand. "I bet you never do, so hear it now."

ALL THE TOUCHING earlier made her jumpy. An hour had passed since she climbed into the bed at the guesthouse—alone. She'd stared at the ceiling for almost every minute of that time.

The guesthouse consisted of a large open space for

the living room and kitchen and separate rooms for
the bedroom and bathroom. She took the bed without arguing and settled in, wearing sweatpants and a
long-sleeve T-shirt under the covers. Her sweater hung
on the back of the chair by the bed. She looked at it,
debating if this was the right time to put it on and step
outside.

The investigator would arrive tomorrow but Harris
was right there. Not even a door separated them. She'd
left that open and could see his head on the pillow on
the floor. He hadn't moved for a half hour. Even now
the sound of his deep breathing floated through the
house. Not snoring. No, this was an oddly comforting
in and out. Almost like white noise.

Careful not to bang the headboard against the wall
or step on the wrong loose floorboard, she shifted and
put her feet on the thick area rug. Pointing her toe, she
stretched out, snagged her sneaker from a few feet
away and dragged it closer. Without taking her gaze off
Harris, she slipped on her shoes, one after the other.

The mattress coils creaked as she grabbed for her
sweater. A few tugs and it was on. Her outfit wouldn't
protect her against the cool night air, but if she was
very quick—did a fast in and out—she might be able
to resolve at least this one task she came to the island
to do.

Up on tiptoes, she crept through the bedroom to
the patio doors. The move put her out of the sight line
from the living room area. Before she pressed on the
handle, she slipped into the bathroom and turned on

the light. Came back out but left the light on. In terms of subterfuge it wasn't perfect but at least seeing the light on might make Harris think she was in there, if he woke up too early.

She opened the outside door just far enough to sneak out. The wind smacked into her the second she stepped onto the patio. She fought to catch her breath and pushed through.

Her uncle had taken the shovel she'd brought to the island. As if she couldn't grab another one. A quick visit with Kramer today provided the solution. The man had a tool for every project and a few she'd never seen before.

She turned the corner of the guesthouse and dropped down to balance on the balls of her feet. Digging through the bushes, she spotted Kramer's rusty shovel just where she dropped it earlier. Only the constant worry of being seen this afternoon prolonged this errand. Now she had the quiet and the shovel. She'd hit the switch that turned off the motion sensor lights out here, which let her move around in the dark, hopefully unnoticed.

A glance back at the guesthouse confirmed that everything remained quiet there. No lights. No movements. No Harris.

Moving faster now, she walked over to the rock retaining wall that separated this part of the property from the small hill that led up to the gazebo then over to the boathouse. Plants and flowers lined the area. Bursts of purple and white dotted the carpet of green.

She didn't need to dig it all up, didn't even have to disturb the plants. The middle section of the retaining wall was her target. Slipping in between the branches of the low-lying bushes, she stepped around the flowers and slid her palm over the uneven rock wall.

She'd skipped the flashlight, which now seemed like a terrible idea. Straining to see by the faint nightlight from the boathouse in the distance, she squinted and felt her way around, searching for loose grout.

She was half sitting in the bush now with one knee in the dirt. She clawed against the stone and jammed the edge of the shovel into one of the cracks. The clunking sounded so loud in her ears, but she knew it barely amounted to scraping.

When the wall didn't give under the pressure, she pushed harder. Whacked the stone as hard as she could. A chunk of stone plopped into the dirt. She slipped her fingers into the opening. This was the space she remembered, a malformed square of about three-by-three inches.

She patted her hand on the cold stone. Touched every surface. When she didn't feel anything, she figured she needed to go deeper into the stone. She shoved the sharp end of the shovel in the hole and moved it around. Still nothing.

She fell back on her butt. The cold ground seeped through her thin sweats but she didn't move. She couldn't feel anything.

The papers were gone. The map. Everything.

Explanations whirled in her mind. Maybe she was at

the wrong place. Maybe someone else found them . . . but why? If the investigators had found something, she'd know by now. There was no reason for anyone to dig in a random spot behind a bush on an isolated island.

Thoughts tumbled through her until she hit on the most obvious one—someone had the documents she'd tried so hard to hide.

She scrambled to her knees. The gagging started a second later. She fought it back. Inhaled deeply as she tried to trick her body into calming down.

She didn't know how long she stayed like that. The shivering snapped her out of her lethargy. The cold had soaked into her, from the air and the ground.

Forcing her muscles to work, she pushed up. She stood there, half swaying as her brain misfired. She needed to come up with a next step, a new place to search, but nothing came to her. Strategy, plans . . . She'd gone completely blank.

Somehow she stumbled back to the patio and stepped inside the guesthouse again. Stripping as she walked across the bedroom, she fell across the bed, turning her head just in time so she could stare at the pale gray wall. Her focus blurred but her heart rate refused to slow down. The beat pounded in her chest.

She had no idea what to do next.

HARRIS OPENED HIS eyes the second he heard the near soundless thump of the door closing behind Gabby twenty minutes ago. He'd been sneaking in and out of houses long enough to recognize the signs. He could analyze every noise without opening his eyes.

Watching her move around out there hadn't provided any insight. She dug and grew more frantic as her hands moved faster in the dirt and rocks. Finally, she'd slumped over. At one point he thought she'd throw up, but she pulled herself together.

Now she lay on the bed fifteen feet away. Her heavy breaths—almost pants—filled the guesthouse. He doubted she even knew she'd made a sound. But all that scrambling . . . He had no idea what that was about. She'd clearly expected to find something out there and didn't.

For the first time since he heard her cries fourteen months ago, he doubted her. Her anxiety hadn't died down. It nearly choked the air out of the room. But this woman carried deep secrets.

He lifted his head and stared into the dark bedroom. His eyes had adjusted to the lack of light while he slunk around the house spying on her wanderings outside. Even with his back plastered against the wall, he'd been able to peek out the window and follow her movements. She was still now. She hadn't moved since she'd flopped down.

He should drift off to sleep and worry about this tomorrow. She thought she'd pulled off her big covert mission. It was tempting to let her believe that.

That was the right answer . . . "Gabby?"

He saw her body stiffen. She didn't lift her head or make a sound.

He said the only words in his mind. "You don't need to hide from me."

Almost two minutes passed without a response. He lay back down and put a hand underneath his pillow. Regret punched into him. He should have shut up and kept up the ruse that she'd conned him. He'd pushed this one too far.

Just as he was drifting off five minutes later, he heard her voice.

"It's not what you think," she said in a voice barely above a whisper.

He opened his eyes but stayed still. "Okay."

"I didn't kill my sister."

"I know." He was absolutely certain of that.

"Remember that feeling." She let out a loud sigh. "Because the evidence is going to say I did."

CHAPTER 6

Gabby didn't say anything to him the next morning. She was showered, dressed, up and out before he even got off the floor. The woman could move when she had a goal. The goal clearly being to avoid him.

Since she didn't want to go into the main house and they were stuck on an island, he doubted she'd get far. But he walked over to the boathouse just in case. The sound of a motor got him moving. He heard a boat pull up to the dock. While he didn't think she'd run, he wasn't taking the chance.

Cool, overcast weather had moved in. Gray clouds filled the sky and the air carried a touch of dampness. He zipped up his sweater and walked faster.

The boat beat him there. Two men moved around on board. One faced away from him, sitting and shifting and collecting what looked like a bag under his seat. This had to be the mysterious investigator.

Harris wasn't exactly looking forward to putting his body between Gabby and some by-the-book guy Stephen hired, even if Wren had interfered in some way. But that was what Harris was there for. Gather intel and keep Gabby out of the investigator's sight. An unspoken—unknown to her—debt weighed heavily between them and Harris vowed to repay it.

"Hello!" The other guy, the one driving the boat, jumped off and secured the lines.

Harris recognized him from the photos Wren provided in his briefing file. Craig Pak. He was in his midtwenties and very sharp. First-generation with Korean parents. A hard worker who left an entry-level lobbyist position to start his own business. He'd taken over a failed boating service and in just two years started making decent money ferrying tourists and homeowners around the area and to the private islands off the coast. Sometimes he led tours, so both locals and tourists knew him.

The guy found a niche and filled it. He already was considered an expert and reliable. Wren also cited Craig as a potential good source of information because he traveled back and forth to the island with supplies and knew Tabitha. She was twenty-two when she died and Craig was only two years older.

Harris was about to break into small talk when the boat's passenger stood up and turned around. One look and Harris knew he was in deep shit. Wren's words came back to him. Something about having arranged for Harris to have help. Knowing Wren's twisted sense of humor, *this* was the help.

Damon Knox. One of the Quint Five. A friend from way back and a total smart-ass. He pretended to be an investigator and worked back channels. He stepped in when Wren needed assistance or someone to play a role.

Damon was good at pretending to be someone he wasn't. And now he was here, on Tabitha Island, pretending to be Stephen's hired hack.

Harris waited until Damon and Craig exchanged some boring chitchat and talked about the weather. After a quick handshake between Craig and Harris, Craig headed off in the direction of Kramer's cottage.

Once out of earshot, Harris glared at Damon. "You've got to be fucking kidding me."

Damon slapped Harris on the shoulder then handed him a duffle bag. "And good morning to you, too, Harris."

Harris dropped the bag by his feet. He had no intention of playing Damon's assistant for the next few days.

"What are you . . ." Harris didn't bother to finish the question. They both knew the answer. "Wren sent you."

Damon winked. "Consider me your savior."

"Not really a word I'd use."

Damon never did anything easy. He tended to pull things apart just to see if he could put them back together again. Not computers or phones—people's lives. Damon liked to read people. Assess, compile intel and make educated guesses. He'd be a star in FBI forensics if he worked there, but his background prevented that type of work. The only way he'd qualify for a security clearance was if Wren faked Damon's background, which he likely did to convince Stephen to hire Damon.

Harris couldn't imagine all the hoop-jumping and loop-closing Wren had maneuvered through to make this—Damon here on the island and in charge—happen. The man really was damn good at fixing things.

"I'm pretty sure my role here has something to do with saving humanity and restoring your tainted dignity." Damon shrugged. "You know. The usual."

"I see your ego is healthy, as always." Harris always admired that about Damon. To most of the world he seemed understated. The kind of man who stood back and watched, waiting for the right time to move in. Only the few who knew him got to see the real man behind the quiet exterior. "And that's quite a job description."

"Actually, Wren said my job is to babysit you—"

"No."

"—and make sure you don't steal anything. When are you going to get over that nasty little habit?"

"It's my job." They could joke, but Harris was not in the mood to be handled. He knew he'd created this problem by trying to liberate the Max Beckmann painting that hung over the fireplace in the main house. The same one looted from a museum in Germany and passed around to everyone but the heirs of the rightful Jewish owners who'd perished, leaving the provenance difficult to prove.

That was what had brought Harris to the island more than a year ago. The family had tried to recover the painting through legal channels. They'd been ignored, spun around and covered with paperwork and demands for more evidence of ownership by government agencies and committees in Germany. Harris had seen it before. He understood being careful, but this type of restitution was long overdue . . . so he leveled the playing field.

This time being there meant Gabby might have a chance of escaping the murder charges that seemed somewhat inevitable. She had a witness and he'd step up if needed. Harris had no intention of going to prison, but he wouldn't let her serve one second either. How he was going to accomplish that balancing act depended, at least in part, on the good friend standing in front of him.

"I thought you had a real job these days." Damon picked up his bag and slung the strap over his shoulder. "Something about insurance."

Leave it to Damon to come up with the dullest career description ever. "I get bored."

"The last time you got bored you walked in on a murder and Wren had to send a boat and a cleanup crew to save your sorry ass."

That explanation shortcut the waiting and hiding. "That's not how I'd describe it."

Helicopters had descended and police combed the waters near Tabitha Island. One of those police boats had scooped him up off the neighboring island— either a fake one or one manned by officers Wren paid off, Harris never asked. But all the mental backtracking he had to do to make sure his equipment had been picked up and all traces of his presence erased had taken some time back then.

Then there was the problem of Tabitha's computer, the one Harris hacked to spy on her. When Wren stepped in to fix a situation he didn't half-ass it. He also didn't leave a trail. To cover Harris's tracks, Wren had spiked the laptop with a virus. More than one, actually. The move protected Harris but potentially buried evidence that could lead to the real killer.

"That's how I heard it." Damon snorted. "Though, when I retell it to the rest of the guys I add a part about you curling into a ball and crying."

"Thanks for that."

Damon's finger tightened around the bag's strap. "I'm an investigator."

"You're actually not." It was a sore subject, but Harris felt obliged to point out the facts. Damon did conduct investigations, but that was different from actually being an investigator.

Damon talked right over him. "It makes sense Wren called me in."

"His fixer skills are working overtime."

Damon scanned the area before his gaze settled on Harris again. "He wants this solved and both you and Gabby cleared."

"Not to point out the obvious, but no one has been able to do that for fourteen months." Stephen had poured a lot of money into getting the answer he wanted and it hadn't worked. Because of the players on the ground, Harris knew this time wouldn't work either, but the goal was to convince him not to try again. To finally free Gabby.

"Lucky for you I'm good at what I do," Damon said.

"And so modest."

Damon started walking. He headed straight for the main house. "The uncle thinks you're working for me. Undercover."

They'd only gone a few steps before Harris stopped them again. "What are you talking about?"

"You're supposed to be here doing appraisals, right? Even the uncle questioned that cover story. What he didn't doubt was my cover story about you being my assistant." Damon whistled. "Man, he hates his niece."

"No kidding."

"The good news is that I get to order you around."

Harris could see it now. Damon would turn that into a sport. "Go fuck yourself."

"I missed you, too."

Harris couldn't ignore those words. He and Damon had joined the group at about the same time. He was thirty-four and Damon only a few years older. For more than a decade they'd been close friends. Lived together for part of that time. Traveled throughout Europe with Damon playing the role of conscience. The guy was antitheft, which made their relationship rocky at times.

When Harris shut down and closed himself off after Tabitha's murder, he pushed Damon away, too.

Harris had been trying to figure out how to repair that damage. Leave it to Wren to shortcut the process.

"I am sorry about going radio silent." That didn't cover it, but it cost Harris something to even say that much. He wasn't a man accustomed to apologizing or accepting blame.

"You mean for skipping town? For not taking my calls? For being a complete dick?"

"All of it." Harris blew out a long breath as he searched for a way to explain it. Gabby was right. The words weren't big enough. They didn't telegraph the shock and despair of watching someone die right in front of him. "I needed to leave after what happened here. Go away and think things through."

"So, you headed off to London and stole a bunch of stuff." But Damon didn't sound angry. The comment didn't carry the heat of an accusation.

"I liberated some items, yes." When Damon started to talk, Harris held up a hand. "For my legitimate job. There's paperwork and everything. Hell, I even worked with Interpol, who is convinced art theft is being used to fund the international drug trade."

"Not your thefts, of course."

Harris ignored the sarcasm. "Drug stuff is an actual crime. I'm not interested in that."

Damon smiled then. "Never change, Harris."

"I don't plan to."

They started walking again. A lawn mower whirred to life in the distance. Harris couldn't see it but he heard the steady hum of the motor. Looking around, he searched for Gabby. He still didn't know how she'd react to seeing him after last night . . . and he wasn't quite ready to tell Damon about it.

"What am I working with here?" Damon asked.

"A falsely accused woman."

He snorted. "Maybe."

Harris was getting a little tired of defending her. He couldn't imagine how frustrating it must be for her to tell the same story over and over and have no one believe her. "I was here that afternoon, Damon. She wasn't in the house."

"She could have killed her sister then snuck out." Damon talked with his hands. "Maybe she came back later and made it look like she was discovering the body for the first time in case anyone was watching."

He might not be an investigator but he sure sounded like one. "What goes on in your head?"

"It's not that strange. People do shit like that all the time. It's actually kind of clever. Sometimes it throws the scent off."

That sounded like something Wren would say. Since Harris didn't want that advice from either of them, he threw in a few more facts. "Maybe but you didn't hear her when she found Tabitha. You can't fake that sound."

"You, the caretaker guy Kramer, and Gabby were on the island when Tabitha was killed." Damon counted the number out on his fingers. "That makes the circle of suspects pretty small."

"I saw both Gabby and Kramer come running *after*

I found the body. Neither of them were in the house."

Harris stopped and grabbed Damon's arm. "No, look. Don't shake your head at me. There has to be another explanation. Someone who was paid and got out before I saw them. Someone who took a boat or swam, like I did. We need to think outside the circle you named."

"It's amazing how often the answer is the most simple one."

Oh, good. Cryptic bullshit. "Meaning?"

"You're suggesting that someone wanted to kill a recluse living on an island, one without an enemy in the world, as far as I can tell. Wanted this murder to happen so badly that he or she came up with this convoluted boat or swimming plan. All while ignoring the fact there were other people on the island at the time."

It sounded ridiculous when he spelled it out like that. "It could happen."

Damon rolled his eyes. "There is one thing you're missing. One more person."

"Who?"

"Wren did some checking. When Gabby's parents died the majority of their estate passed to people who worked for them and to charities. Gabby got enough to pay off her college loans. That's it. Tabitha received the remaining bulk in a substantial trust, including this island."

Damon was winding up to something. Harris could feel it. "And with her gone?"

"Gabby and Uncle Stephen share the trust proceeds,

with the uncle receiving twice the amount that Gabby does."

A piece of Tabitha's estate likely was more money than most people could comprehend. Harris knew the island property alone was worth more than twelve million. Harris could guess at the number for everything, every last asset and bank account, but didn't want to.

He needed to stay focused, especially because he had a new problem. A motive for Gabby to kill. If none of the money went to her it was hard to see a reason for her to kill her sister. But money was a huge motive for a lot of people. It would not be a hard sell to a judge, jury or the public. "So much for the theory that she'd been disinherited."

"Apparently she was until right before her parents' plane crash three years ago, which is why some people suspect her in that, too."

Damn. The evidence did pile up against her without much effort. Even he had to admit that.

But that was about things that *might* have happened. The woman he'd spent time with, listened to as she described her sister as sweet, Harris still couldn't see as a cold-blooded murderer.

He shook his head. "She didn't do it. I'm not buying it."

"Huh." Damon made a strange clicking sound with his tongue. "That was quick."

Harris knew he shouldn't ask . . . was desperate not to ask . . . "What?"

"How you stopped thinking with your brain and started thinking with your dick. You've known her, what . . ." Damon closed an eye as if he were pretending to think of the right answer and didn't know it right off the top of his head. "Twenty-four hours?"

"What the fuck is wrong with you?"

"Put away the fake outrage." Damon leaned in closer and dropped his voice to a whisper. "I've seen photos of her."

Her face. Yeah, that was one thing Harris didn't want to think about. That and her ass . . . those legs. "I'm not the type to get conned by a pretty face."

"Because you're usually the one leading the con?"

"Actually, yes."

Damon nodded. "Then it's good I'm here."

"If you say so."

"For the record, I'm going to start walking again because it seems to be taking two years for us to reach this house. Stop me one more time and I punch you." Then Damon took off at his usual brisk pace. "While you're busy studying her—or at least sleeping in the same house with her—"

"How did you know that?" A knocking started in the back of Harris's head.

"—I'll watch out for you."

For a second Harris wondered if Wren or Stephen—or both—planted listening devices on the island. If so, they might soon get an earful because Harris didn't plan to sleep on the floor for too many more nights.

Yeah, it was stupid and he should stay away from Gabby. Hell, he should back off just to keep from giving Damon a chance to say *I told you so*, but Harris didn't see that happening. When he saw her, all he could think about was what those long legs might feel like wrapped around his waist.

Only her quiet mourning stopped him. That and the guilty prickling in the back of his mind that demanded he leave her alone. He'd done enough damage and was here to repair that, if possible. Trying anything else, lying to her any more than necessary, would drop right into asshole territory.

She might be strong and independent and fully in control of what she wanted in the bedroom—hell, he hoped all of that was true—but she was also broken with grief. She talked about being numb and empty but that was not the woman he saw. If anything, her pain overflowed and washed all over him.

"She didn't do it." Harris repeated the refrain because right then he needed to say it.

Damon made a humming noise. "Let's see if you can keep that charming level of wide-eyed optimism as the evidence rolls in against her."

CHAPTER 7

She'd managed to avoid him all day. Gabby knew there likely was a better, smarter way to play this situation. She didn't have the energy to figure one out.

The map was missing. The same one that led the kidnappers to her parents' home eleven years ago. The drawing of the inside of the house, plus all the notes. She'd buried the packet here, on the property her family used only for vacations and parties. Not their main residence. Not somewhere she'd see the hiding place every day and replay every minute of those lost days.

Back then she'd dug out the open space in the wall. She knew about it. Tabitha knew. Now Tabitha was dead.

There was a connection there, but Gabby couldn't see it. Not other than the obvious one, which was her, but she didn't kill her sister. Someone else dug up the condemning information. It hadn't appeared and her uncle wasn't waving it around. She had no idea what that meant.

Panic raced through her. It fueled every step she took around the wildflower garden her mother had started the year before she died. Sweet peas had started their spring bloom. She could make out bright pink buds and see vines weave through the latticework of the pergola at the back of the garden.

Needing to do something, she squatted down and started ripping out the weeds. There weren't many. She guessed Kramer hadn't gotten to this garden or there wouldn't be any.

The metal closing mechanism on the garden gate rattled off to her right side. She looked up to see Harris step inside the fenced-in area. He stood there among the flowers, wearing jeans and a V-neck sweater with a white T-shirt underneath it. She had no idea how he could make such a simple outfit look so tempting. It took all her restraint not to tear it off him.

Blame the extra adrenaline or the stress, but she kept thinking about him. Not as an appraiser or as someone in league with her uncle. No, when it came to Harris she saw a man. A willing, charming, sexy man. And for once, she wanted to take something for herself.

Her gaze traveled from his beat-up sneakers, up those long legs to his face. One of his eyebrows lifted as he watched her conduct the visual tour. She ignored it. If he could gawk, so could she.

He had to be accustomed to people looking at him. The perfect posture, the confidence that rolled off him . . . that face. No wonder her common sense sputtered out when she saw him.

None of that explained why she kept opening her mouth and dumping too personal information on him, yammering on about things she never talked about. He brought that out in her. This need to confide, to share the load.

One reason for her heightened interest level seemed obvious to her. Unlike so many people who had strolled through her life, he actually listened. At least he acted like he did. He watched her with a marked intensity as she talked. Asked questions. Replayed bits and pieces of earlier talks. That level of connectedness was damn sexy.

Problem was she couldn't trust him as far as she could dropkick him, and she sure had been tempted to kick him once or twice since they'd met.

He stood over her now, blocking the sun and casting a shadow over his face. "Are we going to talk about it?"

With someone else, at any other time, she might pretend ignorance, but she knew what he was talking about. It was hard not to since he'd caught her sneaking around last night and then confronted her about it. "Nope."

He put his hands on his hips. "You have to help me here. Is that what mature people do? Ignore issues?"

Oh, really? "Mature people don't pretend to be asleep."

"Innocent people don't sneak around in the dark," he shot back.

She shielded her eyes with her hand and took a long look at him. "That didn't take long."

"What?"

"For you to flip sides." She stood up, dropping the forgotten weeds and wiping her dirty palms on her pants. "Uncle Stephen will be pleased."

They stood only a few inches apart now. Tension pulsed between them. She could have sworn she saw it blow back and forth with the breeze. But he didn't move. Didn't say a thing, didn't need to because the questioning frown he threw her way said enough.

She was about to walk away, find somewhere else to burn off the extra energy buzzing through her. He dropped his hands to his sides and continued to stare.

Yeah, that's enough of that. She'd reached her end with people watching her every move. She didn't need him, the guy who haunted her dreams last night, to be a part of that list.

She moved to pivot around him when he spoke up. "I believe you."

"Sure you do." But she stopped. Froze there with her shoulder even with his, right at the second before their bodies would have passed each other.

"Tell me the truth so I can help you."

Which truth? She didn't even know which lie he was talking about. They'd piled up until she could barely see over the top of them.

"I needed a little space." She took a few steps and reached out for the latch to the gate.

"You dug a stone out of the wall." His deep voice didn't carry any accusation. He said the words the same way he might recite the weather report, with little enthusiasm.

Her eyes slammed shut as a shiver of fear moved through her. Anxiety washed through every muscle. She kept her back to him. "You were watching me?"

"If you were in my place would you have looked?"

She had to give him points for that. "Of course."

"Then why all the huffing and puffing?"

She turned around and faced him again. "First, I do not huff."

"Debatable."

"Second . . ." She saw a movement out of the corner of her eye. Two figures standing just off the path, right under the clump of oak trees. "Who is that?"

Harris kept his gaze on her. "Don't change the subject."

"I'm serious." She wrapped her fingers around Harris's upper arm and turned him. "There with Kramer."

The guy towered over Kramer. If Harris was six-one, this guy looked to be a few inches taller than that. And lanky. He had blondish-brown hair and wore dark sunglasses. He gave off a too-cool-to-be-here vibe as he nodded in response to whatever Kramer was telling him.

"Ah, yes." Harris nodded. "That's the investigator."

"He's here?" She heard a thunking sound and was pretty sure it came from inside her brain.

This is happening. A new investigator. A new wave of law enforcement. More questions and allegations. Rounds of denials and that look . . . This man inevitably would wear the same look they all got. She could pinpoint to the second the moment in the conversation where every person looking into her sister's death—all of them men—had stopped believing her. Some came in believing every rumor about her. Others took days of reading files.

She dreaded the minute when that doubt would move into Harris's eyes.

"He arrived about an hour ago," Harris said.

She turned on him. "Are you working for him, which would mean working for my uncle?"

"Gabby, listen to me." Harris put his hands on her upper arms and leaned down until they stood face-to-face. "Your uncle did not hire me. I have nothing to do with him. After ten minutes with the guy I decided he was a dick with an endgame. His sole focus is to hurt you."

Her breath hiccupped in her chest. "Would him being a jerk stop you from working with him?"

"No, because I like to eat. But the reality is still the same. I'm not working for him."

Her shoulders fell as the tension ran out of her body. "Well, that's honest."

Harris nodded. "Speaking of which . . ."

"You expect me to, what, just tell you all my secrets after knowing you for less than two full days?" Did he really not understand how much he was asking? She hadn't told anyone about the kidnapping or the map. It was a secret she'd shared only with Tabitha.

"You need to start trusting someone."

She rested her palms against his chest, fought the urge to run her hands all over him. "Do I?"

"How is that lone-wolf thing working out for you?"

She could feel the vibrations against her fingertips as he spoke. His hands cradled her elbows in a gentle caress. That thumb rubbed back and forth over her in a light touch she found mesmerizing.

It took her a second to find her voice. When she did, it didn't rise above a whisper. "Tonight."

His eyes narrowed. "What?"

"You tell me something true and I'll tell you."

The corner of his mouth kicked up in a smile. "You'll tell me what?"

The guy was not dumb. She appreciated that. "Now who has the trust issues?"

"Good morning."

A deep male voice boomed through the solitude and both Harris and Gabby dropped their arms. Here she was, adult and independent and very consenting, and this new guy walking in made her feel like the time her father caught her and Roy Amicker making out in the back of a car. They hadn't been old enough to drive, but they were old enough to get in.

The unwanted guest looked from Harris to Gabby. "Actually, I think we've officially slipped into afternoon."

A slick grin. Those were the first words that passed through her mind. This guy wore the kind of empty smile that said *I'm comfortable judging you.* And she knew that was exactly what he was doing. This look up and down her body may have been quick, but she caught it. Not sexual but appreciative and assessing.

She was not in the mood for one more man on this small island. "You're my uncle's lackey."

His smile looked genuine and amused now. He pointed behind him, back toward the tree. "Maybe I should go out and try to come in again because something about this welcome went wrong."

She felt Harris's hand brush against her back. A fleeting touch, but she got the message. *Calm down*.

"Sorry. Knee-jerk reaction." She tried to wave away the attitude before holding out her hand. "I'm Gabby Wright."

"Damon Knox." He nodded as he took her hand in both of his in a warm shake. "Before you ask the question, I think it sounds like a made-up soap opera name, too."

Okay, there was a charm to him. She made sure to note that and keep it in mind because she couldn't afford to get sucked into the investigator's informal back-and-forth style. "Understood. The only reason my sister never shortened her name is because we would have been known as Gabby and Tabby, which was just too much."

"Your uncle hired me," Damon said, in a voice that sounded more serious now. "I insisted on being paid through the estate, on an order from the court, to remain as neutral as possible."

"But you think I did it." She figured they may as well get that out in the open. Harris insisted he believed her. This guy would never say that.

"I think you're the leading suspect, but that's because I can read. The police think you're the leading suspect." Damon shrugged. "It's all over the file."

"You could sugarcoat it," Harris mumbled under his breath.

Damon looked from Harris then back to her. "Do you want me to, Ms. Wright?"

"Call me Gabby. The Ms. Wright thing has been an ongoing problem for years. I've heard every joke."

Damon frowned. "I don't get it."

"Ms. Wright, as in *right*." Harris made the connection then held out his hands. He didn't say *duh* but it was right there.

Damon shook his head this time. "You repeating the same word doesn't help."

Needing to move on, Gabby took over. "Did you want to question me today?"

"I wanted to know if your sister kept a diary."

The question hung in the air for a second. It wasn't the one she expected from him. She remembered the police asking and officers looking for one, but it struck her as an odd place for Damon to start the questioning. "What?"

"It's kind of an easy question."

"Sorry. I was expecting . . ." It didn't really help her case to start listing off the accusations against her, so she dropped it. "Never mind."

Damon took off his glasses and played with the arm as if he was trying to bend it into another position. He peeked over at Harris. "Did you need something?"

"I'm keeping her company."

Damon's smile came back. "Lucky her."

She didn't know what was happening, but she sensed she might need to duck if the testosterone kept flying. As interesting as a debate between those two might be, she wasn't in the mood to play den mother. "Tabitha wasn't really a diary person. Not a paper one anyway. Not that I remember. She did a lot on her laptop and she loved to read."

"Right, but there wasn't a laptop in the house when the police got here," Damon said, as if he had the entire police file, all however many boxes of it memorized.

Harris shifted. "What?"

Damon didn't even spare Harris a glance as he answered. "It's missing."

That piece never made sense to her. Tabitha didn't keep financial information on the thing. She had professionals who handled her trust. So why would the killer take the computer? "I know, and it's not possible. She lived on that thing."

"You said something about true crime to me the other day?" Harris asked.

There it was. An example of how he remembered a throwaway fact. It impressed her even though she was determined not to be impressed.

She looked at Damon. "That was Tabitha's thing. She was part of this group that informally investigated unsolved true crime cases. They searched for clues and came up with theories." As far as habits went, Gabby thought it was weird, but it fit Tabitha. She liked puzzles, and she really liked the idea of bringing a family peace. "She was really good at it. Read every forensic book there is." That memory stopped Gabby, made it hard for her to catch her breath. "Ironic, isn't it?"

"How so?" Damon asked.

"That someone with that much interest in cases and solving them would become a crime statistic." As soon as the words were out she regretted them. She didn't think of her sister in those terms and she could already see Damon filing the information away for his report.

He kept right on asking questions in a clear, calm tone. "Did she meet in person with this group?"

"Not that I know of. It was online. A pretty big forum, actually, but she also broke off into smaller groups for specific cold cases. Tabitha didn't have that many friends and didn't just invite people over. But she did collect articles. She printed stuff out all the time. All of it should be in the library." She sighed. "Of course, so should the laptop."

"Can you show me where?" Damon stepped back and gestured toward the main house.

"No."

He froze. "Excuse me?"

"I'm not ready to go back in the house yet. Give me a day." God, it had been fourteen months. She had no idea what one more day would do, but she needed to prepare, to wipe her brain clear of the last memory she had of the inside. Tuck the horror away and drown it in darkness.

"Ah, I see." Damon's gaze hesitated on her for a few

extra beats before he glanced at Harris. "Mr. Tate . . . or may I call you Harrison?"

"Harris is fine."

"Why don't you come with me and get started?"

Harris shook his head. "I was going to—"

"It's okay." She rushed to stop whatever Harris planned to say next. That space she said she needed was not a lie. "You go with the investigator. I wanted to say hello to Kramer."

Harris stared at her then nodded. "Then we'll meet up later."

HARRIS FOLLOWED DAMON out of the garden and over to the main house. Harris got as far as the foyer of the big house before he stopped. The hardwood shined and there wasn't one bit of clutter anywhere. The rooms that were visible looked comfortable rather than fancy, but in that paid-a-fortune-for-the-lived-in-look kind of way.

A breeze blew through the two-story opening from a sitting room on one side to a small study on the other. He looked in both directions and saw the windows at the sides of the house were open. White sheers rustled in the wind.

A curving staircase with a railing carved out of mahogany wound to the next floor in front of him. A hall on either side of the grand floating staircase led to the kitchen and dining room. To a downstairs bedroom . . . and to the library. Eventually out to an atrium and an in-house theater.

There was a lot of space to cover but his feet refused to move. All he could do was stand just inside the door. One shift in any direction and the memories came rushing back—the deadly quiet. The smell he couldn't place. The blood.

"You okay?" Damon asked in an uncharacteristically soft voice.

Harris focused and he saw Damon staring at him, the concern clear in his expression. "Not really."

Footsteps echoed on the floor as Damon walked to the base of the staircase and glanced up. When he lowered his head again his expression had changed. He seemed ready to battle. "I need her to move around freely."

It took Harris a second to realize he'd missed part of the conversation or a turn in the topic. "What?"

"You can't follow her around like a lost puppy." Damon exhaled as he crossed his arms in front of him. "I want her to use that shovel her uncle saw her holding, or another one she can find."

Rather than fill in the blanks, Harris ignored the comment. "How are you going to see that when you're standing in here?"

Damon shook his head. He probably winked, too, because he did that a lot, but he wore the sunglasses again, so it wasn't clear what was happening behind his eyes. "It's cute you think Wren didn't set up camera surveillance on the island."

Harris started to question, *but of course he knew.* Wren didn't miss much. "When the hell did he do that?"

"The minute after he saved your ass fourteen months ago. He wanted to see what the police were doing and finding. He mentioned something about needing to 'guide' the investigation." Damon took off the sunglasses and twirled them in his fingers. "Personally, I think he doubted your claims about not leaving fingerprints and wanted to be ready to 'lose' the evidence if needed."

The police had been everywhere that afternoon. The press had descended almost immediately. Most of Wren's energy at that time seemed to be spent on the subterfuge needed to extract Harris. The cleanup, the boat, the people who hid him. But Wren must have been working the crime scene angle as well. That meant he either had people planted in the police department or somewhere in the law enforcement chain.

Harris didn't want to know.

"Tabitha's laptop? Suddenly that seems even more important." Harris hadn't asked for every detail about what was happening in the investigation. He knew Wren followed it closely and that was good enough. But now the pieces mattered. Harris needed to fit them together to form the bigger picture.

"Did you see it that night?" Damon asked.

"I knew about it because I had tapped into it, but I wasn't looking for it when I was here. Honestly, all I remember is the body."

"Well, it's a good thing Wren handled the laptop while you were strolling around on that other island."

Harris could only imagine. "I didn't stroll. To be completely accurate, I swam and nearly drowned."

"It sounds like whatever the two of you did, separately or together, was a waste of time because the killer already had the laptop. Not that it did him or her any good." Damon finally stopped playing with the glasses and shoved them into his shirt pocket. "The laptop being missing is one of those things the police didn't disclose publicly, by the way. I saw it in the confidential report Wren . . . what's the word you like to use? Liberated."

"Shit."

Damon let out a harsh laugh. "I have a feeling we're going to be saying that a lot while we're investigating."

"So, your plan is to watch her to see if her uncle is right." Which would be interesting because Harris definitely planned to keep watching her. He really hoped to be touching her soon. Kissing her.

"There isn't a camera inside the guesthouse, if that's what you're asking."

Jesus. Harris hadn't even thought of that. "Okay."

"Or is there?" Damon smiled. "Fine. There's not, but the holy-shit look on your face was pretty fucking great. It's rare to see you panicked."

"Let's get back to the actual case. Tabitha's true crime fixation thing?" Harris wasn't sure where that fact fit in.

"Yeah, I need to find documents or some background so we can figure out what private chat groups she was in. The main forum Gabby talked about should be easy enough to find. I'm not sure about the rest, but we need to know what she was doing and checking out the people she talked with. She may have found the wrong case or upset someone." Damon sat down on one of the lower steps. "Let's hope the person who took the laptop didn't think to take her actual files."

"I do remember a lot of paper on the floor that night." Harris stared down the long hallway again. "But there must be a million books back there."

"You look a little green."

A tightness banded Harris's chest. Regret, guilt. He had been battling both since he stepped on the island. Shifting artwork around, passing it from one person to its rightful owner, never bothered him. He slept just fine. Watching the life drain out of Tabitha had changed everything.

He dealt in *things*. Moving them around, evening the score, settling old debts. Insurance companies paid out or someone learned a hard lesson in karma. No one paid with their life. "I'm going to get some air."

"Harris, so we're clear. You know I'm going to follow this case wherever it goes." Damon sat with his elbows resting on his knees and an arm dangling between his legs. "I'll protect you because that is always going to happen. Always. But my loyalty doesn't transfer to her."

The words meant something. When Damon pledged his support, he meant it. Harris didn't take it for granted, but he hoped Damon would spare a bit of that loyalty for Gabby. "She's innocent."

Damon shook his head. "No one is."

CHAPTER 8

Gabby didn't go back to the guesthouse or the garden at dinnertime. She wandered over to Kramer's house to say hello. The fact that Kramer and his son, Ted, were putting hamburgers on the grill early tonight was just a bonus.

They asked her to stay and she didn't play coy. She'd been around them, eating with them, for as long as she could remember. Kramer's dedication to first her parents then Tabitha never wavered. He'd worked at the family's home in Bethesda, Maryland, where she grew up. When they died and the house was sold, Tabitha asked him to come to the island with her.

The lives of the Kramers and Wrights were entwined. Her parents paid for Ted to go to the same private high school she did. Back when she had friends, Ted had been one of them. He was a bit younger, but not as young as Tabitha, and spent time with their family.

Kramer was one of the people her parents took care of in their will. There was a trust that paid him and guaranteed him a home and benefits. That was all separate from Tabitha's estate and protected. When the island finally sold, Kramer joked that there was a cottage waiting for him just outside of Annapolis.

Lawyers and financial planners took care of all of it. From the fact Kramer had worn the same baseball cap for two decades, Gabby doubted the man spent much of the money left to him.

They'd eaten a lot of meals together since she arrived back on the island. She didn't have any other family left. Not any members who talked to her. Kramer and Ted never abandoned her. It was the one relationship she'd gone out of her way to keep.

She sat at the picnic table on the small patio and watched Ted fiddle with the grill. He cleaned the grate. Played with the temperature. Clearly grilling was an involved endeavor . . . so she didn't get in the way.

"You hanging in there, Gabby girl?" Kramer groaned as he squatted down on the bench across from her with a beer in his hand.

"Barely." As she'd done for years, she skipped the liquor in favor of the big bowl of chips Ted had put out. Today's variety was sour cream and onion. She'd eat any chip of any type any time. All were welcome in her world. Heck, she could down a family-sized bag on her own.

"This island sure is crowded all of a sudden." Kramer ended the comment by taking a long swig from the bottle.

Ted laughed as he reached over his father's shoulder to grab a handful of chips. "Dad thinks there are too many people wandering around here right now."

She didn't disagree. "He's not wrong."

"Ridiculous." Kramer snorted. "It's all a waste of time."

The endless parade of Stephen's paid employees did get annoying, but there was a bigger issue. One she refused to forget. "If they really can figure out who killed Tabitha, I don't care how many of them come."

"I get that." Kramer reached over and put his calloused hand over hers. "But this group your uncle hired isn't going to figure it out."

She was almost sorry Harris wasn't here to hear that. "What's your theory?"

"Bah." Kramer shook his head. "We've talked about this before."

They had. Many times. She chalked the circular conversations up to grieving, but she wanted to hear his reasoning again. "Humor me."

"Who knows. Probably someone from that online group of hers figured out she had money and came looking for a payday. But they underestimated how tough your little sister was."

Ted sat down next to his father and grabbed another chip. "Someone probably thought she'd be afraid to leave her room. Like she was some kind of shut-in."

Gabby understood the misconceptions about Tabitha and how so many people underestimated or believed the tales that went around about her. That still wasn't the point. "But how did they get on the island?"

"Swim, boat? They are long gone now." Kramer shoved the chip bowl to the side, out of easy reach by either Ted or Gabby. "No one but gawkers come around these days."

She winced. "I'm afraid that's about to get worse."

"We can take it." Ted shot her a smile before he got up to tend the grill again.

"Thanks for coming to help out." She knew Ted had a life. Kramer mentioned Ted had started dating someone seriously, a woman in his office. He had other places to be. He wasn't a longtime Wright family employee. He was a friend . . . one she'd pushed away when she pushed all the other ones away.

He glanced at her over his shoulder. "It's what family does, right?"

"Still, I appreciate it."

"And he likes the paycheck," Kramer said. "The only thing you and Stephen agreed on was paying for extra help to get the property back in shape after all that investigating."

Ted rolled his eyes. "Dad."

"Gabby here is a practical woman. She knows how the world works."

"Speaking of which." Ted set a plate of steaming burgers in the middle of the table. "What's with this art guy? Dad thinks he's working with the investigator."

She tried to concentrate on getting the twist tie on the bag of hamburger buns off. "Probably."

"Then why is he bunking with you?" Kramer asked.

She stopped playing with the bag and looked up at Ted. He smiled at her. Kramer stuck with scowling.

"It's hard to get excited about going back in the main house. Harris told me I could stay with him for now."

"With him? The place is basically yours." Ted's smile dropped. "Gabby, I didn't think . . ."

"It's fine." She ripped a hole in the side of the bag. "I need to get past the block because there is work to do. The investigator thinks there might be a diary tucked away somewhere, which I doubt because police have been in and out of there for months. The paperwork that used to be in there might even be gone."

"Did Tabitha hide things?" Ted asked.

"Reading all that true crime stuff had to make her a little paranoid." That had been the one thing Gabby constantly worried about, that her sister would retreat further and mentally disappear into these horrible crime scenes filled with danger and terrible endings. Gabby never dreamed she should worry about Tabitha actually being attacked. "Truth is, I won't know what she left behind until I'm in there."

"The crime scene guys took care of most of it," Ted said.

Kramer slapped a second piece of cheese on his burger. "Good."

"Enough sad talk. Craig is riding over and picking me up." Ted stole the chips back from his father's side of the table and passed them to her. "We're heading for a night out bar hopping. Want to come?"

It sounded fun . . . except for the drinking, the bar and leaving Harris. Really, none of it appealed to her, but she thought it was sweet for Ted to ask. "No, thanks."

"Craig is a good influence," Kramer said over a mouthful of food.

Ted laughed. "Man, I hope not."

For Craig's and Ted's sakes, she hoped Ted was right. "I always liked you."

IT WAS ALMOST nine by the time she left Kramer's house. Dinner went longer than she expected. Trading stories did that. Time whizzed by and darkness had fallen.

She walked into the guesthouse living room area and just stood there, staring down at the pile of pillows and blankets Harris had used for his makeshift bed last night. They were stacked beside the coffee table now. The room was dark except for the light in the lamp right by his head. He held his cell and she could tell from a quick look at the screen he'd been reading the news.

When he glanced up, her mind jumbled. Outside of the guesthouse, she could keep her thoughts clear and focused. Now inside with Harris, the energy spinning inside her took on a different feel.

She'd expected to be nervous around him. All this subterfuge made a woman tired. But this wasn't about anxiety or exhaustion. The usual internal rush to walk away from confrontation, to go find an easier few hours before bed, didn't hit her.

Jumpy . . . excited. Those sounded more on target with the sensations moving through her.

"Have a good dinner?" Harris asked from his seat on the end of the couch.

She balanced on the armrest right next to him and her heart flipped. She could hear the slight uptick in her breathing. The revving inside her had her shifting around, trying to find a comfortable position on the wobbly perch.

She wanted to blame the way they left things and the expectation that he could not let the conversation between them drop. He'd made it clear he wanted to know about the shovel . . . and her. Not that he'd demanded, but she felt his undercurrent of frustration. She could almost feel the clock ticking down to zero as her time ran out.

"I've known Kramer for almost twenty years," she said as she wrung her hands together.

"And the son?"

That sounded like an interrogation. Interesting coming from the art appraiser guy who hadn't ventured near a painting while he was here. Not so far.

But even that thought didn't stick in her head. She wanted to question him, doubt him, but that wasn't what her body craved. After fourteen months of locking her needs away, of hiding who she was and what she thought and all her dreams, she wanted to unleash. To feel something, anything. With him.

She cleared her throat, trying to hold back the tidal wave of heat crashing into her. She glanced away from him, scanning the room. Seeing the family photos and the stacks of what her father called coffee table books.

The piles of books her mother collected showing beautiful interiors of beach cottages. She'd loved the water. Loved blue and white and overstuffed furniture.

Harris put his hand over hers. "Gabby?"

The simple touch shot through her. Every need flipped into hyperdrive.

"Ted Kramer is two years younger than me. Always been an overachiever. He was a bit of a player a few years back. Always decked out with a touch too much of cologne. The girlfriend is a good influence. He's grown, become more serious and dependable." She figured she'd give him Ted's bio and save Harris the time. "He runs a landscaping company outside of Baltimore."

"Not an ex then."

Good lord. Here she was trying to block out the movie running in her mind of Harris stripping off that sweater and pulling her down on the couch, and he was busy thinking about her with other men. Talk about mixed signals.

"Is that what the clipped questions are about? No, Harris. Never. I put Ted more in the brother category than partner category."

Harris released her fingers and his hand slid back down to the couch cushion next to him. "Does he know that?"

It was the way Harris asked it. With a strange note of darkness in his voice. "I think he'd laugh his butt off at the thought of us being in a relationship. He sees me as an annoying older sister."

"Okay."

"Good." She could actually hear the ticking of the clock on the wall now. She never noticed it being that loud before.

Harris made a face. "Are you ready to pick up the conversation where we left off earlier?"

Man, he was not getting this situation at all. Could he really not read her mood? She was all but sitting in his lap.

For a second she worried she was the only one who felt this head-spinning buzz of attraction. It swamped her. He talked and she watched his mouth. He stared at her and her heartbeat sped to a gallop.

"Actually?" She slid off the armrest. One knee landed on the cushion next to his thigh. She kept going until she straddled his lap, facing him. Not the smoothest move, but it put her where she wanted to be. "No."

He frowned at her. "What are you doing?"

So much for subtlety.

She trailed her fingers up his chest to the base of his neck then over his shoulders. "I want to do something other than talk this evening."

"Gabby?"

Short of feeling him up through his faded jeans she wasn't sure what she needed to do to get her point across. "Harris, please catch up faster than this."

His eyes widened. "Is this a pass?"

Good grief, the man was off tonight. "You can't tell?"

He still hadn't touched her. She was practically grinding on him and he sat perfectly still with his hands resting on the couch, so close to her thighs.

"Gabby, look." He slowly shook his head. "I don't want to take advantage of you."

That was sweet in a wow-you're-not-getting-this kind of way. She cupped his jaw in her palm, let her thumb skim along that perfect jaw and all that sexy stubble. "*I'm* coming on to *you*."

"And you're here, on this island, where it's hard for you to—"

"Harris?" She put a finger over his lips. "Shut up."

She lowered her mouth until it hovered just above his. Before their lips met, he took over. Strong hands landed on the sides of her waist. With a sexy little tug, he pulled her closer. Then he kissed her.

This wasn't a quick get-to-know-you peck. No, he dove in. Controlled and devoured. His lips crossed over hers with a mouth warm and inviting. It was the kind of kiss that pulled her in and sucked her under. Her mind went blank and her body hummed. The need to curl up in him and drag their bodies even closer rocked her.

When she finally lifted her head, all she could think was, *Damn, the man could kiss.* He tasted like he looked—inviting . . . intoxicating.

His hands roamed over her back then slipped to her waist again. His hips cradled hers.

"Shit." He brushed his forehead against her cheek. "I feel like I'd be a dick if I didn't try to put the brakes on here."

His words said one thing but his hands did another. Even as he talked about breaking apart, his fingers went to work on the buttons of her shirt. He had three open and his warm palm rested against her chest with his fingers sliding under the seam of her bra.

Lower. She needed that hand to move lower, for him to really touch her. All of her.

"Do you want to stop?" If he said yes, she silently vowed to dropkick him into the Bay.

"Fuck no." He whispered the words against her neck.

That deep voice vibrated against her, blocking out any ounce of doubt. Her fingers slipped into his hair and she held him there. Tried to find her breath as his tongue swept over her skin.

"I told you I've been numb." She fought to say the words as his mouth traveled along her collarbone. Her whole body shivered at the contact. "Tonight I want to feel something. With you."

He lifted his head and stared at her. His gaze searched her face, but just for a second. Heat flashed in his eyes as he wrapped her tight against him and started falling. He turned her in midair and she landed under him with her back on the couch cushions. She had no idea how gravity or inertia hadn't taken them tumbling down to the floor except that he was in control. Full control.

He lifted up on his elbows and ducked his head to kiss her again. She melted even faster this time. That mouth knew how to take and when to retreat. And when his tongue swept against hers, her brain blitzed out on her.

His body covered hers and the heat pulsed between

them. She shifted her legs to make room for him between her thighs as her hand skimmed down his back. Every muscle, every line, was perfect. His body was lean, and when he covered her, she felt anchored for the first time in a long time. Safe yet desperate for more.

When he started to move she almost thanked him. His mouth slipped to the base of her neck. He sucked on the skin there, making her back arch off the couch. But he kept going. His tongue slipped under the material of her bra to flick across her nipple. The intimate touch had her grabbing on to his shoulders, spearing her fingers through his soft hair.

"God, yes." He said the reverent words as he peeled the top of her bra down and took the tip of her breast in his mouth.

His lips, that tongue . . . pure magic.

Unable to wait another second to feel skin against skin, she tugged on his sweater, pulling it up his back to his shoulders. He lifted his body up from hers and broke away long enough for her to pull it off. Then he was back, with his mouth learning every inch of her breasts as his hands dipped lower.

The button on her pants popped open. "This is one way to stop me from asking questions."

The words crashed through her. It was as if her body had been dunked in an icy pool. Everything inside her froze and shriveled.

One of her hands went to her bra as she struggled to pull it up again and cover herself. The other went to his shoulder. She slammed her fist against him. "What did you just say?"

"Fuck." He closed his eyes and groaned. "Nothing."

She shoved at his chest and moved her legs, trying to kick him off her. "You think this is stalling?"

"I didn't—"

She kicked harder. "Move."

He pushed up to his knees and his arms fell to his sides. "Gabby, please."

"No." She took in his T-shirt, which was pulled up to his chest, showing off his flat stomach. The ruffled hair and the swollen lips. He looked like a guy who stood one small step away from having sex, but he'd blown it when he reminded her this was all a game to him.

She tried to sit up, but his body weight pinned her. "I mean it. Get off me."

"Done." He put one foot on the floor and lifted his body off hers. His hands shot up in the air. "I won't touch you until you say I can."

That was never going to happen. "You're an asshole."

"I'm not arguing with you." He stood on the floor now, staring down at her with an odd expression.

She refused to see the concern and regret shining in his eyes. He'd traveled to the island to collect data, to gather information. He had a job and she was it, and for a few minutes she'd let herself forget that.

"For the record . . ." She tried to hold her voice steady and she sat up and finished fiddling with her bra to get it back in place. "If I want to avoid a conversation. I avoid it. I don't use sex to hide."

His hands dropped to his sides again. "Understood."

The quick acceptance just made her more furious. "I made a pass because I wanted you."

"Gabby, I—"

"And now that's over." She bent over and picked up his sweater. Threw it at him and watched him catch it against his chest. "Get out. Sleep on the grass for all I care."

CHAPTER 9

Harris spent the next morning doing an inventory of the artwork in the downstairs hallway of the main house, mostly to provide cover for Damon, who was snooping around the house. Being the lookout wasn't his usual thing, but it gave him an excuse to stick close to the front door. He hadn't made it back to the library and Damon didn't push . . . yet.

The charcoal drawings and Edward Hopper paintings should have kept his attention. Normally, he'd be running a tally in his head for the estimated values, but not today. Amazing how wanting to kick his own ass made doing any actual work harder.

Last night . . . sweet damn.

Harris shook his head as he turned over the Arthur Dove pencil sketch he'd never seen before and studied the frame. His mind kept blanking out. He couldn't concentrate because he'd messed up big. Gabby's big pass had taken him by surprise. He'd expected her to walk back into the guesthouse, emotionally shut down and head off to bed. He'd been prepared for her to change topics. When she'd curled up on his lap he almost swallowed his tongue. His fucking erection had nearly ripped through his jeans.

Yeah, he needed air.

He put the sketch on the hall table and pushed the screen door open, letting it bang shut behind him. He almost swore when he saw Kramer and Ted standing at the bottom of the porch steps. Kramer held a Weed-wacker and Ted looked up from where he was kneeling on the grass by the flowerbed.

Harris didn't even try to hide his disappointment at not being alone. "Shit."

The rumble of noise whirled to a stop when Kramer shut off the trimmer. "You screwed up last night, son."

Apparently everyone knew he slept alone. Harris really hated the island. "Excuse me?"

Kramer nodded in the direction of his son. "Ted saw you racing out of the guesthouse with your clothes in your hands."

"It's hard to get privacy around here." A man couldn't even fuck up his sex life without everyone running up to talk about it.

It was bad enough he'd had to sneak into the main house last night to sleep. Damon almost shot him from the top of the stairs. Now this. Harris preferred to take his chances with the gun.

"Whelp." Kramer set the trimmer down on the path. "I'm thinking we need to talk."

Ted rolled his eyes as he sat up straight. "Dad."

With his elbow balanced on the porch railing, Kramer eyed up Harris. "No, Mr. Tate here—"

"You can call me Harris since you're about to walk all over my personal life."

"—needs to understand a few things." Kramer glared, as if daring Harris to say no.

Harris almost let the temptation to walk away win. "Go ahead."

"Gabby is off-limits."

That was it. Kramer dropped that little threat bomb and stood there with one eyebrow lifted and the dare still lingering from his defiant tone.

"And?" Harris asked, knowing he would regret not dropping the conversation.

"That's it. One thing. Don't touch her." Kramer nodded and picked up the Weedwacker again.

"He's overprotective when it comes to the Wright family," Ted said.

Kramer jumped right on the end of his son's comment. "And there's only one family member left, so I plan on making sure no one messes with her."

"I'm not going to . . ." Kramer turned on the trimmer and the buzzing sound drowned out anything else Harris might have said. When he held up a hand in mock surrender, Kramer flipped it off again and stared at Harris. "I get it. You work for her. You're loyal."

"You don't understand a thing." Kramer shook his head. "The Wrights weren't like that."

"Like what?"

"Dad." Ted got up and stood beside his father. "That's probably enough."

The conversation had just gotten interesting. No way was Harris ready to drop it now. "Tell me."

"Nah, Ted's right. You're not worth it." Kramer turned his back on Harris and followed the hedge away from the door.

He wanted to end the talk? Fine, but Harris wasn't about to let this be a one-sided battle. "Okay, you've had your say. Now I'll have mine."

Kramer looked at Harris over the hedge. "I don't remember making that deal."

"Gabby is a grown woman. Whatever happens between us is none of your business."

"Tough talk," Kramer mumbled under his breath.

Ted winced. "She did seem upset at breakfast this morning. She didn't specifically say anything, but she wasn't very talkative."

"Is that where she's been going every morning?" Harris figured she walked around the island or spent an hour dreaming up ways to drown him without anyone knowing.

Kramer stepped back to the front of the porch, right in front of Harris. "You don't know much. Do you, son?"

"I know I will work it out with Gabby." Harris didn't know that at all, but he refused to admit that. Not to these two, who he barely knew. It was bad enough he had Damon riding his ass.

"This should be interesting to watch." Ted laughed. "My money's on her."

GABBY MANAGED TO avoid Harris all day. She tried to avoid all of them. Every single man on the island. Their numbers seemed to be growing by the day.

She traveled around the island, and in between ducking and hiding, checking and rechecking, she'd searched for the map and the papers. Someone had taken them or moved them. Since Tabitha was the only other person who knew where they were buried, that meant it had to have been her. There really was no other reasonable explanation, and even that one wasn't all that reasonable.

Tabitha didn't have any reason to dig out that rock. Gabby hated to think the paranoia had gotten to her. She would have called, right? But since the why and when would never be known now, Gabby tried to push those questions out of her mind and focus on what she *could* do.

She pulled everything apart in the guesthouse. Drawers, bookshelves, turned the mattress. Then she tried the boathouse. Tabitha didn't go in there very often but maybe that made it the best new hiding place. A building she rarely ventured into might be the last place anyone would look.

No luck.

Now it was early evening. Past dinner and the sun had started to set as dusk moved in. She'd finished searching for the day and hung around with Ted on Craig's boat before the two of them took off for whatever they planned to do in Baltimore tonight. She intended to walk back to the guesthouse but she saw the fire. She couldn't make out the figure from this distance and in this light, but she'd bet the man at the fire pit was Harris.

Before she knew it, she was there, standing at the edge of the small patio. As she watched, he sat on the bench with his legs stretched out in front of him. No s'mores tonight. He held a water bottle and stared into the dancing flames.

"You just don't learn, do you?" There was no reason to play coy, so she sat down next to him. Only a few inches separated their thighs on the bench.

He handed her the water bottle. "I liked the memory of us here."

Her heart flipped again. The stupid traitorous thing. It needed to stop doing that when he said something kind of sweet.

She took the bottle because it gave her something to do with her hands. "Why are you out here alone?"

"It's been a long day." He rubbed his palms up and down on his legs. "Kramer gave me 'the talk' this morning."

The plastic crinkled in her hand as the water bottle dropped and bounced on the pavers. "What?"

"He thinks you need protection from me." Harris still hadn't looked at her. Didn't look at the bottle where it rolled around next to his foot either.

He continued to watch the fire, follow each cinder as it spun into the wind and up into the sky.

"I'm thinking he might not be wrong," she said.

He leaned back against the bench and turned his face to her. "I screwed up."

"Genius deduction." But she didn't feel any anger. Not there, not in that second when the light of the fire let her see the starkness in his eyes.

"Any chance you'll give me another shot?"

"I guess that depends on whether I need to use sex to evade another conversation." She tried to lighten the mood but she couldn't tell if the joke worked. "Want to ask me a few questions and we'll see if I automatically jump on you?"

His smile didn't reach his eyes. "Cute."

"You asked for it."

"True." For almost a minute he didn't say anything. He looked like he wanted to, but stayed quiet. Then he sat up straighter. "I'm skeptical when people act on emotion. I assume they need something from me or are trying to pull me off topic. Taking people at face value, believing them, is not one of my strengths."

"That sounds healthy."

He reached down to retrieve the water bottle. "Blame my mother. She lied to me my entire life."

As soon as he said the words he closed his eyes. He sat there, passing the bottle back and forth between his palms. Rolling it and ignoring the sound it made as the plastic gave under the force of his hands.

But she sensed the slip, and it was clear that was what it was. It provided a small window into the man behind the sexy smile and killer shoulders. A way for her to get in. "What does that mean?"

"Nothing." He shook his head as he stood up and poked the fire.

Right now would be the right time to let the topic drop. She knew that. His comments hinted at something deep and difficult, but she couldn't walk away. If that were possible she'd be back in the guesthouse and not sitting next to him right now.

That was the point. From the very beginning, something about him pulled her in. Two people who skirted the truth. Two lost souls. Two people with secrets that threatened to split them open. Whatever bound them together attracted and scared her, and it wasn't going away. Not yet.

She continued to watch him stir the embers and send puffs of red sparks flying into the air. "You started this, Harris."

"What I said isn't relevant."

She'd used lines like that her entire adult life. She recognized the trick. "If you want forgiveness, earn it."

He turned around with his back lit by the fire. He hesitated, holding the stick but not moving. Then he blew out a long breath. She could visibly see his chest rise and fall as he pitched the stick to the side.

"She had this secret life." He dropped down next to her with one arm stretched on top of the back of the bench behind her. "She did the carpool and ran forgotten projects to school."

"Sounds like normal stuff."

"Yeah, my dad and I thought she went to work every

day. In a way I guess she did. It's just that instead of going into the doctor's office and being a reception-ist as she said . . ." He stopped as if it hurt to say the words. "She stole things."

"Excuse me?"

"For most of my life it was small stuff, not that I knew that at the time." He sighed. "I found out many years later—everyone did—about the money missing back when she had a part-time job at the preschool. She was let go and no one said anything. Then it was the money from my soccer club. Then things went miss-ing from friends' and relatives' houses. Then a jewelry store. Then another, all without getting caught. The police only discovered the pattern later."

Gabby figured it had to be a cry for help or some-thing similar. "So, she's a kleptomaniac."

"Oh, no. It's so much bigger than that." This time he shook his head. "What she did with those smaller jobs was prepare for her dream career."

She felt a little queasy. "I almost hate to ask."

"She robbed banks."

Gabby almost laughed. The idea was so absurd that he had to be telling a joke, like some tall tale to get her to smile. "What?"

"Sounds ridiculous, right?"

"A little." Way more than a little. It sounded like pure fiction. The kind of story he told to impress a woman in a bar with what a bad boy he was. She'd heard silly lines over the years but never that one.

He wrapped a strand of her hair around his finger. Didn't tug or pull. Just slid the circle he made up and down, smoothed it over his skin.

He believed this nonsense. The thought slammed into her. This wasn't a joke, or if it was he played the role well. His shoulders slumped and some of the color drained from his face. He looked beaten and exhausted. Totally done.

"She kept meticulous notes and it was obvious she planned out the bigger jobs for months, maybe longer, and fed her stealing habit with smaller jobs in the meantime," he said, as if that cleared anything up.

"I don't . . ." God, she just couldn't take it in. Gabby put her hand on his knee and leaned in closer, hoping to be able to read through any act he was trying to sell. "Are you serious?"

"Very. She doesn't exactly own her actions and take responsibility for them, but expert witnesses and therapists who talked with her over the years point to her having this compulsion. This need to keep taking, to ratchet up the danger and live in this chaotic state."

"God, why?"

"A really messed up childhood with a dad who put her to work stealing instead of signing her up for kindergarten." He exhaled. "On the outside she presented one picture of herself—this totally together loving mom—but there was this broken part inside she kept trying to fix with these dangerous thrills."

"Where is she now?"

"In prison." He stopped looking at her hair and his finger and met her gaze. "Will be there until she dies."

Her hand squeezed his leg. "What the hell did she steal to get that sentence?"

"Her accomplice, the driver of the getaway car and likely her secret boyfriend, though she won't admit that part, got into a chase with the police. An officer and an innocent woman driving her dog to the vet were killed in the chaos." He pounded the side of his fist against the bench. Not hard but enough to make a soft thud. "That's how we found out about her other life. The police came to the door."

"I want to believe you're trying to win me over with a sob story, because . . ." She gave up the fight with a groan. "But you're not, are you?"

He shook his head. "Nope."

"I'm not even sure what to say." Her family tree was bathed in death. She mourned losing her parents' trust but she never believed she'd lost their love. The media played up the estrangement but that was more fiction than fact, or it was after those first few lonely years.

She'd lost so much, so many people. But none of them had chosen something as stupid as stealing over her. They died. They were taken, literally ripped away from her.

"My mom, what she did, the lies and how it destroyed my dad, it all plays a part in who I am today . . . in the choices I've made," Harris said in a voice barely above a whisper.

"Have you been to a therapist?" She didn't even know if the question fit in with this conversation, but she felt the need to ask it.

"I don't really need one to figure out why I am the way I am." He snorted. "The cause and effect is pretty clear."

A terrible thought hit her. "Please tell me you don't rob banks."

He shifted in his seat until their shoulders touched. His hand slipped over hers, his fingers entwined with hers. "I've never robbed a bank."

She settled against him, letting the warmth of his body wrap around hers. "I've seen a therapist on and off for years just to figure out how to get up in the morning."

"Was it like that before your parents and your sister?"

She wanted to lie. She prided herself on keeping it together. Through the accusations and all the ugly comments hurled at her, she'd hung on to that. She soldiered through. Admitting that at some point it hadn't been that easy really meant admitting she'd once allowed herself to be vulnerable. She had vowed never to do that again.

But blame the caress of his thumb over the back of her hand or the fire or the intoxicating crackle and smell of burning wood, her defenses refused to rise. Before she could think about it, the words tumbled out. "I always suffered from not-good-enough issues. Weirdly enough, losing my parents changed that. It was as if something shifted inside me and what used to matter didn't anymore. I no longer worried about failing because I was too busy being sick about never seeing them again."

"Makes sense."

"I just want to preserve their memories, you know?" She ached to make them proud of her.

"We all have secrets, Gabby. We all have reasons to grab a shovel and dig in the yard." His gaze searched her face as he talked. "That doesn't make you guilty of killing your sister, and I get that. I know the difference between the secrets we hide out of self-preservation and the sins we deserve to shoulder."

The man knew the right thing to say. The soft words, the understanding, it broke through. She was thrown back into the same state from last night. She needed to be touched and held. Not by just anyone, but by *him*. "Any chance I can lure you back to the guesthouse?"

"So long as you understand I'm a bad bet." There was no amusement in his voice. "Sex, I get. Heat, attraction, bodies—all good. But if you're looking to believe in someone, I'm not your guy."

He was actually warning her off. It would have been cute if she didn't want this so much.

"Can I trust you not to say something annoying while I get your clothes off?" she asked.

He shot her that sexy smile that melted her resistance and more than a few brain cells. "I think I can control my impulses for that long."

"That's good enough for now."

CHAPTER 10

Harris blocked out every word, every doubt. The voice at the back of his head shouted for him to stop. She deserved better. She needed to hear the truth. All true, but he didn't exactly lie to her. *Not exactly.* She knew he was holding back . . . they both were.

His emotions volleyed back and forth as they made the slow walk to the guesthouse. The stay-away-from-her side won by a mile but he couldn't make himself break away. He'd spent so much of his time knowing her—most of which she didn't know he existed—floundering in a quicksand of guilt. Before they exchanged one look he'd already failed her.

Every argument and bit of common sense told him to step back. To put a wall between them. But the minute he thought about the solution, he abandoned it. His need for her veered into the wild and uncontrollable. Maybe if they had this one time he could find some sort of equilibrium. Either that or the guilt would plunge him under once and for all.

He had no idea how they made it across the lawn without tripping. The walk started out fine. Hurried, but fine. No touching. Then the back of his hand brushed against hers and he practically climbed on top of her. He wrapped his arms around her. His hands roamed all over her. By the time they got to the guesthouse they were locked in a blinding kiss.

He pressed her back against the door, held her there with a hand on either side of her head. Need pounded inside him and he poured it into the kiss. No holding back. The air between them thrummed with electricity. And when her fingers went to the button on the top of his jeans he almost lost it.

"Inside." The pent-up feelings for her had him barking out the order.

Her mouth went to his neck as she reached behind her and turned the knob. The door opened and they almost fell through the opening, but he caught her just in time. He held her, walking her backward. They knocked against a table and thumped into the wall. A lamp tipped and rocked on its base but thanks to some miracle didn't fall over.

Through it all he kept kissing her. He couldn't stop. Her mouth lured him in. Her scent and those hands.

He tugged the bottom of her shirt out of her cargo pants. His fingers fumbled with the buttons until she pushed his hands away. She had the material open and dropping to the floor while he worked on her pants zipper. He lowered it tick by tick as they passed through the doorway to the bedroom.

Her weight shifted while she kicked off one sneaker then the other. Then she was sitting on the edge of the bed with her hand running over the front of his jeans. She'd gotten the button open, but they balanced on his hips.

"God, Gabby. Do it." He wanted the zipper down and his clothes off.

He didn't even need to say the words. She leaned forward and pressed a kiss against him. Outlined his bulge with her fingers. Caressed him through the material until he sucked in his stomach on a sharp hiss. Then she did it again.

Looking down was like every fantasy come to life. He skimmed his fingers through her soft hair. Watched as her mouth worked and her hands traveled over him. She was open and honest in this. For a person who shut down and closed herself off, she didn't hide now.

So sexy.

She lifted up long enough to kick her pants off. She sat there, wearing only a simple white bra and the sexiest little pair of bikini underwear he'd ever seen. He itched to strip it all off her, but there was no way he was skipping this part.

Her hands slid inside the waistband of his jeans as she tugged the zipper down. The pants slipped over him. He was so hard, so sensitive, that the rough scratch of the material had his hips pushing forward.

Hot and wet, her mouth covered him, surrounded him. She squeezed the base of his shaft and licked the tip. The mix of touching and tasting had his vision blinking out.

"Gabby . . ." That was all he could get out. A soft whisper of need.

His fingers slipped through her hair as he held her head close. He didn't want to break contact. Then she licked her tongue up his length and his knees buckled. Standing above her he had the perfect view of the curve of her neck. The light danced on her skin. He could see the inviting shadow between her breasts.

God, he wanted her.

Unable to hold back, he put his hand under her chin and lifted her head. Her lips were wet and puffy. So damn sexy.

"Your turn." He almost didn't recognize the rough sound of his own voice.

She nodded but didn't say a word. Using her hands and legs, she scooted up higher on the bed, making room for him. He didn't hesitate. He stripped his jeans the rest of the way down his legs and took the boxer briefs with them. Naked now, he crawled up the mattress. In between her legs.

Kneeling there, he ran his fingertips over her upper thighs and along the elastic band of her bikini bottoms. Every inch of her intrigued him. Her skin was so smooth, so perfect. A mix of lean muscle and incredible softness.

He reached under her and skimmed his palms over her ass. She lifted her hips as he peeled her underwear off. Then he lowered his body, slipped down until his chest touched the mattress and his mouth swept over her. He blew a shot of warm air over her and her hips started to move. Her hands fisted in the comforter on either side of her.

Lying there, she was open and ready for him. He could smell her. He slipped a finger inside her then out again and saw the wetness on his skin.

"Harris, please."

He wanted to make her beg. Hear her chant his name. But he was never going to last that long.

He needed her with him, as gone as he was. To get her there, he lowered his head. Slipped his tongue over her, inside of her. He used his fingers and his mouth, taking turns as he caressed her.

Her legs fell open and a sweet moan escaped her throat. The sound echoed through him, testing his control. He couldn't wait another minute. He needed to be inside her, plunging into her, feeling her close around him.

He lifted up on his elbows. Trailing kisses over her stomach then up until he reached the edge of her bra. He couldn't believe he'd left it on this long. He unclipped the hooks as he licked and kissed a trail to her neck. His hands worked between their heated bodies as his mouth met hers. The kisses mirrored the touches, wild and full of need.

His heart raced in a frantic beat. It hammered hard enough to throw off his breathing. He was panting, his hands moving over her. He cupped her breasts and kissed that soft space behind her ear. His body caught fire just as the heat rose off hers.

She caught his face in her palms. "Condom."

The haze cleared for a second. "Right."

He struggled to remember where he was as he loomed over her. The strange bedroom . . . where he put the condoms . . .

"Bedside table." She pressed a line of kisses up his neck as he hung there above her.

"Okay." Not that he could move. Her legs were locked around the back of his. Their bodies rubbed together, skin against skin. Energy pulsed inside him until his hands shook.

"Yes." Her head dropped back on the mattress. "Now, Harris."

That got his attention.

With a knee balanced on the bed, he maneuvered around her. Stealing a quick glance at her was a mistake. It broke what little concentration he had. On her back with her arms palms up by her head. She was waiting, and he needed to move his ass.

The drawer rattled as he pulled it out. A quick check and he had the condom. He fumbled, trying to get it open. Somehow he managed it. He rolled it over his length as he moved back between her thighs. Her knees were in the air now with her feet flat against the mattress.

So damn inviting.

Slipping his hands under her thighs, he pushed her knees closer to her chest. He took his erection in his hand and brushed the tip over her, opening her. Back and forth as the muscles in her legs visibly shook.

Watching her run her hands over her stomach nearly

killed him. She understood her body and what she needed. She didn't shy away from this feeling, and he loved that. Loved how good she felt as her inner muscles closed around him.

He pushed into her nice and slow, celebrating every inch. When she reached out and grabbed his hips and pulled him in tight, he didn't fight it. He sank inside her in one deep, long stroke. Sensations rippled through her and he felt every one. Her shoulders lifted and her hips bucked.

His body took over then. He pumped inside her. In and out in a natural rhythm that didn't require a signal from his brain. This was about feeling, about watching her body move.

One of her arms dropped over her head and her mouth opened on a soft sigh. He didn't stop. A clenching sensation took over his body. He felt his release rushing through him and wanted to get her there first.

He slipped his hand down and touched her. Pressed his finger against the spot he knew would drive her wild as his body moved inside her. She gasped and her eyes opened. Her hands slid over his ass and up his back. Traveled over his shoulders then her fingernails dug in. She held him in a tight grip as she brought his body closer.

The friction of skin over skin drowned out every other thought. He moved, she moved. Their breathing mixed. Their legs tangled.

Those long legs encircled him. Her ankles locked behind him. Her body stiffened right before she came.

Those tiny inner muscles clamped down on him and he saw white.

It was his turn then. His body moved and his mind went blank. Wave after wave of excited need ran through him. The energy built up until it exploded. He emptied as his hips continued to buck.

After, he just lay there on top of her, enjoying the way her body fit against his. The softness to his hardness. The smell of him on her skin. The dampness between her breasts and on his back.

The sex was so damn good.

He liked looking at her, arguing with her, matching wits against her. But this . . . this was fucking amazing. So much for thinking they could do this once and be over. If anything, his need for her slammed into him even harder. He waited for a fresh smack of guilt and regret for lying to her, for not coming clean. It hadn't hit him yet, but he knew it lingered inside him somewhere.

He pulled out of her, but he didn't want to. He could stay there, rocking his body against hers all night. She hadn't complained. Her fingers still brushed over his shoulders and her tight hold didn't ease. But he outweighed her and they needed a second. A breath before they rushed into round two, or worse, broke apart with her deciding once was enough.

He forced his body to move. He didn't go far, just pushed up on his elbows and balanced his chest over hers.

He smiled down at her. "Hey."

Her gaze toured his face as her finger slipped over his scruff of a beard. "Hey, yourself."

He remembered her warning back at the fire pit. "You'll note I didn't say anything."

She frowned at him. "Huh?"

"You told me not to be annoying during sex."

She laughed then. At first it was a small bit of happiness but then she let go. She laughed until she bent her head and rested her forehead against his chest.

"You okay?" But he loved it. He'd seen her smile, but not nearly enough. A loss of control seemed so out of character that he hoped it was a good sign. Maybe she'd crossed some invisible barrier.

She lifted her head and kissed him then. A hot, sexy kiss that said she'd loved the sex as much as he did. "I'm pretty great."

"I hope that means I can stay the night." That might be pushing it, but she made him feel powerful. He was pretty sure he could swim to DC no problem right now.

She wrapped her arms around his neck. "Just try to leave."

TWO HOURS LATER, after a second round and a shower, they lay entwined on the bed. She was on her side with him spooning her from behind. The position both drove her wild and made her feel safe.

Heat radiated off him and soaked into her bones. She was relaxed but rode the edge of being anything but. If she had any energy or could move a muscle she might turn over and slide over him. It was so tempting.

She shifted a bit and his arm tightened around her waist. They were naked, because why bother to put on clothes now. He mumbled something against the back of her neck before placing a kiss there. The touch was enough to send a new tremor spinning through her.

He warned her that he didn't do feelings. That he was not the guy a woman should risk anything on. Sex was about sex. She got the message, appreciated the warning. Hell, she felt the same, so they seemed like the perfect match. But tonight was not about the touch of a man without feelings. He didn't keep his body and mind separate. There was nothing selfish about how he acted in bed.

Thinking about him and back to the story he told about his mom . . . she tried to make sense of it all. She understood that he didn't share easily. She could tell that about him from the start. But he'd opened up, run the risk of her not believing him.

She knew he expected they'd both share their secrets, but he only got a one-sided deal. Not that she'd promised, because she really hadn't. She'd gone out of her way not to utter the words. But now, lying there in the dark, the need to say something pummeled her. She'd held in her secrets for so long. This one nearly destroyed her family. She didn't know how to tell all of it, but her brain begged for her to share at least a part.

His weight grew heavier against her and she knew

he was drifting off to sleep. If she waited just a few more minutes the moment would pass. He'd be asleep and then she could try to rest. If only she could turn her mind off.

"I didn't plan my own kidnapping." There it was. She'd made the statement over and over during the years. She'd told police and private investigators. Two lawyers and her family. She'd screamed it at her parents until they just stopped listening.

Harris didn't say anything. Didn't pepper her with questions. His legs shifted and his body felt more alive. Yeah, she'd woken him up. Now the question was if she could go through with it. Baby steps. God, she wanted to tell him all of it because she needed him to know she wouldn't intentionally hurt her parents that way.

"I joked with friends about this movie I'd seen and how I could fake a kidnapping to get my trust and break free of my parents' control. It was stupid teen crap, kind of a my-parents-are-worse game. Big talk, but not real talk. Not to me."

Harris made a humming sound. "But to someone."

"Friends of friends heard. They were the ones who planned it." She'd never guessed the stupid ramblings of bored kids could change everything in her life, but that was exactly what happened.

She'd been dependent on the money and all the benefits it brought. She never debated how privileged she was because that was obvious, but her parents weren't the must-make-more types. Her father was uncomfortable with the money and her mother didn't really want any of it. She would have been happy to keep designing houses, which was exactly how she met Gabby's dad.

"These other kids knew my schedule and when I was home from college and the general blueprints of the house because they'd been there for a party I had when my parents were away." The party they forbade her to have, not caring that she was in college now and it was sort of expected.

Thinking back now, if she'd only listened . . . wasn't that always the way?

Harris made a humming sound that vibrated against her skin. "That's the evidence that was used against you."

"I drank a lot back then and would talk big." She'd started at sixteen because she thought it was cool. That was one downside of being her mother's child. Her mother liked to drink and Gabby learned that skill by watching. "I started young and didn't stop. Well, I did after the kidnapping. Consider it a scared-sober thing."

Harris dropped a kiss on her bare shoulder. "Did you know in advance they were going to take you?"

"No." She didn't sense any doubt in his voice, so she continued. "I think they started it as a joke but then more people got involved and it spun out of control."

His thumb rubbed up and down on her stomach. "Did they hurt you?"

Getting beaten up didn't matter. The ones who went

through with the kidnapping weren't actually her friends. She barely knew that group and they insisted the injuries were necessary to make the ruse more believable. She begged them to stop all of it, but there was that one guy who seemed to be in charge. The one who called her "spoiled rich girl" and made it clear he thought she deserved being hit. Later, he insisted she ordered them to hit her to be realistic.

"They destroyed my parents' trust in me. That was the worst part. I didn't do it, never would have, but there was a piece of my mom and dad that always doubted." It was the one time in her life where the darkness nearly overwhelmed her. She'd searched for reasons to stay alive and couldn't really find any. That scared her right back into therapy.

Harris's hand spanned her waist in a reassuring touch. "You were gone for days."

"Being taken turned out to be the easiest part to recover from."

He turned her over until her back rested against the mattress and he balanced over her. "And all this has something to do with the shovel."

"Yes."

He didn't ask anything else. Didn't push.

He was letting her tell the story her way, in her time. This was all she could do now. There was so much more. The pain and the betrayal. The begging and the map. But that could wait. Truth was, the spark of attraction she felt for him ignited into a full-fledged flame, and she didn't want to lose that.

"I'm going to kiss you again." He started to lower his head.

She put a hand on his shoulder because she needed to see his face when she asked the next question. "You're not going to insist on knowing everything about me and what happened and every fact?"

"No."

"Really?" He acted like he didn't care but she got the sense something else was going on. Like, he was giving her time and space, two things she needed but never expected.

His eyebrow lifted. "Do you need that from me in order for us to sleep together? Because I really want to keep doing this."

"In other words, I can keep some of my secrets but then so can you?" She already knew the answer to that. He put on a good show but underneath something else bubbled and churned.

"Yes."

His matter-of-fact response was oddly reassuring. Other men would deny or out-and-out lie. Not Harris. He wasn't like other men. He was so much better.

"Then get to it. The kiss, I mean." This time she pulled him down to her. "We'll figure out the rest later."

CHAPTER 11

Harris managed to push away the lingering need to know more about Gabby and focused on how good touching her the night before had felt. He was actually in a good mood as he walked across the freshly mowed grass.

The second he saw Damon standing on the main house's front porch everything changed. Harris had seen that expression before, the mix of smart-ass and you're-toast look on Damon's face, and it never ended well.

"About time you woke up," Damon said as he stared at Harris over the top of his coffee mug.

At least today Damon looked a bit more like an investigator and a bit less like a guy with an impressive T-shirt collection but little else to his name. The dark pants matched the dark mood circling around him.

"It's not even eight." Harris knew because he'd forced his body out of bed exactly a half hour ago.

Staying there, going another round with Gabby, had been a huge temptation. It didn't help that she'd been sprawled across the bed naked. When he got up to shower she grumbled about too much moving in the morning and smashed her face into the pillow. He took that as a sign that she might not be a morning person.

He needed a bit more sleep, but there was a lot of work to do. Damon had pushed off the alarm and security people Stephen hired. He didn't want any of them messing with the equipment Wren already installed on the island. Worse, Damon had already texted to say they needed to talk. It was either wake up or run the risk of Damon knocking on the guesthouse door.

"It's exhausting, right?" Damon asked as he leaned against the porch post.

Harris did not want to ask. Even thought about pivoting around Damon and going into the house or, better yet, heading to the opposite end of the island. But Damon would never let it drop, so . . . "Just say it."

"This game of musical beds. Are you going to keep changing every night?" Damon made a "huh" sound. "If so, I thought Wren and I could start a betting pool."

"First of all, kiss my ass."

Damon nodded. "That's a fair response."

"Second, I'd like to point out that when I did try to sleep here, in the same house as you, you threatened to shoot me." Damon had scared the crap out of Harris the other night. Started yelling, hit the lights.

"You tried to sneak in and knocked over the coat rack. I should have shot you just on principle." Damon made a tsk-tsking sound. "I mean, what self-respecting thief makes that kind of racket?"

"Keep your voice down." Harris did a quick look around, half expecting Kramer or his son to pop up out of nowhere. It wasn't until he saw the two of them over by the pool, walking around it and nodding while they inspected it, that Harris felt comfortable talking outside about this topic. "And it's former thief."

"It's weird how I keep forgetting the *former* thing." Sarcasm dripped from Damon's voice.

"I've gone legitimate." Harris thought maybe if he said it often enough others would believe him. He didn't consider what he did now stealing, after all. It was a matter of balancing the scales. If some Nazi stole art in the forties, he could try to fix that now. If a rich asshole used his influence or took a painting to settle a debt, Harris could make that right.

Truth was, stopping cold never worked for him. He'd tried. Almost getting caught on this island and arrested hadn't scared him straight. Neither had the other time Wren had to step in and bail him out.

He'd been on this road a long time, at first intrigued by his mother's obsession and then compelled by the adrenaline rush and his own driving need to fill a void inside him by taking risks. His current job provided cover, which made it easier to do his behind-the-scenes work. He'd established himself as the go-to person to track lost art. It was the part where he sometimes stole it back that his friends seemed to question.

"I am standing here instead of sitting on a beach in Hawaii because you can't go fully legitimate," Damon said.

Harris couldn't exactly deny that. "Blame Wren."

"I have been. He calls every day for a check."

"Controlling bastard."

Damon nodded. "Right?"

"What was your text about?" The sooner Harris got an answer, the sooner he could track down a cup of coffee. He had a feeling this was going to be a multi-cup day.

"So . . . we have a problem."

Harris knew those words would come out of his friend's mouth. "I'm barely awake and I can name three."

"Well, some of us didn't get much sleep but I'm betting your night was more fun."

Harris wasn't the type to kiss and tell, but come on. "I can a hundred percent guarantee that."

"Wren sent the security video. I now have a hookup and I've been going through the days since Gabby arrived on the island."

It was the way Damon said it, all slow and calculating. As if he was trying to test Harris. If so, Harris was pretty sure he'd fail because he was too tired to school his reactions. "Okay."

"Her late-night activities . . ." Damon hesitated. "Do you really not know where I'm going with this?"

The dramatic pause thing seemed extra annoying without coffee. "Spell it out."

"She got up one night and dug a stone out of a wall. Acted pretty upset that there wasn't something hidden there." Damon set his mug down on the porch banister. "But I think you know all of that. See, the Harris I know wouldn't miss a woman sliding out of bed. He'd hear it and follow her."

Well, fuck. "You seemed to suggest a second ago I was slipping."

"Look, I'm here to help you, asshole. I know you've got this new outlook where you cut me out and—"

"No." Harris needed to shut this down right now. Needed to step up and own this part of the mess he created. He hadn't hurt Tabitha. The way he mangled the crime scene had been half accident and half an attempt to cover his own ass. The latter would always haunt him. That guilt plagued him and he shut down. He ended up pushing away one of the people he'd always counted on and trusted.

It was a knee-jerk reaction. Having a mother in jail did that to a guy. Starting at age fifteen he'd seen up close and personal what that kind of ending did to a family. His father hadn't said a decent thing about a woman since. He skulked around, ran through marriages and girlfriends and lived his life alone.

While that overreaction didn't make sense to Harris, he did understand the need for caution. That wasn't about women. It was about anyone. Trusting led to emotional destruction. He kept his circle of friends small and tight. And when it came to Harris, he'd blown it.

"I fucked up in not calling back, for taking legitimate jobs overseas and traveling in between work assignments so I was never in the same place. Running to fight off the urge to go back to my old ways." Harris couldn't find the right words so he went with the ones that came to him first. "You didn't deserve that."

"Are you agreeing about how you're an asshole so I forget Gabby and the wall?"

Harris couldn't help but smile at that. Damon was so practical, so to the point. "A little."

Damon nodded. "It's a good trick."

"About us . . ."

"Don't make it sound like we're dating." Damon's smirk telegraphed how much he was enjoying this part of the conversation. "I just need you to recognize that I'm the absolute smartest, best-looking and most talented friend you have. You can even say your best friend, just so I can rub it in to Matthias and Wren."

"I like how self-deprecating you are."

Damon's mood sobered. "I know the last fourteen months sucked. You got your ass handed to you here and went into a tailspin." He stopped for a second then continued. "Next time, reach out or I'll slam you into a wall."

"Done." With that, Harris knew they were all right. Damon didn't hold a grudge. He'd aired his frustration, it was out, they'd dealt with it. Now Damon would move on.

Harris wished he had the move-on skill.

"Now back to your messed-up sex life," Damon said.

"Let's not do this."

Damon snorted. "You once pissed all over me because you didn't like the woman I was dating."

"Dude, she stole from you. Like, four hundred dollars and a watch." It was two years ago and the whole scene made Harris wonder if Damon had a sense of self-preservation when it came to women.

"Whatever." Damon waved off the concern as a big smile spread across his face. "Back to your hot girlfriend."

Harris heard the footsteps then. He looked over his shoulder, following Damon's gaze to see who was coming. There was Gabby, wearing jeans and an oversized white oxford. The outfit was simple and her long hair was tied back.

She'd never looked sexier.

She whistled as she got closer. "You're talking about hot women? Anyone I know?"

"You do know how to sneak up on a guy," Harris said.

"You're not exactly quiet." She stopped right beside Harris. "Like, at all."

Harris shot Damon a quick glance. "So I've been told."

Damon didn't ease up on the whole leaning-there-trying-to-look-casual thing. He managed to pull it off because his personality came off as oddly relaxed. For a man whose personal history had all the calm of a cyclone, it was an interesting trait. "You're just the woman I wanted to talk to this morning."

"Really? You two seemed pretty intense there for a second." She looked back and forth between Harris and Damon. "Should I come back?"

"We're done." Harris took her comment to mean

she'd been watching. He should have known. The sensation of being under a microscope lingered on this island. "Damon here asks a lot of probing questions."

Damon nodded. "They teach you that in investigator school."

She pounced. "Speaking of that—"

"Nope." Damon stood up straight. "We're not going to sit around and talk about my credentials. It's a nice trick, Gabby. The whole thing where you make me the subject, but no."

Gabby's eyes widened. "You're a little paranoid."

"Only a little?" Harris asked.

"Probably more than most." Damon stepped back and opened the front door. "You should both come inside."

All the amusement faded from Gabby's face. She went from light and sunny to wary. "I . . . don't . . ."

Before Harris could say anything, Damon jumped in. "Gabby, I'm not unsympathetic."

She sighed at him. "Let me stop you because I sense you're about to say something really annoying."

"I can't erase what happened in this house or how you feel. I honestly wish I could step back in time and make that afternoon never happen." Damon kept holding that door open as he talked. "But it did and the only way I know how to help your sister now is to try to find the person who did this to her."

A crackling silence followed his words. Harris knew Damon made sense and that Gabby was smart enough to see that. But sometimes what a person needed to do battled with what they could conceivably do. Taking this step, breaching the doorway and walking inside, asked a lot. Hell, he hadn't been able to walk back the hallway and search the library yet, but he guessed that was about to end.

Gabby inhaled, doing nothing to block the loud sound of air whizzing in and out of her. She rubbed her hands together as she stood there so still. Her gaze traveled over the front of the house, up to the second-floor windows. Finally, she nodded. "Fine."

Her voice was soft and a bit wobbly. Harris put a hand on her lower back for support. "Are you sure?"

"He's right. You're right." She seemed breathless and gasping for air as she spoke. "I've been going over this and around it. It's time to go through."

Damon didn't move away from that open door. "Any time you need to step out, you do it."

"Thanks." Still, she didn't move.

Harris waited next to her, touching her. The house once meant something to her and her family. He didn't know how to bring the good memories back. The bloodstain had been removed but the nightmare would linger, likely forever.

She took the first step. Then another. Her sneakers thudded on the porch as she walked up with halting steps.

Damon nodded in Harris's direction. "You can also hold his hand if you want. That sort of thing doesn't bother me."

She glanced up at Damon as she passed him. "You're an odd man, investigator."

"Call me Damon, and, yes, I am."

THE WALK INTO the grand entry of the main house consisted of some of the hardest steps she'd ever taken. Familiar smells hit her. The cleaning liquid used to keep the banisters shiny. The flowers blooming in the window boxes that then carried their scent into the house.

The house was old and full of creaks and groans. When the wind swept through from one side to the other the paintings on the wall would rattle and her mother would start her annual speech about how impractical it was to have a house right on the water. Tabitha, so carefree back then, would run into the rooms, opening even more windows.

They'd had crab feasts here. They once hosted an office picnic on the grounds. Then there was that fund-raiser for literacy. The memories bombarded her as she stood there, eyes closed and reliving them all.

At some point she slid her hand into Harris's and now they stood there as if waiting for the house to tell them something. She could hear the steady beat of music and realized Damon had the radio on in the office right off the entry. She glanced over at the desk. It was covered with papers and two laptops. A jacket hung over the back of the chair and his cell sat on the top of the pile.

"Are we going in there?" She could handle that room. Her father had used it. He'd pretend to work and she'd find him in there, smoking a cigar right through the open window so her mother wouldn't know. Of course, she always did.

Damon shook his head. "The library."

The words, so innocuous, ripped through her. The numbness she'd cultivated, the same lack of feeling that had helped her survive, cracked. Pain seeped through her in this insidious slow drip. If it had slammed into her, she could run outside, but that wasn't how it worked. Not this time. It spilled through her, touching everything.

She squeezed Harris's hand and he pulled her in closer to his side. It was an unspoken comfort. His presence, just being there, gave her someone to lean on.

She heard a scuffing sound and realized she'd literally been dragging her feet. The distance between her and Damon increased as they walked down the hall. Her speed slowed. Harris didn't seem in a rush to get there either. He visibly swallowed and more than once she saw him blow out a long breath. It was as if her anxiety transferred to him.

Damon reached the door and did a double take when he looked how far behind him they were. "We can take as much time as you need."

Forever. She needed that long, maybe longer, to get over the choking sensation in her throat. The way her airway closed a little more with each step she took.

She put a hand to her throat, wanted to claw at the buttons on her shirt, but all she felt was skin.

Right before they reached the doorway, Harris stepped in front of her and turned around to face her. "If it's too soon—"

"Harris."

He ignored Damon's warning tone and kept talking. "This is about what you need."

Then it hit her. He was wrong about this one thing. This really wasn't about her. It was about Tabitha. This was where she lived her last moments. This was where she lost everything. So, if there was a diary to find or notes that would lead to something substantial, maybe a breakthrough in her case, Gabby would go in. She owed her baby sister that much.

"I'm okay." She was anything but, but saying the words helped. She repeated them in her head until it became a mantra.

Harris lifted their joined hands and kissed the back of hers. "You're so much better than that."

The pain in her stomach made her want to double over, but she fought it off. Her therapist's words came rushing back. This was about the fear and pain, and she needed to flip that around and use it to fuel her. Overcome it and take back control.

Every joint ached. Every step tore through her muscles, but still she walked until she got there.

At first she just hovered in the doorway. Her gaze traveled over the room and landed on the empty spot over the fireplace where a Beckmann painting once rested. The matting had been ripped during Tabitha's attack. After a court-approved repair, the masterpiece now sat in her uncle's house, but only as a temporary holding place while the estate battle waged.

Harris and Damon stared at her while she scanned the piece of furniture and fought off the flood of family memories. Keeping her eyes up—off that floor—she looked from bookshelf to bookshelf. Her gaze hesitated on the doors at the opposite side then dipped down. She shut her eyes, half expecting to see Tabitha there, but saw only carpet. Not the familiar gray one. This one was new and blue.

She ventured in. Dropping Harris's hand, she went to the stacks of books on the table. A mix of classics and genre fiction. Tabitha had read it all. Gabby smiled as she picked up a spy novel from the top.

"Put that down." Damon's shout shot across the room.

The book smacked against the floor. The next minute he was standing next to her.

"What the hell is wrong with you?" Harris asked Damon as he put his body between hers and Damon's.

"Don't move for a second." Damon looked around the room. His gaze flicked from the books to the french doors to Harris's face. "Were you in here earlier?"

"What?"

Harris looked as confused as she felt. The desperate gnawing in her gut as she walked into the room gave way to something else.

"The books are in a different order than when I was in here last night." Damon pointed at the bookshelf.

"That photo has been moved, as has the curtain that goes in front of the doors to the patio."

Harris shook his head. "What are you talking about?"

"Last night I set up the room. The new inside sensor alarms haven't been installed, so I was extra careful just in case."

She glanced down at the books. "Maybe you remembered the order wrong?"

He scoffed. "No."

"You're saying someone broke in here." Harris's voice vibrated with what sounded like anger. "How did you not hear someone running around?"

"Because no one ran anywhere. The person was quiet and also really careful."

She had a million questions, but the shiver running through her made it hard to ask any of them. She went with the most logical problem first. "So, what do we do now?"

Damon shrugged, as if a break-in wasn't big news. "At least this narrows things down."

"What kind of answer is that?" she asked.

"The only people on the island last night were the three of us."

Harris shook his head. "Someone else could have gotten on by boat."

The boat. That piece of information helped restart her brain. "Right. It wasn't just us. Ted and Craig went to Baltimore. I'm not sure what time they came in, but I saw Craig's boat leave when we got up this morning, so they were back at some point last night."

Harris and Damon looked at each other before Harris spoke up. "You think someone came back with them?"

"Maybe it's time I had a talk with Ted and Craig," Damon said.

"They wouldn't do this." When both men stared at her with blank expressions, she tried to explain. "There's no reason. They've both had access to the island and the house. They were friends with Tabitha. Heck, they're two of the people she saw on a regular basis." The way Damon and Harris kept staring made her nervous. She had to clamp down on the need to explode at them. "What is it?"

"Do you think the fact they were friends with Tabitha makes it less likely one of them would hurt her?" Damon asked.

"Of course."

Harris winced. "People generally are killed by people they know. Not strangers."

These two had an upsetting answer for everything. "That's not possible. Not in this case."

Damon nodded. "Okay."

As reactions went, she thought that one might be worse than the unblinking stares. "You don't believe me."

Damon sighed. "I believe *you* believe what you're saying."

"Don't do this." A new wave of anxiety hit her. "Please don't falsely accuse them. I don't want anyone else to have to deal with that."

"Whoa." Damon held up both hands as if he were

trying to placate her. "I'm going to ask questions. That's all."

Harris just stood there, not saying anything. That made her twitchier than the idea of her friends being questioned—again. She turned on him. "Now would be a good time to tell me if you and Damon are actually working together."

"Gabby," Harris said in the voice someone might use to calm an upset child. "The man is trying to do his job."

Panic boiled over inside her. Being there, a new break-in . . . Harris's half answers. She couldn't deal with all of it right now. Not with them watching her and assessing every move.

"For the record, that's not an answer." The words rushed out of her then she started walking. Down the hall, into the entry. Out into the sunshine.

HARRIS WANTED TO chase after her, but what could he say? He'd been lying to her from the start. Sure, they had a mutual-deception thing going, which made absolutely no sense since they had shared never-tell-anyone type secrets. But he hadn't been honest about knowing Damon or telling her about his own role in what happened fourteen months ago. At least one of those truths seemed like an impossible climb.

"I've realized one thing," Damon said from right over Harris's shoulder.

"What?"

"You kind of suck with women."

Harris nodded as he watched Gabby get farther away on the path. "With this one, yeah."

"Let's hope she's not on the video."

Harris spun around to face Damon. "What are you talking about?"

"I told you Wren put cameras on the island. It's why I didn't bother locking the front door last night. Well, that and because I couldn't guarantee Gabby wouldn't kick you out of bed again." Damon hesitated, likely for dramatic effect. "But my point is one of those well-hidden, invisible-to-the-naked-eye cameras will show us who came into the house."

Harris closed his eyes. He knew it wasn't her. There was no way she snuck out after they had sex. He refused to believe she'd tired him out to go hunting again. "Damn."

"If she got away from you once, she could have done it twice."

It was as if Damon was in his head, reading every thought. Harris hated that. "It wasn't her."

"We'll know soon enough."

CHAPTER 12

Damon insisted on immediately questioning the Kramer men. Harris wasn't about to miss that. Tagging along also gave him a chance to put a little more breathing room between him and Gabby. The idea of letting her cool off before they talked sounded good to him. He just hoped they were talking hours and not days.

They tracked Kramer and Ted to the pool. They'd been standing there, walking around and checking gauges, pumps and water levels for over an hour. Harris figured they had to be done soon or at least need a break.

Damon didn't waste any time. He started talking as soon as they stepped onto the flagstone patio running along one side of the infinity pool. "I need to talk with Ted."

"No," Kramer answered without looking up from rummaging through his toolbox.

Ted rolled his eyes. "Dad."

"Neither of you actually get to say no," Damon said, talking right over Ted.

Kramer looked up then. "Are you FBI? Do you have a badge?"

This was going well. Harris couldn't imagine what usable information they could get out of this conversation. "He's got you there."

Kramer continued to balance on his haunches as his focus turned to Harris. "And why are you here?"

Good fucking question. "As a witness."

It was the best excuse Harris could come up with. In a way it fit with the cover they'd already established. No one believed the art-valuation story, even though it was sort of true. At this point it might make more sense to dump it, but at least he was actually qualified to perform that sort of work. This investigation stuff was well out of his area of expertise.

Kramer frowned. "What does that mean?"

"I'm a neutral party. I listen in and provide testimony in case there's a question later." Harris ended the comment with the same fake confidence he'd been practicing his entire life. It must have worked because Damon only shot him a quick glance.

Kramer made a show of exhaling and half groaning as he stood up. The wrench he dropped into the toolbox made a loud clanking sound. "Don't you think it's time you admit you two are working together for Stephen?"

"You like to ask a lot of questions." Harris switched strategies. Forget reason. He flipped into attack mode. Putting people on the defensive tended to change the conversation. "Is it just the answering that's an issue for you?"

"What's your problem, son?" Kramer asked.

"Okay, that's enough." Damon walked on the edge of the pool. Only inches from falling in. "Where were you last night?"

Kramer threw out his arms. "We're on an island. Where the hell do you think I was?"

"That's a fair question." It was the same one Harris kept running up against. The island meant limited movement. People couldn't get off a boat and blend in. Anyone visiting would be seen, which meant they had to be a known quantity . . . unless they snuck on like he did. That meant skills or training or a hell of a will to get in and out.

"It really is." But Damon continued to stare at Kramer. "Now try answering. Did you leave the island?"

"I had dinner, checked on the boat slip, like I always do, then watched some television until I fell asleep around nine." Kramer flicked his hand, as if waving them away. "Now you can leave."

"Alone?" Damon asked.

"Son, do you see other people on the island?"

Damon looked at Harris. "He's a joy to talk to."

"I'm happy you're the investigator." Harris did much better with jobs that didn't include humans. Security systems, blueprints, plans filed with the city—he handled all of that with ease. The fewer people involved in a job, the better.

He didn't take on partners. That was the one thing that tripped up his mom and shined a spotlight on her after years of getting away with it.

Ted balanced the pool skimmer against the edge of the pool. "Let's shortcut this since it's probably my turn next. I left the island with Craig last night. We went to a few bars and had some dinner in Baltimore. We got back here after one and I told him to stay. He left about seven this morning."

"You two slept at your dad's place." Harris didn't have to phrase it as a question because he knew. He'd seen Ted go in and out of the cottage every day.

Ted nodded. "Yeah."

"And your dad was there when you got back last night?" Damon asked.

Kramer stepped in front of his son and aimed all of his ire at Damon. "What's wrong with you?"

"Someone broke into the main house last night," Damon explained.

"Probably him." Kramer switched his attention to Harris as he pointed. "I don't trust you."

That wasn't exactly news. Kramer hadn't exactly been a one-man welcoming committee, so Harris wasn't surprised. "You've hidden it well."

Kramer reached down and closed his toolbox. When he stood up again he had it in his hand. "Are we done?"

For a few seconds Damon stared at Kramer, looked him up and down. "For now."

"Excellent." Kramer pushed past Harris and walked across the patio and into the grass.

"I'm sorry about that." Ted sat on the edge of one of the teak deck chairs. "He wants all of this to go away."

It sounded reasonable enough but Harris didn't quite get it. "What about you?"

"Tabitha is dead. It's hard to say we should all move on when her murder is so unsettled."

Damon stood at the end of Ted's chair. "What can you tell me about Craig?"

"Craig?" Ted stumbled over the name then fell silent.

Points to Damon for leading with a question Ted didn't expect. Harris appreciated the strategy. "That's what he said."

"For the record, you sound like an investigator right now," Ted said.

Damon nodded as he eyed up Harris then looked at Ted again. "He could use some work, but yeah."

"Craig is a great guy. He grew up not far from here, spent a lot of time on the water as a kid. We all did. He went out and tried to do the day-job thing, following his dad's footsteps and all that, but he knew it wouldn't work. He missed the open water and managed to make that into a career." Ted looked at the patio beneath his feet. "Actually, I think . . . well, that doesn't matter."

"You know you can't just drop that comment, right?" Damon asked.

Ted hesitated for a few seconds but then started talking. "It's not my place to say, but he had a thing for Tabitha."

Damon's stiff stance eased as confusion crossed his face. "What?"

"Did they date?" Harris asked at the same time.

"Tabitha didn't really date anyone in the sense of going out to movies and such. Craig spent a lot of time here." Ted shook his head and looked around, as if he were uncomfortable talking about any of this. "He was devastated when she was killed. We all were, but his reaction seemed even more, I don't know, personal?"

"Did you talk with him about Tabitha and how he felt about her?" Damon asked.

"Not really." Ted shrugged. "I mean, come on."

Harris didn't remember anything about Craig in Wren's reports except for a few lines. That likely meant the police overlooked him, which could mean an opening. "Was he here that day?"

"I don't think so. Who knows?" Ted shook his head. "I'm probably not the one to ask since I wasn't either."

"Let's try it this way. Did anyone else know about Tabitha and Craig's relationship?" Because Gabby hadn't mentioned it and there was nothing about that in the police report, and there would have been because "the boyfriend" always became a person of interest.

"You're blowing this up bigger than it probably was." Ted looked from Harris to Damon. "He had a crush. I think she reciprocated it." When no one said anything, Ted started talking again. "Look, she was beautiful, like Gabby. She had a life. It was just a very structured one. People assume she was agoraphobic but she wasn't."

Harris looked at Damon. "He means a fear of leaving the house."

"I read," Damon said without breaking eye contact with Ted.

"My dad blames her parents. After what happened with Gabby . . . well, they suffocated Tabitha. Armed guards, no friends, schooled her at home with tutors. She was young and it had an impact."

"Do you believe Gabby arranged for her own kidnapping?" Harris asked, dreading the answer.

"Hell, no." Ted made a face like he couldn't believe Harris even asked. "Guys, you are looking in the wrong direction. Craig and Gabby? They both loved Tabitha. We all loved Tabitha. She was really lovable. No, this was a random thing or someone in her online group."

And there it was. The mention of that group again. A piece of the puzzle that had taken on much more significance over the last few days.

"What do you know about the group?" Harris asked because he had to.

Ted shrugged. "Nothing, really. She talked about the cases and showed me posts. That sort of thing."

"Lots of dangerous people in the internet." Damon finally stepped back from the end of Ted's chair. "Craig probably drives some of those people around."

"He didn't bring a killer here, wait for him to stab her then ride back to Baltimore with him." Ted swore under his breath. His expression said he was done. "Is there anything else?"

Damon shook his head. "No."

Mimicking his father, Ted got up and picked up the tools he'd been using. He brushed by Damon and left the patio. More like stormed. His feet fell in heavy, loud steps as he dragged the pool skimmer behind him.

Harris stood next to Damon and watched Ted go. "There seems to be a lot of support for this online forum idea."

"Wren is compiling all the records right now."

Of course he was. "I'm guessing he didn't get a search warrant to collect all the internet data."

Damon's eyebrow lifted as he looked over at Harris. "Do you get one when you break into people's homes?"

Since there was no way to win that argument, Harris skipped it. "So, tomorrow we go through video and paperwork."

"That is the plan."

Necessary work. Harris got that. But the idea of poring over files and chat forum transcripts made his eyes cross. "Boring."

Damon smiled. "Do you want me to find a vase for you to steal instead?"

"Maybe."

Damon patted Harris on the shoulder. "Go find Gabby."

That sounded like a pretty great idea, but Harris didn't understand why Damon was suggesting it. "I thought you were the one who warned me about getting too involved with her."

"I figure you'll fuck it up on your own."

"Thanks for the support."

Damon shrugged. "What are best friends for?"

CHAPTER 13

Gabby glared at the clock—midnight—then went back to staring at the ceiling. She vowed to paint the walls of the guesthouse after tonight. If she ever saw the color eggshell again she might get violent.

It was cool outside. She could hear the wind rolling off the water. She was pretty sure it was ninety degrees in the bedroom. She wanted to glare at Harris, blame him for heating up the mattress, and not in a good way. Heat thrummed off him. Probably had something to do with his size and how he sucked up most of the space. She would have pointed that out to him but they hadn't said a word all evening.

They'd eaten dinner with Damon and Ted. Not her choice, but Damon insisted. Ted clearly hadn't liked it any more than she did because he barely looked up from his hamburger all meal.

She folded her arms over her chest then let them slide to her sides again. She was locked in a battle with the most uncomfortable bed in the world. It had been fine before tonight but now . . . no.

Harris let out a big dramatic sigh. "I wonder if this is what it's like to be married."

"You're not funny."

He rolled to his side and faced her. "Hey, I'm just trying—"

"What?"

He put a hand on her stomach. "I'm not the enemy here."

The soft touch erased some of her anger. She knew she was being unreasonable by blaming Harris for everything that had gone wrong on the island during the last few days. For asking questions that needed to be asked and for pushing her to analyze all she thought she'd known about what happened here fourteen months ago. Despite all the frustration and confusion, she could still recognize she was the problem right now.

This thing where he talked in that hypnotizing voice or treated her to a gentle caress and her defenses tumbled . . . she didn't get that at all. She'd dated men before, some good and some pretty terrible. She'd experienced good sex and had no trouble taking care of that issue herself, if needed. It wasn't as if he wiped away her past and every insecurity with a mind-blowing orgasm. She didn't believe life worked that way.

But he did have this *thing*. Being around him calmed her. Engaging in banter, seeing how the verbal sparring excited him as much as it did her, ignited this dormant need inside her. She craved the energy and the challenge. Loved the rush she got when he kissed her and when his fingers slid through her hair.

All of it, wanting to be with him and the vulner-
ability that came with that, sent her into a full-body
shake. It scared her and rocked what she believed to
be true about herself. Left her open to feeling something for someone again after she'd committed to a
lifetime of keeping her emotions shallow.

"You're still lying to me," she said to the quiet room.

God, she didn't even know why she cared. If the
time with him was about sex and burning off some of
the spinning inside her, they really didn't need to talk
that much.

He was driving her to distraction. Just by lying
there, a few inches away with his warm breath blowing against her cheek. She couldn't keep her shield up
against him and she hated that. Mostly, she hated that
the feeling only went one way.

His thumb moved back and forth over her stomach.
"Honestly though, have you told me everything?"

"No." Of course not. She couldn't . . . shouldn't.

He tucked a hand under his pillow and raised his
head higher. "Then what's the difference?"

She turned into him then. Flipped on her side, letting the sheets fall low on her hip, and stared at him.
"I have no idea."

He looked at her as if she'd lost it. "Okay."

"I'm in the mood to be irrational." And that wasn't
far from the truth. Part of her wanted to poke at him,
get him riled.

A smile appeared on his lips and disappeared just
as quickly. "Is that really your answer?"

"Yes." She reached out and dragged a finger over the scruffy start of his beard. "How did we both get so messed up?"

"Years of practice."

Since she thought that was his serious answer, she didn't fight him on it. "Probably."

"Listen." He moved closer and draped his arm across her waist. "I never talk about my mom, but I told you."

"Please tell me you didn't do that just to have great sex." He wouldn't be the first guy to use that tactic. She'd been fed lines over the years. Some idiots tried to use the kidnapping to get close to her. As if that wasn't one of the worst moments in her life.

Harris's story, shocking as it was, felt genuine. She believed him.

He ran the back of his hand down her cheek. "I told you about my mom because I wanted to tell you."

That voice. It broke through her every single time. "That's why I shared about the kidnapping. People look at me a certain way, like a victim or a criminal. I didn't think you'd see me as either. You know the world isn't made up of only black-and-white choices."

"Any chance you'll tell me the rest of the kidnapping story?"

He knew. Of course he knew. They were both survivors, walking wounded. She'd recognized that from the start and a part of her reached out to him.

For the first time in years an automatic "no" didn't

slam into her head as a response to the kidnapping question. The idea of sharing the burden brought her relief, not panic.

Tabitha was gone. She would understand. But a promise was a promise.

"Maybe when you tell me what you're really doing on the island, I'll finish the story." He might know art but that wasn't why Stephen brought him to the island. It was the bit of truth that lingered behind every action, every moment, she shared with Harris.

He was paid to be here and handle things. It could be that she was the *thing* he was brought here to handle, and that thought made her stomach flip over in horror.

"What if I told you I came here, now, for you? To help." His thumb traced the outline of her mouth. Smoothed over her lips.

"I have no idea what that means." She didn't want to break the contact so she whispered the words.

His gaze searched hers. "You ever make a mistake and feel like you'll probably spend a lifetime trying to fix it?"

That question . . . it meant everything. The relief that soared through her didn't make any sense, but there it was. Chalk it up to the hope that he really got her. No one had ever totally understood her, not even her parents. "You just described my entire adulthood."

He leaned in and touched his lips to hers. A soft press that barely amounted to a kiss, but she felt it spiral through her.

"You are beautiful," he whispered against her mouth.

"Now I really do think you're saying things to get me into bed."

"We're already in bed."

He really kissed her then. Treated her to a long, dragging kiss. One that had her shifting on the bed and curling into him. When he lifted his head her hands were pressed against his chest and not even a whiff of air separated them.

"Then maybe you're just trying to get my clothes off," she said as she kissed her way over his chin.

He slid his hand under her T-shirt. "How long would that take exactly?"

"We should try it and see."

He rolled to his back, taking her with him. Her body slid over his and she loved every hard angle. Their clothes didn't provide any barrier to the combination of heat and delicious friction. His hands slid under her shirt and kept going. Warm palms cupped her breasts. He caressed with a gentle kneading and her skin caught fire.

She lifted up just long enough to rip the shirt over her head and off. By the time it fluttered to the floor she was on top of him again. She speared her fingers through his hair and held his head there for her kisses. She didn't hold back or play it cool. She kissed with all the pent-up emotion she'd been burying and ignoring all day.

In that moment, doubts blew away. This was about him and her and a heat that had her aching for more.

As they kissed, his hands plunged into her pajama shorts. He tugged her up higher, until her softness rubbed against his growing bulge. She wanted to ride him. Just climb on top of him and let her inhibitions fall away.

Her hair cascaded around her shoulders when she lifted her head. It brushed over his shoulder and he caught a handful of the strands and balled them in his fist. With a soft pull, he brought her mouth back down to his. This kiss seared through her. She actually felt her temperature rise and her skin flush.

They needed a condom. The thought ran through her head and stayed there.

She stretched, trying to reach the nightstand drawer. An unexpected flash caught her attention. At first she thought it was the reflection from the television, but they didn't have one in this room. She looked at the picture on the wall then to the window as her brain battled back from the edge.

A mix of orange and red broke through the black night. She blinked, shook her head. Tried to figure out what she was seeing. A light, but not steady. It peeked around the right side of the main house. Fog had descended and blocked her view. Wait . . . not fog.

Then it hit her. "Fire."

Harris laughed as his hands landed on either side of her waist. "I agree."

"No, Harris." She scrambled to sit and ended up straddling his waist. "The house is on fire."

BY THE TIME they threw on clothes and rushed to the main house, Kramer was already there. He stood by the line of shrubs outlining the porch and yelled instructions to Ted. Harris couldn't hear over the crackling of the fire as it burned away this home that had already withstood so much.

Smoke raced up the back right side of the house and curled into the air. Flames licked at the Tudor beams. The fire hadn't spread to engulf the upper floors, but it was only a matter of time. The house was old and sturdy, but it could go up in an explosive ball of flames.

And Damon was in there.

Harris pushed that thought out of his head. It was either that or not be able to function. He needed all of his strength and concentration to get through the next few minutes. He didn't wait another second. Kramer was talking about running a line to the pool. They didn't have time for planning. They needed to act.

Leaving Gabby standing there, Harris ran around to the side of the house. Pieces of the house burned and fell, igniting the grass and flowers in an orange glow. Flames ate through the wall. Heat thrummed off the building, creating an invisible wall that he could not pass without gear.

His mind raced as he tried to remember his walks around the island. He'd spent part of every day looking and searching. Call it an occupational hazard, but that meant taking a mental inventory. Right now all he could think about was the hoses in the gardening shed near the back of the house.

A line of fire danced along the porch banister where it met the back of the house. He'd just decided to run through it, take the chance he could beat the fire before it spread farther when he saw Damon walking toward him on the grass. Hoses dragged behind him.

Relief soared through Harris. Air punched out of him on a gasp. The idea of Damon being in there, trapped or worse, had strangled him in panic ever since he saw the flames. But now they could work together. They met under a window at the side of the house.

"The sprinklers are on but they need help," Damon yelled over the roar of the fire.

Harris couldn't think about the age of the house or when the sprinklers were installed. They needed to stop the spread of the fire. Harris followed the line of the hose to where it stretched out of the shed. They were hooked to something and he didn't bother to check. He hoped Damon had handled that.

"Now."

Damon's yell and the crash and bangs as the fire devoured part of the house echoed all around Harris. He pushed it all out and turned on the hose. Water shot out and he fought to aim it at the roughest spots. He heard shouting all around him and the sound of footsteps. When Gabby stepped up next to him, he fought back the fear for her safety. A lump clogged his throat but he nodded to her.

Embers somersaulted in the breeze. Smoke blew over them, into them and around them. A white haze seemed to cover the island.

Still, they battled. Harris's fingers locked on the hose. His arm muscles ached from holding the stream steady. Together with Damon, Kramer and Ted, they fought the fire. The joint attack from hoses, water buckets and the sprinklers turned the growing flames into a flicker.

The whole thing felt like it lasted for hours, but Harris knew it hadn't been that long. Dark soot stained the side of the house, but the upper floors and entire front seemed unscathed.

When the last of the fire disappeared, Gabby sat down hard in the damp grass. Harris tried to drop the hose but his fingers refused to unclench.

"Here you go." Damon came over and peeled Harris's palms free. He put a hand on the side of Harris's head. "You okay?"

Harris nodded. "Were you asleep?"

"I was in the front office."

Harris's memory flashed to the layout and the room by the front door. "Away from the fire."

"I got lucky."

Harris looked at Gabby. She sat stunned and un-moving. Kramer had put a jacket over her shoulders. The entire yard was in shambles. Ripped-up lawn and grass slick with water. White pieces of something floated in the air. Harris assumed it had something to do with drywall or paint.

"This can't be an accident." Harris looked at Damon. "Did you hear anyone in the house?"

"I'd drifted off."

"We need to start locking doors and setting the alarm." Someone kept getting into the house and causing damage. Likely someone standing on the island right now. That fact filled Harris with a killing rage.

Damon glanced at the hole in the side of the house. "Too late. The fire started in the library. If there was paperwork to be found, it's probably gone now."

That all made sense in the context of what had been happening on the island. Tabitha's killer was covering tracks, making it even harder to connect the dots. There was no other explanation. Setting fire to the property couldn't be about money. Sure, there would be insurance but the property unscathed had to be worth more.

After greed, there were a few other reasons for this kind of human damage. Hate, love, revenge. One of those fit. Harris scanned the faces in front of him, trying to pick up on any thread, find any hint of why someone would take this risk.

Gabby stood up. She walked past him to the front of the house. Stood there, right by the steps, and stared up at the impressive structure. Her shoulders were back and squared. Her feet apart. Once again, danger crept around her and she didn't show any signs of breaking. Harris admired the strength on one level. It worried him on another. He knew what it was like to walk around empty, to keep his mind busy so that he would never feel anything. He wanted more for her.

"Hey." He stepped up behind her and put a hand on her shoulder. "I think you should—"

She whipped around and fell against him. Buried her face in his neck.

The move stunned him. For a second he stood there frozen, then he wrapped his arms around her, enclosing her in a fierce hug. His lips went to her hair. The mixed scent of smoke and shampoo hit him.

He wanted to tell her everything was going to be fine, but he was tired of lying to her. Nothing about what was happening here was fine.

"I won't leave you." The words slipped out, but he didn't regret them.

"Promise?" Her arms tightened around him as the word vibrated against his skin.

"Promise."

CHAPTER 14

No one got much sleep that night. The fireboats arrived after the flames had been doused. An inspector and her team spent hours searching through the charred remains of the library. The sun had risen before they left.

Armed with a cup of coffee and operating on less than an hour of miserable sleep on a porch chair, Harris approached the main house. He'd showered at the guesthouse, but now he was back and ready to figure out the next step.

The smell of burned wood and metal tinged the air. The smoke had cleared and architects, handymen, builders and a host of other professionals would soon descend to clean up and repair. Harris figured they had three days—tops—before they lost control of the island. That meant less than three days to solve Tabitha's murder or risk Gabby being a perpetual suspect. Or worse, in jail thanks to whatever trumped-up charges Stephen could create.

Harris walked into the house, no longer too haunted to walk around freely. A new danger lingered. The front of the house had escaped the blaze but still looked like a war zone. All the fire and rescue people had stomped through it. There were muddy tracks on the floor. Tables were moved. Two hoses lay in the entry.

He made his way through the hall to the library. The wallpaper darkened and peeled the closer he got to the room. In the doorway, he saw it. The devastation. The room had been transformed into a black-and-gray wasteland. A few of the bookcases closest to the patio doors appeared relatively unscathed. The rest of the room looked like it had been leveled with a blowtorch.

Black streaks stained the ceiling. The table had been reduced to ash. Curled ends of burned books and papers littered the floor. And Damon stood in the middle of it all with his hands on his hips.

"Should we be in here?" Harris asked as he sipped on the steaming-hot coffee Ted had made for him.

"The inspector said it was safe but not recommended. I took that as a yes." Damon bent down and picked up a soggy blob that was once a mantel clock. "Her report will say the fire was intentionally set, but that's not a surprise to any of us."

"And once again Gabby will be blamed." Harris could see it on the news now. A new scandal for Gabby Wright. Another unexplained moment of horror in her life that the media and gossip blogs would twist.

She lived in a cloud of suspicion and Harris couldn't understand why. Even now, no one had pointed a finger at her, but he knew it was coming. From the tense way she'd walked around Kramer's cottage this morning with her head down, keeping to herself, she expected the bright light to shine on her once again.

"Good thing you were sleeping with her when this crime happened." Damon's eyebrow lifted as he stared at Harris. "It would be really helpful if you were awake."

"We were." This time he could actually provide her alibi. His identity would be a problem only if someone really dug. Even then, Wren promised to keep his name and past secure and Harris didn't doubt Wren or his abilities. Having a professional fixer as a friend paid off.

"That was quite a scene last night," Damon said as the remains of burned books crunched under his shoe. "Was that your first fire?"

"Not even the third, which is not a good topic, by the way." Damon looked up from scanning the floor. "But I meant you and Gabby in that very public clench."

Only Damon would use a fire to dig for personal information. The guy had balls. Harris gave him that much. "It's called comfort. The poor woman has lost everything. Her parents, her sister. Now someone is coming after her, or at least this house."

"Poor woman?" Damon snorted. "You talk like she's your grandmother, not the hot chick you're sleeping with."

Not exactly the topic Harris wanted to tackle first thing in the morning, but Damon wasn't giving him much of a choice. "And you act like that's your business."

"According to Wren, everything you do on this island is my business."

Harris could almost hear Wren issue that order. "He is totally a pain in the ass."

"If he didn't bail us out and keep us from jail every year or two his controlling assoholic tendencies might matter, but they don't."

"That fixer thing is helpful. One of his better traits." Harris couldn't have imagined what the last fourteen months would have looked like without Wren's help.

"I also love how quickly he grabs the check at dinner." Damon reached for a book on one set of now-battered and tilting shelves only to have the paper all but disintegrate in his hand. "Rich people, gotta love them."

"I've tried to break him of that habit."

"Yeah, don't. I'm cheap but I like to eat." Damon turned around to face Harris again and clapped. "Okay, good talk. Are you done stalling?"

Harris had a feeling that wouldn't work, but it was worth a try. "I guess you had a point and I missed it."

"Your relationship with Gabby is a problem. It clouds your judgment."

"It's not like that. We're . . ." *Shit*. Harris didn't even know what to say next. It wasn't as if he could deny they were together. Maybe not *together* together, but the sex did count. So did the way they shared secrets, but he had no idea how to label that.

Damon put a hand to his ear. "Yes? I'm waiting to hear what brilliant thing you'll say next."

Well, then they both were because Harris wasn't sure how to describe his relationship with Gabby. *Conflicted* and *confusing* were just two of the words that came to him. She knocked him off balance, made his dick hard and his brain malfunction. The combination had him treading water.

All that was true but he went with the safe answer. "We understand each other."

"That's hot."

Yeah, that fit, too. "Weirdly, it is."

"I'm not asking for a play-by-play here. I just want you to admit that you care about her."

That was not a word Harris was ready to throw around. "She is a human being."

Damon brushed his hands on his pants before moving on to the next bookshelf and studying what little recognizable items were left on it. "More stalling. That's adorable."

"I'm not—"

"Stay on topic."

"Which is?" Harris tried to set the mug down but he couldn't find a solid surface to do that.

"You are here because you have unfinished business that's kicking your ass. Guilt is making you stupid." Damon gave up the search and walked over to Harris then. "Your dick isn't helping matters."

All true, which he hated. "Did you just never learn the concept of tact?"

"You want to know who killed Tabitha." Damon lowered his voice but not by much. "That's why I'm not on a beach and you're not stealing a painting off some fascist's wall overseas."

"I liberate artwork."

Damon rolled his eyes. "You are so fucking annoying."

"Which is why we're friends."

"That's interesting. Not a surprise but it's nice to finally hear you admit it," Gabby said from the doorway.

The unexpected sound of her voice had both men jumping. Coffee sloshed over the side of Harris's mug as he whipped around to face her. The liquid burned his hand and had him swearing under his breath.

Damon recovered first. "Well, hello."

She smiled and treated them to a little wave. "Surprise."

"How long have you . . ." Jesus, how much had she heard? Harris replayed the entire conversation with Damon in his head and winced. "Okay, we need . . ."

What? He had no fucking idea what.

She glanced at Damon. "Is he going to finish a sentence?"

"I'm not sure."

Just what he needed. The two of them working together against him. Harris couldn't imagine verbally battling them both.

While Harris continued to reel, she pressed on with her conversation with Damon. "How long have you two known each other?"

"We just met," Harris said, rushing to keep his head in the game.

Damon shrugged. "For more than a decade."

Fucking hell. Harris turned to Damon. "What are you doing?"

"Come on. She is a smart woman," Damon said. "Unless you want to sleep in the pool tonight I'm thinking you need to be a bit more careful with your answers."

She smiled at him. "I'm starting to like you, Damon."

"That will wear off." Harris would bet on that.

"Unfortunately, that's probably true." Damon looked from Gabby to Harris. "Okay, you two lovebirds have a lot to discuss, including the fact Harris and I were roommates for—what?—a few years. It was before we realized grown-ups needed privacy. And he's got a neatness thing that drove me nuts. So fucking annoying."

"Jesus, Damon." At this rate, Damon might spill every last secret. Harris could almost hear it.

Gabby put a hand in Harris's face. "You stop." Then pointed to Damon. "You should keep talking."

"I will, but this thing between you two—whatever it is, because Harris doesn't seem to know—will have to wait. The bigger issue is the house, the videos and the paperwork."

Gabby's hands dropped to her sides and she started to frown. "Who exactly are you?"

"Huh." Damon shook his head. "Harris, you want to take that one?"

Harris rarely didn't know what to say. He always had the right phrase ready. A cover he could fall back on. It was part of why he'd been successful liberating artwork and delivering it from one place to another. He had a Plan B handy. Today's Plan B was the truth. Between the fire and the sex and the secrets and Damon's shit-eating grin, this was where they were.

Harris took a deep breath and plunged in. "We are here investigating Tabitha's murder. I really am an art appraiser, but he has law enforcement skills."

She looked at Damon. "Well?"

He nodded. "True."

That was annoying. He finally told the truth and she fact-checked it. "Why are you asking him?" Harris asked.

She rolled her eyes. "Keep going."

In this deep, Harris dove even deeper. "Stephen thinks we're working for him. We're not."

"Then who's paying you? The insurance company or the court? Who?"

All fair questions. It was not as if he could just drop Wren's name and end the discussion. It likely wouldn't mean anything to her, but it would cause trouble if she started asking around. "An interested party."

She shook her head and shot him a "gotcha" look. "I was with you until right there."

"There are people in this world who insist on knowing the truth. Who want answers to difficult questions." Harris realized that summed up most of his friends. All of the Quint Five possessed that trait. The driving need to solve puzzles, especially if those puzzles dealt with human lives. "A mutual friend of ours is one of those people. His girlfriend works for this place called the Doe Network. She helps to find answers for families with missing relatives."

"Was she connected with Tabitha?" Gabby asked.

"No." Harris didn't actually know if that was true. "I mean, it's possible Tabitha was on her organization's website, but I don't know. I'll ask." Gabby blinked a few more times than was normal, so Harris dropped that topic. "But we're off track here."

"Good summation," Damon said in a tone that suggested Harris had blown it.

"I'm still confused," she said.

Before Harris could go back and clean up his comments, Damon started talking. "Bottom line, we think your uncle is a dick and that you're more than likely innocent."

More than likely? "Damon."

"What?" Damon shrugged. "That's a positive statement."

"It's okay." She put out her hand when Harris started to say something else. "Better than I usually get, actually."

Damon stared at her for a second with his eyes narrowing. "What were you digging out of the wall?"

She glared at Harris. "You told him."

"He saw it. Our mutual friend has surveillance equipment on the island. Really well hidden, but it's there." Harris didn't see any reason to hide that fact. She wasn't the one running around causing trouble. And if she did decide on another midnight digging session, she might actually ask him to come with her. Clearly this three-mile stretch of land was not as safe as they'd hoped.

Her face lit up. "Then you know who started the fire."

"I like your practical side." Damon winked at her. "I was actually going to review the video but then Harris came in here talking about . . ." This time Damon shook his head. "Something."

"Let's look." She glanced around the floor and to where the table used to be. "Wait, where?"

"You may not like what you see." Thinking about who could be on that tape worried Harris. She'd been abandoned by so many, some willingly and others not. She didn't need another body blow.

She made a huffing sound. "You do understand my family history, right? It's hard to shock me at this point."

Wrong. Something deflated inside Harris. "Don't ever say that."

She frowned. "Why?"

He slipped his hand under her elbow and guided her back into the hallway to the office Damon had been using for days. "It invites trouble."

Ten minutes later, Damon had the video cued up. He ran it off his laptop, but Harris knew Wren had reviewed it first. Since his cell hadn't started ringing, Harris figured the video didn't provide many clues. Wren would be barking out orders if it did.

Now it was their turn to pick the video apart.

Harris and Gabby hovered over Damon's shoulders.

The laptop screen was divided into eight small boxes, each one showing a different part of the island. The timestamp indicated the video had taped last night.

The images were grainy but easy to make out. The buildings. The front porch of the main house. The darkness. Wren should have installed the sensor lights he had at his house. That would have made all of this easier.

The images flipped by at timed intervals, showing different angles. Gabby pointed as one flashed on the screen. "There. Stop."

Damon slowed the images down, focusing on a figure appearing by the retaining wall by the pool as if rising out of the water. Tapping on the keyboard, Damon followed the person's trail then sat back hard in his chair. "I see a person in a hoodie."

"Not Kramer." That was the part Harris picked out. Kramer had a specific walk. He didn't run and didn't stand up perfectly straight. No, this person moved with speed and agility. Harris tagged him, and he was pretty sure the person was a younger man.

Gabby frowned at him. "You can't think that Kramer would set fire to the house."

That was exactly what he'd thought. The guy had access to everything. It made sense that he could come and go unnoticed. "Disgruntled employee who has always been on the fringes of a wealthy family. They pretend he matters, but he's never really invited into the inner circle." When she continued to stare at him, Harris shrugged. "It happens."

"None of that is true."

While he appreciated her near-automatic response to protect the people she cared about, Harris wasn't really in the mood. "He's an employee, Gabby. Don't think he doesn't get reminders of where he stands in the Wright family every single day."

"I understand that. I'm not trying to paint my parents as saints, but they weren't ogres either." Damon looked up at her, and with both men watching her, she seemed to grow more nervous. She shifted around as the words rushed out of her. "I know the rich-people stereotypes. Trust me, I went to school with a bunch of them. They're hanging off the branches of my family tree. But my parents didn't really live that life."

Damon winced. "They owned five houses."

"Okay, yes. I don't deny how lucky I was, how lucky they were, when it came to finances. I'm not looking to play the victim here. But if my mom had her way my dad would have turned it all in and she would have gone back to being an interior designer. That's how she met my dad. She helped him buy a couch."

"That is a strangely romantic story," Damon said as he spun his chair fully around to face the two of them.

Frustration pulsed off Gabby. Her desperation to convince them played in every word. Harris understood her devotion to her family. With his background, he didn't suffer from the same issue, but he could recognize it in others. His worry was that it clouded her judgment here.

"My parents weren't perfect. Believe me. But they

did love Kramer. He got money when they died. More than I did." There was not a hint of anger in her voice. If that fact hurt her, she hid it well.

"*He* didn't fake a kidnapping," Damon said.

The skin tightened around her mouth. "Neither. Did. I."

Her response didn't leave a lot of room for debate. Harris believed her. He also knew there was something else going on, possibly a bigger piece that she kept hidden. The digging. The secrets. Hell, even the undying support for the family that didn't back her with equal fervor. Something wasn't right.

"Male, probably in his late twenties." The desk chair squeaked as Damon turned back to the screen. "That leaves us with Craig, Ted, someone hired by your uncle to cause trouble or some random attacker."

Harris knew Damon skipped a step. "You can't tell a person's age by the hoodie."

"The reveal had more dramatic effect with the age, so I added it."

Gabby stepped closer to the screen. "Where are those cameras?"

"Outside," Harris said.

She snorted. "That's not helpful."

"I wasn't trying to be."

She turned away from him and squinted at the screen. "Okay, then what about the day someone messed with the library?"

Damon shook his head. "I checked that this morning. Same hoodie."

She asked the right questions. Harris liked that about her. She pushed and poked at the facts until she understood them. Harris was starting to think she had an equal ability to bend those facts when needed. He believed her comments about Kramer. That was how she saw things as a kid growing up in the house, but who knew how Kramer saw it.

But the second after Harris thought about Kramer, his mind circled back to Tabitha. This all started and ended with her. Gabby, the woman who insisted she didn't feel anything, granted a lot of devotion for the people she knew. But Tabitha was her ultimate soft spot.

Then it hit him . . . if Gabby were going to lie for anyone, she would lie for Tabitha.

"The person sneaks in at night," Gabby said, as if trying to put the pieces together in her head.

"And knows exactly where to go." To the place Tabitha spent the most time. Again, Tabitha. Apparently more than one of the Wright daughters kept secrets. Harris wanted to know if they were the same secrets. "Whatever Tabitha hid she likely kept it in the library, and the person who killed her doesn't want it found."

"What's 'it'?" Damon asked.

Harris tried to reason it through—the kidnapping, the seclusion, the murder. He couldn't see how they were related, not with a decade in between, but there was one person in the room who might. "Gabby?"

She shook her head. "I don't know."

But that voice. Harris heard the bobble. He saw how her hands shook as she rubbed them together. "For the record, this would be a good time to talk about why you were digging."

Her eyes closed just for a second before reopening. "It's not my secret to tell."

Damon watched her now. "What does that mean?"

"She's protecting Tabitha. The rock and shovel were never about *you* and the kidnapping, right?" He had no idea what it was about, but the same word kept screaming in his head—*protection*. At first he'd thought the shovel incident was Gabby covering up her secrets. Now he was convinced she was keeping someone else's.

"Tabitha is dead. She didn't set the fire or search through the library." Gabby backed up toward the door to the office. "You two should stay focused."

Harris watched her run right into the open door then maneuver around it into the hallway. "You never struck me as a runner."

"Really? That's weird because I've been running my whole life." That was all she said then she slipped out.

Harris didn't go after her because he wasn't sure what to say. Pushing her might force her to shut down.

"You're not really going to stand here, are you?" Damon glanced up at him. "You can't be that much of a dumbass."

"She's—"

"On the verge of opening up to you despite the way you bulldozed into that conversation."

Damon was right . . . not that Harris intended to admit that. "Try not to burn the rest of the house down while I'm gone."

Harris just stepped into the hall when Damon piped up again. "You know, if you did care about her, which I know you don't because you're so honest and everything, but if you did now would be a good time to show it."

"Love-life advice from you?" Harris couldn't think of a less likely place to get it.

"Only one of us standing here has a *love* life to worry about."

CHAPTER 15

Gabby could barely hold it together. She paced in front of the guesthouse couch. She'd come so close to spilling it all. Harris asked a simple question in that reassuring voice and her world broke apart. It was as if the ice inside her cracked and shifted and a small bit of light shined through.

That was why she bolted. She needed to walk away and regroup. She'd kept this secret for years. Turned her life upside down to maintain it. Changed who she was and how she viewed her family as a result. To then just blurt it out . . . and for what? A man she barely knew?

She walked faster, tripping over the area rug then kicking it aside with her sneaker. The energy bouncing around inside her demanded release. She wanted to scream and shout and run. Flee.

God, why had she come back here? She should have let the court rule against her and walk away. Not try to solve the murder or protect her sister one last time.

Her gaze went to the bedroom and her duffle bag on the floor. She didn't own a lot of things. Stuff, collectibles, no longer mattered to her. Once "things" were taken away she realized how little they meant. What she missed was her family. What she called up in those dark moments were memories of the good times.

That was how it had worked for her. Her parents stopped the flow of money all those years ago and she morphed from how-dare-you furious to panicked to afraid. When she hit acceptance and no longer demanded her parents listen, they let her back in. All those tales of her being cast out weren't quite true. They cut off the money and made her reprioritize. It turned out to be a gift in that way, but every other aspect of what happened was a nightmare.

Without a knock, the door opened and Harris stood there. He didn't breach the entry. He hovered in the doorway, watching her. Those intense, intelligent, all-seeing eyes looked dull. His body, usually so alive with confidence and energy, seemed listless.

She knew why.

"When did you figure it out?" She expected a flood of pain to engulf her, but the sensations bombarding her didn't knock her down. For some reason, even more light poured in.

"Standing in the house, right as we were talking." He still didn't step inside; it was as if he were waiting for permission. "But, honestly, I'm not sure what I know."

"I'm trying to figure out if what you just said makes sense." That was her out. She could shrug him off and change the topic.

They'd forged this arrangement where they told each other things few if any other people knew, but also held back. It was this unspoken agreement. A tentative trust that made sense to them but probably wouldn't to anyone else.

They matched on that level, both buried in a past that defined them. For him, his mom . . . and whatever secrets he had so far refused to share. For her, the biggest decision she'd ever made. The one that changed everything.

He stared at her, not speaking, for a few more seconds. He finally walked inside and closed the door behind him, shutting them out to the rest of the world.

"You haven't been hiding *your* secret. You've been hiding hers." He took a step toward her then stopped. Half a room separated them when he spoke again. "Gabby?"

There it was. The ultimate truth. The same one she never dared to tell.

Before she could deny it, the dam inside her broke. All the memories tumbled out. The shock and the disbelief. Tabitha's begging. For once, Gabby didn't try to stuff the emotions back in. They rolled through her, knocking her off balance.

Reaching down, she felt for the couch but touched the table. That was good enough. She sat, waiting for the interrogation to begin. For Harris—art appraiser, junior detective or whatever he really was—to rip apart the pieces of the story she'd told him. It had all been true, or at least a version of the truth, but she'd left the most staggering parts out.

For once he didn't speak. He didn't launch into a joke or throw out a sarcastic remark. Didn't pretend he knew more than he did or try to lie his way through a list of questions. He stood there with his arms hanging loosely at his sides with his face wiped clear of all emotion. No judgment but no pity either.

The quiet waiting worked. She tiptoed into the silence with a simple fact. "She was only twelve."

Harris nodded, as if willing her to say more. She looked away instead.

With her head down she watched her hands. Saw how red they were from how she twisted them together. She dropped them to her sides and grabbed on to the table. Her palms ached from the harsh grip, but she didn't let go. This moment called for some pain.

"Even back then, before everything happened, she was really sheltered." That was an understatement. Their parents' form of correcting her behavior was not to let Tabitha be a child at all. "My parents thought money corrupted. They had this tremendous life, but it didn't stop my mom from drinking too much. Didn't stop me either, and I was sixteen at the time."

"Sounds like the usual teen stuff." They were the first words he'd said since he dropped the bombshell that started them down this road.

"Maybe, but when you're surrounded by all these people with all that money and all that entitlement, you can start to think life owes you something. You figure you can relax and wait to collect the trust fund. I knew so many people like that." She had been that person. Sure, she went to college, but it was all for show at the beginning. She depended on her parents to give her the means so that her *real* life could begin.

When Harris didn't say anything, she filled in more details. "After my freshman year of college, the year I almost flunked out because I viewed classes as optional, my parents made it clear the majority of their money would go to charity. That I shouldn't expect a handout. They thought the family tradition of passing wealth down to the next generation was a terrible idea. That it produced limited people."

Harris made a noise that sounded like an agreement. "They might not be wrong about that."

"I get that now, but my nineteen-year-old, private-school, vacations-all-over-the-world self was pissed." She hated the person she was back then. Such a stereotype. Not as bad as some, but not responsible either. "That's when it happened. The movie I saw and the joking about staging a kidnapping."

Harris came the whole way into the room. He didn't stop walking until he was on the couch perpendicular to her with his knee touching hers.

"It really was just talk, but Tabitha heard. She was always around because my parents didn't really let her go anywhere else."

"But you could go out and go to college and have parties?" he asked in a soft, coaxing voice.

"Right. See, they made their mistakes with me and

were not about to do it with her." Uncle Stephen had called her the bad seed. Gabby hated to think she was ever that bad. "My father said that pretty often. Uncle Stephen picked up on it and believed I was the problem child in the family, though I really wasn't. Selfish and entitled, sure. But not someone who caused her parents a lot of grief."

Harris nodded. "Until the kidnapping."

"She was trying to help. Her instincts were off." Gabby was jerked back into that moment, the one where Tabitha admitted what she'd done. On the floor, crying. Begging Gabby not to hate her. "She drew this map of the house and gave up the alarm codes."

"Oh, Tabitha." Harris closed his eyes.

"She was twelve and sheltered. She didn't know. At that age you have stupid crushes on older boys and one of them took advantage of that." That piece of shit Gordon. To this day Gabby tracked his movements. She hated that he'd married and moved on. He got away with manipulating Tabitha and planning it all. "This guy, the one in charge, flirted with her and told her she was pretty, which she was, but she didn't really know that because she'd had so little contact outside of the family."

Harris put his hand on top of hers. She could feel the anger zipping around inside of him. Tension pulled at the corners of his eyes and snapped his shoulders to sharp attention. He didn't even know Tabitha and he hated hearing that she'd been used. That was who he was. He might think he was only interested in sex—

no strings—but the guy reached out. In this case, both physically and emotionally.

"I was tied to a chair and blindfolded. At times they put headphones on me and other times they took them off. I had no idea how much time passed or when it would all end. The pleading didn't work. Neither did threatening them." Her voice choked off.

His warm hand closed over hers. The now familiar feel of his thumb rubbing over her hand, caressing her, broke through. She grabbed on to that lifeline.

"I was gone and at some point Tabitha realized it wasn't a game and I wasn't playing."

Harris leaned in closer. "Did she tell your parents?"

"No. She panicked. Shut down. Apparently hid in a closet for days, or that's the family rumor." Gabby purposely blocked those details to get through her private hell. She had to be selfish and not take on Tabitha's guilt and pain, too. "I was gone but by the time I got back she'd changed. She was so quiet."

Harris made a humming noise as he traced a lazy pattern over her palm. "You figured it out and you protected her."

Who knew that simple touch could be so reassuring? It was as if his fingers telegraphed his belief in her. The hold took some of the long-festering hurt away.

"Growing up I did the big sister thing and ignored her sometimes and told her to go away other times."

"But, Gabby. Come on."

She knew what else he wanted to say. That there

was no excuse. But after being told how she'd messed up in the family for so long it was one more fact that gave the accusations credence. In her head she'd failed Tabitha. She hadn't pushed her parents back or rescued Tabitha from the suffocation. For a long time she looked at the kidnapping as her penance for not living up to everyone's expectations of who she should be.

"The accusations about me staging the whole thing took hold. The kidnappers hadn't really thought it through and they fought instead of making the ransom call. They panicked and yelled at each other. When a bunch of them went on a beer run, one let me go. Kept me blindfolded and dropped me on the side of the road, but I was free."

"And since I've read the accounts in the news, I know none of them are in jail, which pisses me off." The simmering fury was right there in Harris's voice.

"Getting the police to believe friends of friends kidnapped me and messed it up, but I was innocent, was not an easy sell. Almost immediately, Uncle Stephen confessed to having doubts." She wrapped both hands around Harris's and held on. "My parents tried to support me, but then they lost faith, too. I can't blame them since my story did bounce around. It was hard to be convincing once I admitted to joking about a kidnapping."

"Tabitha never told them the truth."

"When she was sixteen she finally confessed to me. She was so different by then. Her carefree childhood gone. I couldn't imagine how she'd survive that level of scrutiny and the massive disappointment they would all level at her. It was one thing for the family to turn on me. I could take it. In her state, I didn't think she could." She closed her eyes, hearing her sister's pleading. "So I convinced her not to speak out."

"You played the role of bad guy. Permanently." He shook his head as a note of disgust moved into his voice. "And your parents never questioned. Never realized."

She had been so angry for so many years about that. It was one thing for her to protect Tabitha. Gabby viewed that as her job . . . But no one stepped up to protect her. "It was easier."

"Not for you."

God, yes. That was it. No one made it better for her. Saying it, even thinking it, made her selfish so she stuffed it down deep inside for so long. But that was the point. She still harbored all this frustration and anger, ran from the money and the Wright name, because no one bothered to believe in her.

"What did she bury in the wall that you were so desperate to retrieve?" Harris asked in his calm, compelling way.

There was no need to hide this part. She'd unraveled the lie. Whatever vow she'd made to her sister now lay in tatters. She knew that should eat at her, possibly destroy her, but all she felt was this crashing wave of relief. A sense of having the pounding weight lifted, if only for a short time.

"We both did it. She showed me the map she drew and copies of notes she had with the guy who was in on it and duped her." He'd been dumb enough to write it down. The papers had other handwriting on them. She assumed someone might be able to use it to connect the map to all the perpetrators, but that could also trickle back to Tabitha, so Gabby didn't want to use the documents. "I wanted to burn it all. She insisted we bury it in case the police did come for me one day and I needed the proof of my innocence."

Confusion moved into his eyes. "You were digging it up to take to the police or to clear your name?"

"No, I wanted to destroy it all, once and for all. Make sure no one ever saw it." Finally bury the past so that she could try to move on.

"And whatever happened to this ringleader?"

"Long gone. It's not him doing this. There's no reason for him to do it." Gordon was smart enough to stay out west. She would know if he ever lost that sense of self-preservation. So long as he stayed on his turf, she wouldn't shake up his world. "Saving Tabitha meant saving the rest of them, some of whom I didn't even know because I never saw their faces or heard them talk. To this day I know two guys who were in on it but not the rest. There really is no reason for any of them to be worried. I've proved with a decade of silence that I have no interest in pursuing this."

"The next time you try to tell me that you don't feel anything, I'm going to remind you of this moment."

She felt shattered, literally blown into pieces. She didn't want to remember anything about this talk. "I don't understand."

He lifted their joined hands and kissed the back of hers. "A woman who goes to those lengths to save her baby sister isn't numb. If anything, you might feel too much."

"Don't make me into a martyr, Harris. I set the entire kidnapping in motion by being a spoiled brat." That was the piece she had to live with. Who she was back then.

"By being human." He rested their joined hands on his thigh. "You're willing to cut Tabitha a lot of slack. Maybe do that for yourself."

"If I thought back then that throwing her butt in juvenile hall would have saved her today, I would have done it." That truth hit her the day they buried Tabitha. All those attempts by her parents to keep Tabitha safe might have gotten her killed. She had skills, but not the ability to ward off an attacker with a knife.

"Of course. Because you're decent and loving."

"Harris, don't." All that emotion she claimed not to feel rushed to the surface. The tears she'd held back pooled in her eyes.

He brushed a hand over her hair. "You're a survivor. It's one of the sexiest things about you."

"You still think I'm sexy after all that? I feel like a washed-out dishrag." Probably looked like one, too. Her muscles ached as if she had the flu. From the dry mouth to the ache in her stomach, she'd been wiped out. Offering all of that information left her dizzy and ready for a three-year nap.

But she could see warmth and, yes, affection in

his eyes. It thrummed off him. Not pity. No, this was something deeper, bigger. Something that didn't make her shrivel up and feel pathetic. This came from strength and it empowered her in a moment when energy had abandoned her.

His hand slipped down and his fingers wrapped around her neck, keeping her there with a gentle hold. "It's taking all my restraint not to take you to bed right now."

A very different sensation moved through her. "Don't."

Some of the tension pinging between them vanished and he started to pull away. "Okay."

"I mean don't restrain yourself." She put a hand on his knee and let it travel higher. "Act on it."

CHAPTER 16

She felt free. Gabby couldn't remember the last time her heart soared when someone kissed her or her stomach jumped when a man's palm traveled up her thigh. Both happened now.

After sorting through old horrors, a new feeling settled in her. Hunger. For him.

She leaned over, letting her mouth hover over his cheek. She didn't touch him at first. She inhaled. Let the charged distance pull them in deeper. Then the room spun around her. He had her off the coffee table and on his lap. His hands traveled over her back as their lips met.

The kiss shocked her as it had every time. He didn't linger. He dove in and took over. Told her with his lips that he wanted her and couldn't hold back.

The need coursing through him was the sexiest thing ever. He didn't play games or hide the way his body readied for her. His erection pressed against her thigh as his fingers clenched and unclenched against the material of her shirt.

The baseball style T-shirt he wore had her concentration cutting out. It fit snug over his biceps and chest but hung loose near his belt. It showed off every bulge and every line. Highlighted his lean stomach and gave her a peek of the elastic band of his underwear sticking out of the top of his jeans.

This man made unsexy white cotton hot. Hell, he made everything look good.

She had no idea what he really did for a living. He studied the artwork in the main house with a lot of interest, but that could all be for show. It didn't matter to her because here, now, on the couch with her thighs pressing against his, clothes and careers were the last thing on her mind.

Her fingers went to the buttons on her shirt. She got the first undone, then the second. At the third he leaned forward and pressed his mouth against her skin. Nibbled a little bite then sucked on the skin where he'd just inflicted the sensual torture.

The move made her weak. She grabbed on to his forearms for balance as his mouth toured her chest. Just as his lips dipped down and his tongue slipped along the edge of her bra, he shifted again. He licked up her neck then went higher. When he hit that sensitive space behind her ear and blew a hot breath across her skin a tremor ran through her. She almost jackknifed off his lap.

"That is so fucking sexy," he said with a deep voice that vibrated through her.

Without missing a beat, his hands slipped to her waist and held her steady. She refused to give in that easily. She rocked her hips from side to side, grinding her body against his until she heard him moan.

Those long fingers tightened on her waist and he brushed his lips over hers. "Much more of that and this will end early."

That was all the incentive she needed. Oh, she wanted to savor every minute, but there was something so tantalizing about watching him squirm. About seeing that admirable control seep away from him.

"How does this feel?" She rotated her hips, pressing the V of her thighs against his length.

"You are playing a dangerous game."

"You." She kissed his neck. "Should." Her mouth moved to his chin. "Teach me a lesson."

Her mouth met his and an explosion of need fired off in her brain. Heat flushed through her as his tongue met hers. Her arms wrapped around his neck and her fingers slid through his hair. She pulled his body closer, aching to feel his chest rub over hers.

Through it all, her hips kept moving. She practically rode him through his jeans. Lifted her hips up and down, sliding over his bulge, tempting him. Destroying her control in the process.

His breathing kicked up and a desperate panting filled the room. When his fingers skimmed under her shirt to the clasp at the front of her bra she almost shouted for joy. She needed his touch. Wasn't sure how she'd survived the last fourteen months without any meaningful human contact.

He peeled the cups of the bra down and stared at

her. He did not try to hide the heat in his eyes or the appreciation in that smile. His gaze roamed all over her. Then he bent down and took her nipple in his mouth.

Her head fell back and her body tensed. She could hear his kisses, feel them. Smell the need building between them.

She lowered her head until her mouth grazed his ear. "I want to ride you."

"Fuck yes." He mumbled the words against her breast.

She was convinced he'd make her wait, keep torturing her with that tongue. But in one fluid move, he rose to his feet with her body wrapped around him. She linked her ankles behind his back and let them drop down to his butt. As her body adjusted to fit against his, she grabbed fistfuls of his shirt and dragged it up his back.

She fumbled to get him naked as they walked. He headed for the bedroom, kissing her with each step. She marveled at how he could concentrate. If she had to lift a pillow right now she wasn't sure she could do it. All of her energy had centered on getting her shirt open. Now she put it into getting his off.

The kissing, the touching. Hands sliding over each other as their breathing failed. The tension pounding between them ratcheted up. She'd lost the ability to think. All she wanted was his hands on her and her legs open on the bed.

"I'm going to make it last." This time she bit down

on his earlobe. Sucked it between her teeth until he hissed.

His shoulder smacked into the doorjamb, but the uncharacteristically clumsy move didn't stop him. He bounced and kept going. He fell back on the mattress, turning and twisting so his body took the brunt of their weight. The move left her sprawled on top of him. A sexy friction had them both gasping as they moved over each other.

"Gabby." He put his palms on the sides of her head and pushed her hair back. "I'm going to make you beg."

That was exactly what she wanted. "Get to it."

He lifted up just long enough to push his shirt the rest of the way up and off. He flipped their bodies before the material hit the floor. One second she stared down at him; now he hovered over her. His heat seeped into her. His energy melted into hers. The wild frenzy of hands and stripping and clothes hitting the floor came next.

With her shirt and bra off, he brought his chest down against her. The sensation ripped through her. She couldn't touch him enough or get him undressed fast enough. Her hands hit against his as he tried to unzip his pants. He got it partway down and she took care of the rest. She'd use her teeth if she had to.

Just when she resolved to do just that, he sat up. He rose over her, straddling her. His hand spanned her stomach. He stared at her pale skin against the tan of his. Once again she wanted to know who he really was and where he'd been. That skin tone. Who'd given it to him? The woman whose choices shaped him. The countries he'd seen. She didn't have the breath to ask, but what little air she had managed to drag into her lungs rushed out again when his hand traveled lower.

Without a word he unfastened her pants. Slipped one button after the other out of their holes. Dragged the material down with one tug. She wanted to help him kick off her shoes, but she couldn't spare the energy. Her breathing stayed shallow and her gaze followed those expert fingers as he did all the work.

One shoe thudded against the floor. Then the other. He threw the pants off the bed. When he leaned down she held her breath, not sure what he planned next. The top of his pants hung open and his bulge pushed against the briefs underneath. She was about to reach out and caress him when his eyes met hers. Heat simmered between them. That same attraction that had sparked between them the minute she saw him shot off the charts.

She wanted him. Not just here. Not just for a day or two. She wanted to get to know him. To have the right to touch him whenever she felt the need.

She couldn't say the words. Even having the thoughts sent a spike into the moment. She blinked, trying to figure out when pure sex had morphed into something deeper. But before the panic could take hold he kissed her through her underwear. Rubbed his cheek against her then fixed his mouth to her. Pushed her legs up and open and dropped down between them.

His fingers slipped under the elastic band of her underwear. Kept going until the tips skimmed over her. The brushing, back and forth, had her hips lifting off the bed. Her head flipped from side to side on the comforter as his hand traveled under the silky cloth. She heard a ripping sound but it barely registered. When his mouth touched her bare skin, she seriously thought about never wearing underwear again.

She said his name on a soft moan. "God, Harris. Yes."

His fingers danced over her and his tongue swept inside her. She had no idea where her clothes went and didn't care. This moment was about him and her and how much they needed to come together.

Looking down the bed, she glimpsed his dark hair on the top of his head. Saw him concentrate on pleasuring her, and she wanted to return that feeling. Slowly, she closed her legs, brought her thighs tight against the sides of his head, and her hand reached down. She grabbed a handful of hair and gave a little tug.

He looked up. Her wetness clung to his full lips.

He really was the sexiest man she'd ever seen. Attractive in way that men and women would notice. Sleek and comfortable in his own skin. Alive with energy and wild when his clothes came off.

"Get on your back." She heard her rough voice give the order.

For a second he lay there . . . then he smiled. That sexy grin lit up his face as he crawled over her body. This was not a subtle climb either. No, he brushed his chest over hers. Slid a knee up her inner thigh. This was a takeover in the best sense of the word. He let her lead, but he made it clear this was what they both wanted.

And she couldn't wait another second.

She waited until he was eye level with her then she pushed him on his back. Getting him there didn't take much effort. Keeping him there took none. But he wasn't the submissive type. His hands found her breasts and he teased and caressed them. His fingers circled her nipples as she reached over for a condom.

He'd skipped putting the box in the drawer. It was out on the table now, and she was grateful. She didn't need one more distraction. The man under her proved interesting enough.

Taking his hand, she guided it down her body. Straight to the center of her again. He didn't need a lesson in this. A finger slipped inside her. Went deep before plunging in and out. It only took a second for her hips to match the rhythm.

She wanted to drop her head back and let the sensations pulse through her. But she wanted something else more. Her hands wandered over his thighs. She rubbed her palms up and down his legs until he couldn't stop moving them. She circled and tempted but never touched the one place that strained for her.

"Damn, Gabby. Do it." He growled out the order.

That made her want to tease him even more. Her fingertips drifted over him, skimming the hair on his legs then dropping between them. When they traveled back to his stomach, he grabbed her wrist. The hold didn't hurt. It wasn't even that insistent.

She was able to break it without trouble and flatten her palm low on his pelvis. "Who's begging now?"

"You sure you want to play this game?" He asked the question through harsh pants.

She could not think of a more inviting thing. He didn't think about surrendering. She doubted the word ever entered his mind. But he did want to play.

"I want you inside me." Her mind couldn't think about anything else.

Need flashed in his eyes. "Put me there."

She patted the bed, searching for the condom. Moved the comforter to the side. Lifted up a bit on her knees, sure it had slipped underneath her. When she glanced at him again, he held the packet between two fingers.

"Need this?" he asked.

"You do it." Because she wanted to see him roll it on. Watch him touch himself.

The man did not waste time. He tore the packet open and had the condom out in record time. He slowed down for the rest of the show. Started to roll it on then stopped. He took her hand and wrapped his around it. The two of them guided the latex on him. Inch by delicious inch, it slipped over his length until he was fully sheathed.

By the time they finished, he was rock hard and she needed to end the torment. The game had backfired on her. She'd wanted him to beg, but now she all but pleaded with him to move his hand.

Lowering her body down, she guided him. Felt his length slip inside her, stretching her. She kept going, pushing him deeper. Her inner muscles grabbed on to him and tightened. She couldn't feel where he stopped and she started.

Without thinking, her body started to move. She pushed and pressed. She rode him in time with a steady beat in her head. The same one that hammered in her heart.

His hands slid over her and her head fell back. The pulsing started deep inside her, that clenching that warned her about what was to come. The tightness wound and coiled inside her. She felt the waves of pleasure build and plunge faster.

Her brain turned off and her body took over. This was raw and filled with need. Every part of her that ached before burst to life now. As her body rose over him and his hands traveled over her she felt wild and free. Open and so clear.

When her hips started to buck, he lifted his legs. His feet slid along the comforter as he curled around her, cradling her.

"Gabby . . ." he said as his head lifted off the mattress.

Tension pulled at the corners of his mouth. She could see he was on the edge, waiting for her. But she prolonged the pleasure. Clenched her lower body even tighter and let the waves hit her.

He swore as his hands clamped down on her waist. He dragged her down as he lifted up. They met in the middle for a kiss that sent a new shot of excitement through her. His breaths grew shorter and his eyes closed. When he dropped back onto the bed, she knew he was right there. His mouth opened and she let go then. Gave in to the pleasure that hovered just out of reach as he came.

Their bodies pressed together as the orgasm ripped through her. So much for control. This knocked her off balance and had her gasping. She grabbed on to his shoulders to keep from toppling over.

The final waves robbed her of her strength. She fell against him. Hot and covered in a slight sheen of sweat, she lay on top of him. His body rose and fell on rough breaths and she held on for the ride. When he finally stopped moving, she snuggled in. Her legs fell to either side of his hips and she didn't move. She wasn't sure she could.

"Damn." His voice sounded reverent.

She was right there with him. She would have agreed but keeping her cheek on his chest felt too good. They fit together like the perfect puzzle. He didn't notice the slight bulge of her stomach or the way her thighs had a bit too much jiggle. Or if he did, he didn't seem to care because he caressed and kissed her there enough.

This, him, today and every day since they'd met, he made her feel worshipped . . . loved.

What the hell? Her eyes popped open just as she was drifting off. A winding panic started deep in her stomach. Had she become so needy that she was desperate to call any affection love?

The thought made her stomach flip over. "Harris?"

He laughed and his whole body shook. "There is no way I can go again right now. I'm not twenty."

His amusement eased some of the anxiety welling inside her. "You're a very impressive thirty."

"You're a little off, but we'll go with that number."

"Thank you." She wasn't sure why she said that except that his ready acceptance of the Tabitha situation and her role and all of the messed-up drama in her family made her feel welcome in his arms. It was an unusual sensation not to be judged.

His arms tightened around her. "I should be thanking you because that was . . . damn, woman."

"I mean for listening."

She could feel him smile against her hair. Man, everything about him was tempting and adorable. Except for the few things that made her want to strangle him.

"Thank you for telling me."

She lifted her head and looked at him. Those beautiful eyes were clear. No confusion or frustration. Most of all, no anger or pity. He accepted her for her. She almost didn't know what to do with that information.

"You keep looking at me like that and you're going to get lucky again very soon." She placed a quick kiss on the scruff of his beard. Liking the roughness, she did it again.

"Honestly? I'm not a guy who believes in luck."

Not the most romantic thing she'd ever heard, but okay. She was actually a little disappointed, but tried to hide it. "Fair enough."

He put a hand under her chin and held her gaze. "Or I wasn't until you."

"Well, that's better." She lay her head back down, hiding her smile from him. "Just wait until you get your strength back."

"How about now?"

She kissed his chest. "Now works."

CHAPTER 17

The next afternoon, Harris stood with Gabby and Damon near the front porch of the main house. They'd eaten lunch and stayed outside for as long as possible to let the smell of smoke clear. Now they had a meeting. Gabby just didn't know it yet.

She'd just announced her intention to clean up the shed following the fire. Harris didn't volunteer to help because he knew they had other plans. Just as he thought it he saw two heads poke up from the bottom of the hill near the boathouse. Two men, one young and one old. Both unknowingly under surveillance.

He nodded in the direction of their guests. "We have company."

"Who could be . . ." She spun around to look and her smile faded. "Oh, no."

Just then Stephen and Craig came into view. Stephen wore his usual dark suit. Craig was explaining something that had Stephen nodding. Mostly, Harris noticed the small suitcase. He sure as hell didn't think this meeting would extend to an overnight visit, so he had no idea what that was about.

"He's here about the fire," Damon said.

"You don't need to pretty it up." Gabby crossed and uncrossed her arms. She'd morphed from the vibrant, confident woman last night to unloved niece in less than two minutes. "You mean he's here to blame me for another mess."

Harris didn't care why they showed up now. He just wanted both men on the island for a short time. "It's convenient."

She looked him up and down with a strange look on her face. "Do you know what that word means?"

"Sometimes people think they're collecting information when really they're subtly being interrogated." That was the reason Harris and Damon had the conference call with Stephen early this morning. The reason he left the DC office he practically lived in these days as rumors of an impending divorce swirled around him and arrived in record time. They'd specifically asked him to come and check the property before the reconstruction phase started.

From the way Gabby rolled her eyes she looked less than impressed with Harris's response. "No offense. But neither of you are what I'd call subtle."

Damon put his hand against his chest in mock pain. "That hurts."

"I can be very charming," Harris said at the same time.

She broke out the eyeroll for a second time in less than a minute. "That's not the same thing."

Stephen and Craig reached them. Neither smiled.

Harris guessed Craig had been fine until he had to walk and have a conversation with Stephen. That man sure did know how to suck the life out of a party.

"Gabrielle." Stephen provided that less-than-cheerful greeting before nodding to Harris and Damon.

"I thought you preferred to go by Gabby," Damon said.

Her gaze did not wander away from her uncle. "Which is why my uncle called me Gabrielle."

Harris decided to take control of the introductions. "Craig, you know everyone, right?"

"I do." Craig's gaze shifted to the house. "Are you guys okay?"

Harris was about to answer but Gabby jumped in first. "We got lucky."

Stephen made a sound somewhere between a snort and a scoff. On him it sounded refined and extra annoying. "I'm sure luck had nothing to do with it."

"Now, that's a lack of subtlety," Damon mumbled under his breath.

"Excuse me?" From the red face to his refusal to give his niece eye contact, Stephen looked ready to blow.

That possibility didn't work for Harris at all. Gabby was off-limits and Harris needed a few minutes with Craig and Stephen or the meeting would mean nothing.

He gestured toward the house. "We should take a look at the damage."

Craig held up a hand. "I can come back and—"

"Craig, I doubt Stephen will want to stay on the

island very long." It was the best argument Harris had for having the two of them stick around, though he couldn't blame the kid for wanting to run. Even standing outdoors the tension threatened to choke them all.

"I'm prepared to be here for however long it takes." Stephen made that announcement then headed for the house. Brushed right by Gabby without saying a word. Didn't really recognize anything but the house looming in front of him and his rush to get in there.

"At least stay for a few minutes." Damon put a hand on Craig's shoulder. "I have some questions."

Craig frowned as he glanced at his watch but started walking. "Ah, sure."

They all headed in then. Harris hung back until he walked even with Gabby. He didn't say anything. He wasn't sure she would even hear it. Her shoulders had stiffened and her hands stayed balled at her side. That energy that usually pulsed through her had faded until her skin looked dull and her eyes flat, devoid of all emotion.

She had retreated into her shell. He recognized the move now. He had no idea how to reach her, so he settled for resting a reassuring hand on the small of her back as they walked.

Only her steps slowed when they walked into the house. Stephen zoomed down the hall to the library. He hesitated before going in, tripping a little on what was left of the door's threshold, and visibly straightened his shoulders.

Craig didn't limit his gawking to the library. He

looked around at the items on the walls and peeked into other doorways. When he got to what remained of the library he took a deep breath. Harris wasn't sure of the significance, except that he would know as they all did that this was the room where Tabitha died. While some facts were kept out of the news that one wasn't.

By the time Harris and Gabby got there, Stephen stood in the middle of the room. He turned in a circle, scanning the damage. His gaze finally landed on Gabby. "Why this room?"

"You're asking me?"

"Yes, Gabrielle. I am." Stephen let out a furious exhale that matched the sharpness of his voice. "Do you have any idea what the renovation is going to cost?"

The last of the fight seemed to drain from her. She threw up her hands. "There is no reason for me to set fire to the house."

Harris felt sick for her. On one level he understood the uncle's frustration. The man knew part of the story but not all of it, but his absolute dismissal of Gabby ticked Harris off. "She inherits it, doesn't she? Why would she burn it down?"

Stephen walked over to the bookshelf. "We'll see."

"Okay, yeah." Craig edged his way toward the hall. "Maybe I should go."

Nice try, kid. As if Harris would let Craig leave now. "And miss the family drama?"

"Let's all go into the dining room for a second." Damon didn't give anyone an opportunity to argue. He made the suggestion then started walking.

He led the impromptu march down the hall and through the other side of the house. Except for a few scorch marks on the ceiling and some water damage, this part of the property hadn't sustained much damage.

A long table stretched along the center of the room. With windows on two sides, the room was bright. The light bounced off the pale yellow walls. They each took a seat with Stephen at the head of the table and Damon and Harris sitting across from each other. Harris had pulled out the chair next to him, thinking he could reach for Gabby's hand if things got rough.

Before anyone else could start, Stephen folded his hands together on top of the table and stared at Damon. "Where are you on the investigation?"

"Someone broke into the house and searched the library," Damon said. "I'm assuming the person didn't find what they needed because they torched the library after that."

Stephen's fingers clenched together. "Where were you during all of this?"

"Sleeping."

Stephen's fingers turned white, almost gray. "That's your answer?"

"Yes." Damon threw a notebook on the table but didn't open it. He pointed the tip of his pen first at Stephen then at Craig. "I'm going to need alibis from both of you."

"Me?" Stephen sounded appalled by the idea.

Confusion swept across Craig's face. "Wait, why?"

"Right? It sucks to be hauled in and questioned for

things you didn't do." Gabby dropped that little verbal bomb with a load of sarcasm.

"Relatively few people travel to and from this island. I need to account for all of them," Damon said.

Except for his hands, Stephen hadn't moved one inch since sitting down. His back remained board straight and the flat line of his mouth didn't budge. "I need to understand why you, a trained professional, didn't hear someone breaking in."

The accusation was tough to miss, but Damon didn't take the bait. He sat there answering every question lobbed at him with a straightforward, totally Damon-like response. "I slept through the first intrusion. I heard the second and ran downstairs but didn't see anything but fire. It raced up the drapes, which explains why the flame took off so quickly."

Stephen scoffed. "So you failed to apprehend the person even though you were right there."

Harris noticed Stephen had perfected the scoff. He brought it out almost as a reminder that he viewed his status as being above everyone else's. So, Harris took a turn. "He could have been killed in the fire."

Harris knew Damon didn't need his help, but Harris couldn't stay quiet. He'd sat there, taking it in, listening to Damon dole out comments in a dry tone, but Harris was reaching the end of his patience with good ol' Uncle Stephen.

Stephen waved a hand in Gabby's general direction without bothering to look at her. "Talk to her about that."

"You just don't stop." She sat back in her chair with her arms crossed in front of her. "What is your problem with me? Just say it."

"Do you really want to go into this right now? I can lay out why I have my suspicions." Stephen unleashed on her in a voice filled with fury before turning to Harris. "And you. You're here but as far as I can tell you don't add anything to this endeavor."

Good. That was exactly what Harris wanted. He was fine being the target. He glanced at the cell on his lap, the one tucked out of sight under the table, and knew he needed a little more time.

"I didn't set the house on fire, if that's what you mean," Harris said, half hoping to tweak Stephen even more. The guy balanced right on the edge of his control. It might be helpful to see what he did when he lost it.

Damon nodded at Harris before joining in the conversation again. "Craig? You were on the island the night of the first break-in."

Damon's loud voice seemed to startle Craig. He jumped in his seat. "I was?"

"You and Ted went to Baltimore," Gabby said.

"A couple of days ago? Yeah. Just the two of us came back. We didn't bring anyone and I didn't see anyone." Craig shrugged. "I can give you a list of my regulars and some names of tourists and others I've taken around over the last week."

So helpful. Harris didn't know if that was a genuine offer or clever subterfuge. "Do you go up to the main house when you're on the island?"

Craig's eyes narrowed. "Why would I?"

The answer amounted to a dodge and Harris was not in the mood. "That's kind of why I asked the question."

"And last night?" Damon asked. "What was your schedule?"

Craig looked from Harris to Damon. His gaze shot back and forth as he answered the questions. "I did some runs and then went home."

"What time?" Harris asked.

"I was back by ten or so." Craig responded then looked at Damon. "And before you ask, I was alone."

"This is a waste of time." Stephen stood up. "I need to get contractors and inspectors out here."

Harris took a cell out of his pocket and slid it across the table to Stephen. "Make the calls."

"I have my own." Stephen tapped on his pants pocket as if to prove his point.

Gabby's eyes narrowed as she looked at Harris. For a second he thought she might blow the cover that she didn't even know was happening and ask some questions, but she didn't. She turned back to Craig. "You might need to do some extra runs to get people in and out."

"Of course. Whatever you guys need." Craig stood up and moved toward the doorway to the hall. "I'll head out now, if that's okay. I have some scheduled runs today."

Damon looked at Stephen. "You going with him?"

"Do you have an issue with me being here?"

Stephen just did not cut anyone any slack. He held

his strictest scrutiny for his niece but no one got away unscathed. Harris didn't understand that choice. Life was hard enough without going through it as a complete asshole.

"The more people on the island, the more likely it is we'll be tripping over each other and trampling on evidence," Damon said.

For almost a full minute Stephen and Damon engaged in an informal staring contest. They both said their view then waited. Neither moved and the silence suggested no one else should either.

Stephen finally blinked. He shifted his weight as he took the cell out of his pocket. "I'll catch a ride back. I want to speak with the fire inspector."

Gabby sighed at him. "I doubt she'll talk to you until the report is done."

"There's information she might need before she can reach her conclusions," Stephen shot back.

"Is the goal to make sure she's poisoned against me?" she asked.

"You brought this on yourself, Gabrielle. You don't get to act like the innocent party now."

"That's enough." Harris stood up and physically put his body between hers and her uncle. He was fucking done with this. If Stephen wanted a punching bag he should go buy one. From now on, so long as Harris was around, she was off-limits. "Craig, do you need anything else?"

He shook his head. "No. We should go."

The kid looked as uncomfortable as everyone else

felt. His expression said *get me out of here* and Harris didn't think that had anything to do with the murder or the fire.

Stephen reached the doorway and turned to take one last look at Damon. "You're here to do a job."

"I'm aware of that."

"Good." He spared Gabby a quick look of disdain then left.

As soon as both men left the room, Damon was up and out of his chair. He stepped up to the window and pulled back the sheer. He didn't hide, but he didn't step into the open either as he watched the men walk away.

Harris slipped the cell out of his pocket and looked at the screen. "That went well."

"Uh-huh. What's really going on?" she asked.

Harris dropped the cell on the table. Damon held one up.

"We cloned their cell phones." The strategy proved quicker and easier than getting subpoenas. Checking the cells gave them windows into both men's lives. Their schedules. Their texts and eventually their emails.

Gabby stared at the cells. "What?"

"The point was to keep them in here just long enough to get their information." He and Damon had worked that out this morning. Wren could collect a lot of data and either dump it on them or have his people do it, but Harris thought Gabby needed to be in on this. She needed to get her hands in there and dig. It was the only way she'd ever move past the revolving door she'd gotten stuck in.

She picked up the phone nearest to her and stared at the dark screen. Then she looked at Harris. "You did that? The supposed art appraiser."

That was not really a place Harris wanted her mind to go, but the answer wasn't difficult. "That is a real job."

"He can also shoot, do a decent showing with hand-to-hand combat and defuse a bomb, if given enough time—admittedly, he's slow at that." Damon made a face. "You're better off running."

Okay, that was more than Harris wanted to share. Going down this road could lead to trouble. She knew he wasn't quite who he appeared to be. She didn't have any clue about his role the day of the murder or his work in liberating artwork. Harris preferred to keep it that way. Once those facts came out, she'd be gone. This—them, whatever it was—would be over. He wasn't ready for that and refused to analyze why.

"And you know something about cloning phones." This time she sounded more fascinated than upset.

He shrugged. "My skills are endless."

She didn't look away from his gaze. She held it, watching him with a new sort of interest in her eyes. "I'm starting to see that."

Harris had no idea what to think about that.

Damon came back to the table and grabbed the phones. "Is this a sex thing?"

Count on Damon to ruin a moment. Harris should not have been surprised. "What is wrong with you?"

"Just wondering." Damon sat down and started fiddling with the cells.

Gabby watched him for a second before turning to Harris. "So, you have the phone information. How does that help you?"

"We track the calls but more importantly the phone information gets us into the email information."

"Legally?" She winced as she asked the question.

Harris frowned at her. She had to know better by now. "Don't be ridiculous."

"Maybe I shouldn't hear this." She shook her head. "What's the term? Plausible deniability."

She likely wasn't wrong, but Harris didn't have any interest in shutting her out. She deserved answers and he worried those answers would upset her. She may as well be prepared. "We want to back our way in. See if either of them is talking to anyone about the island or Tabitha."

"But you'll end up seeing other stuff."

Damon lifted his head. "You mean porn?"

"I mean privileged communications." Gabby raised her voice as she talked. "Stephen with his lawyer. Stephen emailing everyone he knows to talk about how much he hates me."

Damon threw her a blank look. "Do you care?"

"Wouldn't you?" she asked.

"Not really."

Yeah, that was enough of that, too. Harris tried to

guide the conversation back to topic. "With Tabitha's laptop gone and now most of the paperwork in the library destroyed in the fire, we need to be able to recreate any contacts she had."

"Including Craig?"

Harris knew he had to tread carefully. He and Damon might question Craig, but she didn't. That made tiptoeing through his life a bit harder. They had to be tactful and they had to be sure. "He's one of the people who can come on and off this island without trouble. He has access. He has the means. He knew her. She wouldn't have questioned him or fought him coming into the house."

"The person who attacked her seemingly walked right in. She didn't have defensive wounds," Damon explained. "That likely means she knew her attacker, which makes the suspect pool very small."

She shook her head. "You can't be serious."

He'd read the reports. The wound part was an issue. "Would you rather we lie to you?"

She leaned forward in her chair, at first talking to Damon, then she turned to Harris and put a hand against his outer thigh. "You're talking about someone I know, someone I trust or at least am related to, being the one who killed my sister."

He slid his hand down to cover hers. "Gabby, no matter what we find your life is probably not going to be the same."

It was an obvious point, but Harris felt like he needed to say it. Maybe because it applied to him now. None of this, what happened back then and what was happening with Gabby now, would leave them unscathed.

"But my sister will still be dead."

God, it ripped him apart to hear those words come out of her. "Yes, but we may know why."

She nodded. "Do what you have to do."

CHAPTER 18

It had been a long day and it wasn't even dinnertime. The sun still rode high in the sky but approaching clouds were threatening rain. Gabby guessed tomorrow they'd wake up to overcast skies.

Stormy weather suited her. The main house had a tarp and temporary covering over the fire-stripped parts, but she didn't worry about that. The house was a thing. Fixable, replaceable. Her mood reflected her latest round with her uncle. Her emotions kept bouncing. Dramatic highs with Harris. Paralyzing pain with her uncle.

He'd never been an easy man to like. He judged too quickly and had a rule for everything. Teen girls were pretty far out of his comfort zone. For some people having a niece might make them change, be better or more loving or softer. For Stephen she had always been a confusing puzzle who didn't obey his orders and made his baby brother worry. That was long before the kidnapping and the plane accident and Tabitha's murder. Those events had taken an already hard man and broken him. Wiped any and all emotion right out of him.

She understood that she had become his target, rational or not. But while she mourned everything else, it made her ache for what could have been.

She walked over to the kitchen area, wanting to forget about the newest confrontation with a bag of chips. Get lost in the salt and fat. She might eat the whole damn bag. It sure wouldn't be the first time.

The paper rustled in her fingers as she grabbed it off the shelf. As she looked down to open the bag, the door slammed. Her head popped up and the bag fell to the floor with a crunch.

There he was. Uncle Stephen, or a version of him. This one had a loosened tie and a wild look in his eyes. She'd never been physically afraid of him, but his words could land a wallop.

He'd planned to leave then changed his mind and insisted on staying the night on the island to inspect the house and made it clear he expected a briefing from Damon. She had walked away from all of that for a few minutes of quiet and snacking in the guest-house. She had no idea Stephen followed her.

"What are you—"

"I am done with you." Rage made his voice shake.

A strange energy thrummed off him. The sun beamed in through the window but he gave off a dark vibe. He wasn't shouting but she got the sense his body shook from the force of holding it back.

It was as if a tidal wave of fury moved through him.

He saw her and it exploded. He never looked disheveled. He was the guy who wore a suit to a kid's birthday party at a water adventure park. Today the suit looked right, fit well, but there was something off. That in-control remoteness had given way to something else.

"Why are you here?" she asked.

He didn't answer her but started walking. He paced around, watching her. "How is it possible you ruin everything you touch?"

She didn't turn her back on him. She faced him head-on as they performed this odd dance. A good five feet separated them but she started to wonder if that was enough. "I didn't—"

"Shut up." He came to a stop with his hands on his hips. "Do you even know what you've done?"

She couldn't even tell which supposed sin he was ranting about. "Nothing. That's the point."

"We need to end this, Gabrielle." His voice rose with each syllable. "This, the destruction, has gone on for far too long. To this family. To my marriage. Enough."

Marriage? She'd heard about a trial separation, but hoped the whispers were wrong. The few distant family connections she had said her uncle and aunt were still living together and trying to make it work. "Is Aunt Lena okay?"

His face twisted in disgust. "See, you get that worried look. Your voice sounds genuinely concerned. But there's nothing inside you."

The words ripped through her. They didn't just sting

this time. They shredded her. She sensed that was the point. He wanted her to pay and he was tired of it not happening.

"They are all dead because of you." The words came out with a note of awe. He shook his head as if he'd just realized all he'd lost.

But what about her? She wanted to scream that question at him. He'd been allowed to mourn. People believed his pain. No one wanted to hear anything from her. Her being at a funeral earned a scowl of disgust.

Before she could say anything else, he moved on. "The evidence is clear."

He talked without looking at her now. It was as if she were not there and he held the conversation with the air.

"There is no evidence." She knew that with absolute certainty because she hadn't done anything to Tabitha. She would never do anything to Tabitha.

"Because you burned it. That's what this was, right?" He barked out a harsh laugh. "The investigator was getting close, so you burned it all down."

He'd twisted all the facts until they didn't even look recognizable. As he talked his expression changed, as if he were figuring out a problem in his head.

It didn't take a genius to figure out she was that problem. "Uncle Stephen, listen to me—"

"You gave up your right to call me that." He shook his head. "I warned your dad. I told Colin to be careful. Not to let you back in. To keep you away from Tabitha."

The warnings to her dad. Keeping her sister away

from her . . . It was old news but still too much. Gabby tried to swallow and couldn't. She debated trying to run past him but feared he'd catch her.

She fell back on the only fact that still bound them. "I am your niece."

"Not anymore."

Air punched out of her lungs. Everything inside her shriveled and her knees buckled. She wanted to slide to the floor and stay there.

She also wanted to lash out. To punch back and hurt him.

"How can you say that?" She looked at his pinched face and closed expression and anger swept through her. People who barely knew her believed her. Harris, Damon, Kramer. But not her own uncle. For the first time the power of that betrayal hit her. *He* had failed *her.* "Get out."

He took a step toward her. "You can't order me."

The door swung open and Harris stood there with his hand still on the knob. "You should listen to her."

Stephen barely spared Harris a glance. "This is not your business. Go back to the house."

"Okay, we'll do this the hard way." Harris grabbed her uncle around the neck. Pressed his throat right in the bend of his elbow and squeezed.

"What are you—" Stephen's voice cut off.

"I'm choking you. Thought that was obvious."

Her mind scrambled. Nightmare scenarios about this going too far or her uncle suing Harris ran through her head. "Harris, please."

Stephen kicked out and scratched at Harris's arm. All the moving and shifting and fighting didn't have much impact. Harris stood there taking it all, only moving his head to avoid getting hit in the face.

"Calm down." Harris didn't ease up on his hold. "Now."

After a few more minutes of trying to break the grip, Stephen slouched against Harris. He was breathing heavy and his gaze darted around the room. After a few tours it landed on Harris's bag and the very male underwear sticking out of the top of it in the bedroom.

His fingers tightened on Harris's arm. "You're staying here with her?"

"The sleeping arrangements aren't the issue right now. Your attitude is." Harris gave the older man a little shake. "Apologize to your niece."

"Go to hell." Stephen practically spit out the words.

Harris didn't look even a little impressed. "Wrong answer."

Her uncle stared at her. Even in this state, he managed to glare. "Call him off, Gabrielle."

She'd been a spectator, out of words when Harris walked in. Still stunned by the way her uncle barged in, acting like he belonged here and could say anything without worrying about consequences. Then there was Harris. Sexy and surprisingly rough when he needed to be Harris.

He put his mouth right near Stephen's ear. "The official name for this is rear chokehold. I restrict your breathing and if I'm really careful you only pass out."

"Let go of me right now." Stephen's voice sounded firm and sure but the color had drained from his face. "You're fired."

She almost laughed. Only her uncle would try to pull that right now.

"You didn't hire me." Harris looked up at her and rolled his eyes before returning his attention to Stephen. "So, let's try this again. Are you ready to talk in a civil manner?"

After another round of scuffing the floor and trying to get leverage, Stephen gave up. He honestly never stood a chance. Harris was much younger and in better shape. He also seemed determined to play the role of hero, which was interesting for a man who claimed not to get involved.

Stephen's shoulders finally slumped and his grip on Harris's arm eased. "Fine."

Harris hesitated. He held on until she nodded to let her uncle go.

Once Harris did, Stephen spun around to face him. Adrenaline or fear had his eyes wide and glassy. "Have you lost your mind?"

Harris shrugged. "You're still alive, aren't you?"

"And now you two are together." Stephen eyed up Harris's bag again then stared at her. "Of course you are. You figured out a way to handle this and get what you want."

He looked so eager to say whatever horrible thing was in his head. She debated kicking him out and contacting her attorney to keep him away from the island.

But she wanted to know whatever was the big news he felt compelled to share. "What are you talking about?"

"Do you even know who you're sleeping with?" Stephen pointed at Harris but kept his gaze on her. "He's working with the investigator. He's here to find out information on you."

The excitement in his voice suggested he wanted to knock her down with the news. But it was too late. "I know he's with Damon."

"You call him Damon?" Stephen yelled the question.

"Damon and Harris. They're working together. I know all about it." She'd already accepted this piece. A part of her always knew it to be true. They'd just finally confirmed it. Now that they had, they were trying to figure out the island's secrets.

"You are unbelievable." Stephen shook his head. "I guess if you sleep with them they'll look the other way, or that's your hope. Your father would be horrified by your tactics."

Harris grabbed Stephen. Harris's fingers tightened around the older man's neck. "You are really close to being choked again."

But the damage was done. The words were out there. In addition to all the sins he'd thought she'd committed Stephen had now added a new one. She could barely count the ways she'd disappointed him. The list was too long.

She'd tried to get through to him. Kept the slightest contact because all of her family was gone and she was desperate to reconnect. But to what? He'd severed every tie. He picked every word to inflict maximum damage. He refused to believe her, despite all her hopes that he would one day.

Enough.

"He's staying in here. With you," Stephen said, stating the obvious.

She wasn't ashamed of that fact and wasn't about to pretend to be. "Yes."

"You're sleeping with him. That makes you a—"

"No." This time she was the one who took the step closer. "Stop right there. After all the unforgivable things you've said and done to me over the years, do you really think calling me names matters? You hate me. I get it. Well, Uncle Stephen, I don't like you either. You want us not to be related? Fine. As of today just pretend we aren't."

"And then there's the part where I'm five seconds from kicking your ass." Harris moved his hand and tightened his grip on Stephen's shoulder until he winced and squirmed and tried to get away from him. But Harris held on.

Stephen made a squeaking sound as he tried to move away from the punishing hold. "You are fired."

Harris sighed. "You can say it a hundred times, but I still don't work for you."

It took a few tugs, but Stephen jerked out of Harris's grip and stood up straight again. "Then I'll let your *friend* fire you. Damon is on my payroll."

"Good luck convincing him of that." Harris opened

the door and shoved him toward it. "And stay out until she tells you that you can come back in."

Stephen didn't say anything. He was too busy storming across the lawn toward the main house.

Numbness filled her now. A gray hollowness as her mind blanked out and she moved on automatic pilot.

Before she could grab the chips off the floor, Harris was in front of her with a hand on her arm and his face just inches away. "You okay?"

A wave of dizziness moved through her. "Art appraiser, my ass."

He shot her one of those sexy smiles. "I told you I have other skills."

"Apparently." She needed to sit and regroup but she only got as far as the armrest of the couch. She plunked down and forced her mind to focus.

"I thought he was going to . . ." Harris shook his head. "I didn't want him touching you."

"He wouldn't hurt me. Not physically." She didn't even know where that came from since she was no longer sure it was true. When he'd stepped toward her, in that moment, he looked like he was prepared to do whatever he needed to take her out of the family for good.

"Your optimism is impressive but wildly naïve, Gabby. Everyone is capable of violence if pushed far enough. Don't underestimate that."

"He's my uncle." She had to believe some bond still existed. That it wasn't that easy for him to erase her forever.

Harris cupped her cheek in his hand. "He's unraveled. You're right. He's not your family anymore." He briefly closed his eyes before opening them again. "Shit. I could have phrased it better."

But he was right. The words matched her uncle's actions. "No, I get it."

"His behavior kind of makes you wonder what he would do if Tabitha ticked him off, doesn't it?"

Gabby couldn't let her mind go there. Not now. She wasn't thinking rationally or ready to take on that mental battle. "You're jumping to conclusions."

"Just thinking out loud."

"Thank you." She took his hand in hers. "What you did was pretty chivalrous."

He lifted her to her feet and wrapped his arms around her waist. Let his hands rest against her lower back. "I get the idea you don't need to be rescued very often."

She toyed with the zipper on his sweater. "I've learned if I wait around for a savior to ride to my rescue I'd be waiting a long time."

"Maybe it's time you let someone in."

Her gaze moved up from his sweater to his face. She tried to read his expression, to figure out what exactly he was offering, but she couldn't get a fix on him or his emotions.

She could play games or ignore this. God knew she had enough to deal with at the moment. All smart thoughts. But when she opened her mouth for once she said what was inside her. "You already are."

His eyebrow lifted. "That's big talk from a woman who professes not to feel anything."

But he didn't run. Hope soared inside her at the thought and she didn't know why. She'd started down a road she wasn't sure she wanted to travel. "Does it scare you?"

"I'm not going anywhere." If anything, he pulled her in even tighter.

This was too much. Too fast. Too something.

Her mind raced as she tried to come up with something neutral to say. "Should we check on Stephen?"

Harris shook his head. "I'll text Damon and warn him, but otherwise let Stephen find his own woman."

The word spun inside her. "Is that what I am to you?"

"You are right now."

She inhaled, trying to calm her mix of jangled nerves and festering rage. Her uncle set off both inside her. The burden that weighed on her for so long eased when she saw Harris. She'd been so wary of relying on anyone for so long. So quick to push people away and keep things informal. With Harris she wanted more.

"Do we need to get back to work?" She'd never be able to concentrate, but she could move papers around. Anything to keep her hands and mind busy.

His arms dropped to his sides and he headed for the door.

Disappointment rammed into her, but she managed to stay on her feet. She scooped the bag of chips off the floor and glanced up in time to see Harris throw the lock. "What are you doing?"

"Guaranteeing some privacy." He picked the bag out of her hand and threw it on the counter behind her. "Giving in to the need to touch you."

His arms slipped around her and he pulled her close. All that frustration and uncertainty drifted away. Here it was between the two of them and nothing her uncle said mattered. "Do I get to touch you back?"

He winked at her. "I'm counting on it."

CHAPTER 19

Two hours later Harris and Gabby walked together toward the main house. The sun had all but disappeared into a bank of puffy gray clouds. Harris still fumed. He didn't hate many people because he usually didn't care enough to waste time on that sort of thing. But he hated Stephen.

Harris had hung back at the guesthouse after the standoff. The plan was to be there for her and make sure her uncle's words hadn't taken hold. Harris never expected *he* would need the time alone with her. His hands actually shook when he'd held her. A moment of comfort had morphed into something big and much scarier and then their clothes were off.

He'd spent so much of his life cultivating relationships that benefitted him but didn't intrude on his life. The one exception was the Quint Five. He would do anything for those men and the small group of friends they'd formed. Other than with them, Harris didn't do deep.

He enjoyed sex. The release and the heat calmed

him. But he'd kept his partners casual, even forgettable. They had fun together for a short time but neither of them looked for anything more.

But he didn't feel casual with her. He was invested. This amounted to more than sex for the sake of having sex.

The topic wasn't one he wanted to discuss or even admit to. Instead of examining it, he settled for brushing his arm against hers as they crested the hill.

Damon stood on the porch. He looked as if he were waiting for them. He didn't hold his usual coffee mug or any paperwork. He leaned against the porch post surveying first the land, then them.

He waited until they joined him to step back into the house. "Did you have a nice visit with your uncle?"

"Did he threaten to fire me?"

"Both of us. He's charming like that." Damon nodded in the direction of the building down the hill. "He's at the boathouse with Kramer, by the way."

They all kept walking. Harris and Gabby followed Damon into the study off the entry. Papers littered the desk. Stacks of files covered the top of the printer. He had dragged in a small table from the kitchen and two hardback chairs.

The space had been turned into a war room. Harris knew Damon spread everything out in here because there was a lock on the door. With Stephen staying upstairs for whatever amount of time he remained on the island, they needed to be careful of exposure.

Gabby continued to the far side of the table across the men. She pushed a few files around to read the labels on them. "Harris tried to kill him."

"Interesting tactic." The lightness in Damon's tone suggested he was impressed and more than a little supportive of the approach.

Harris shrugged as he pulled out a chair and sat down. "I only threatened to choke him until he passed out. Different thing."

"And a totally reasonable response."

The amusement was evident in Damon's voice, but Harris didn't find anything funny about the toxic family scene he'd walked into. "You didn't see him come after Gabby. You probably would have shot him."

Gabby's head popped up. "You have a gun here?"

"What the fuck? Go back." Damon put his hands on the back of the leather desk chair he'd rolled over and leaned in closer to Gabby. "What did he do to you?"

That was more like it. Harris counted on Damon having that reaction and he didn't disappoint.

"It's fine. Everyone, calm down." She waved off the concern and went back to studying the documents in front of her. "My uncle has said much worse things to me."

"That's pretty appalling." Harris wanted to use other words to describe what he viewed as a fucking tragedy but he had vowed to stay calm. Getting all pissed off wouldn't do her any good. But now she was staring at him and he didn't know why. "What?"

She smiled at him. "Nothing. You actually sounded like an art appraiser there for a second."

He'd never met anyone—man or woman—who took his casual acquaintance with the truth on certain subjects so well. It was as if she trusted him with her body and her secrets but nothing else. He was completely sure how he felt about that.

But, at least for now, he planned on maintaining the cover story. "Again, it's a real job."

"Yeah, you keep saying that. I don't disagree, in general." She pointed at him. "I just don't think *you* do that job."

Damon pulled out a chair and sat down. "You two are cute."

Harris decided to derail this topic, and fast. He turned to his friend. "Did you find anything?"

"Good pivot." Damon gestured to the paper explosion on the table. "And, yes. A mound of data."

Gabby flipped through a stack of documents in front of her. "What exactly is all this?"

"Internet records. Phone records." Damon held up two empty coffee mugs. "I made coffee."

Harris looked at the tray next to Damon. It looked like he put together a few mugs, the coffeepot, a tub of sugar and a banana. An interesting and not all that helpful mix. "We're going to need a bigger pot."

Gabby picked up a back statement. "I'm not sure what I'm looking for."

"That's how this works." Damon shot a notepad and pen flying in her direction on the only clear space on the table. "You dig and read and try to make connections. Some will be obvious. Some will be based on a feeling."

"That's what your sister did on those crime forums." So much of finding clues depended on sorting through minutiae.

Gabby's hands landed on the table and the paper in her hand crinkled as it folded. "It was more than that. You know that, right? She worked with this team and they did reports for law enforcement and true crime television shows. She's worked with the Innocence Project and others."

The unexpected burst of defensiveness took him by surprise. "Do you think you need to sell her to me?"

"I want you to see her as more than a statistic." Gabby's voice took on an added urgency. "She was flawed and confused and sometimes scared, but she was funny and sweet and absolutely dedicated to the idea that every family deserved answers about their loved ones."

Harris stretched an arm across the table and slipped his fingers over her clenched fist. "I'm sorry I never got to talk with her."

For a second no one said anything. She stared at him and he stared back, willing her to understand on this issue they were on the same side.

Damon smacked his open hand against the top of the table with a sharp whack. "Papers."

With the silence broken, Harris nodded and dug in. "Right."

They worked for the next three hours without interruption. Every now and then one of them would hold up a document and ask for help clarifying it. They all made lists on their notepads. Harris didn't know what was important so he highlighted anything that jumped out at him. They reviewed, analyzed and correlated. Each of them collected a stack they wanted to keep close and share with the others.

Music filled the room from whatever service Damon used on his computer. They stayed in there with the door locked. Stephen never tried to come in, but Harris had seen him walk onto the porch just before footsteps sounded on the stairs.

Ted and Kramer worked just outside the window, piling wood and discarded items from the fire in a big bin. The weather had gotten cooler and a storm threatened from farther out on the water. Kramer walked at his usual pace but called out orders, sending his son scurrying as they raced to miss the rain.

But Harris had found something. Maybe important, maybe not. It was one of those anomalies that jumped out and demanded attention.

He glanced over at Gabby. She had her hair pulled up in this convoluted knot on top of her head. He'd watched her do it. Just a pen and her hands. She didn't use a mirror or anything. The whole thing proved his theory that women had spooky voodoo powers men would never understand. The end result was pretty stunning. She managed to be compelling without trying. Casual yet elegant with that sexy long neck and inviting mouth.

"Tell me what you know about this team she worked with." His voice broke into the quiet room. Both Damon and Gabby looked up at him.

She made a humming sound. "Not much. It was online and they went back and forth on crime theories and suspects."

Damon leaned over. "Why, what are you looking at?"

"Here are some transcripts for online chats. I can see the members going back and forth, talking and testing ideas." They spent hours going through every detail of a cold case. Harris admired that level of dedication to anything. "And then this happened about ten months before Tabitha was killed."

He turned the transcript copy around so both Damon and Gabby could see. With the tip of his pen, Harris pointed to a line about halfway down the page.

Gabby picked the page up and scanned it again. "I don't know what I'm supposed to be seeing."

"A new member." After months of debating with a set number of members, someone else came on the scene. "Crimesleuthing."

Damon whistled. "That's quite a username."

That was not the part Harris found most interesting. He glanced at his notes and he laid out the theory. "He or she starts right before Tabitha's birthday. Talks to members on open forums, gets invited to the much smaller private group." That alone might not be significant, but that wasn't all. "There are chats between Tabitha and this person, just the two of them, right up until she died."

"Looks like the night before," Damon said.

Gabby hadn't eased up on her double-fisted grip on the papers. "You got this from Tabitha's internet information? The same information we're going to pretend was legally obtained."

"Yeah, let's pretend we did." If they started waiting for probable cause and subpoenas they'd never get anywhere. Worse, they'd tip off anyone who was watching that there was movement in the case and where it came from.

"It looks like we have a new unsub." Damon stretched as he reached for the coffeepot, which had already been refilled three times since they all sat down.

"Unknown subject," Harris said, explaining the technical term.

"I know. I watch television." Gabby frowned at him as if to say he was the one who lingered two steps behind, not her. "You're thinking this person stalked Tabitha and then . . . what?"

They shouldn't add two and two and get seven. Harris didn't want her jumping to conclusions or filling in blanks. That meant he needed to keep the expectations low. "She's careful but identities can be cracked. We may have a guy who figured out who she was, how much money she had, and came to find her. Or it could mean nothing."

Gabby's frown only deepened. "You think someone snuck on the island all those months ago and then did it again the other night just to burn down the library?"

Admittedly it sounded ridiculous when she spelled

it out like that, but he did see an opening for how it might have happened. "If the person thought there was evidence proving a connection to Tabitha, that could explain it. Your inheritance issues have been in the news. How hard would it be to dig around and figure out the island might be sold or at least have a new owner soon?"

"I'm never going to live here." She visibly shivered as she made that declaration.

"Unless you've said that to a reporter and it's all over the internet, this person likely wouldn't know that." But Harris understood. Being there temporarily and limiting the time spent inside the main house made the visit tolerable. She could pick an end date in her head, think of a future somewhere else. But moving onto the island meant living with the memories every single minute. Harris hadn't been able to do that in his own life.

He'd relocated across the country to keep from getting entangled or ending up as his mother's lifeline to the outside world. So, he got it.

"So now we get more records from this forum and try to trace this guy." Damon leaned back in his chair. "I also want to search through the data collected from the cloned phones from Craig and Stephen."

Gabby eyed up the darkening skies outside and the almost empty coffeepot. "It's going to be a long night."

She needed a break. For him and Damon this was work. It centered on trying to clear her name, and without anyone knowing he was even involved, Harris's. But for her this was about investigating friends and family. Emotionally it had to tug and pull at her. Knowing the truth sounded good unless the truth meant more heartache.

"You head to bed." Harris looked around at the stacks on the floor they hadn't touched yet. "We'll organize what we have, then I'll be there."

She looked like she was going to argue but then she nodded. "Okay."

He stood up. "I can walk you back."

"I'm fine." But her eyes were starting to droop and the rest of her hair slipped out of that makeshift knot on the top of her head.

Harris found the look pretty adorable, but she did need sleep. "Since I almost strangled your uncle this afternoon, I'm not sure that's true."

"It's a full island." She stood up and sighed at them in the men-are-so-difficult way she'd perfected. "Uncle Stephen and Kramer were over by the fire pit earlier. Ted and Craig went to the boathouse to pick up something Ted spilled when he was working in there earlier."

As a show of independence or defiance or whatever, it sounded like she planned on fighting this to the end. Unlucky for her, so did he. "Is that information supposed to make us feel more secure?"

"I'll be fine."

Damon folded his arms behind him. "You can kiss. I won't watch."

She frowned at him. "You're kind of nosy."

"Right?" But Harris thought it sounded like a damn fine idea.

He maneuvered her out of the study. After a quick look at the staircase to see if Stephen had come down, Harris opened the front screen door and guided her outside with a hand on the small of her back. A second visual scan of the grounds for trouble convinced him that the island was quiet. He could see the fire pit blazing and hear male laughter.

He could watch every step from this position as she walked to the guesthouse so he decided to let the subject drop. But not the kiss.

He leaned down and caught her mouth with his. That fast the exhaustion drained away. Every muscle burst to life. When he lifted his head he thought about suggesting they go back and test out that table in the guesthouse. The thing looked sturdy enough to hold them both. But then he saw the strain it took for her to keep her eyes open and he dropped the subject.

"I'll be down soon."

She reached up with a hand around the back of his neck and gave him a kiss that suggested she might not be that tired after all. "Wake me when you get in."

Harris reentered the study a few minutes later. He didn't realize he was whistling until Damon stared at him with one eyebrow raised. That was enough to cut off the tune.

"So, Uncle Stephen." Damon hadn't changed his position. He still leaned the chair back to the point of tipping and folded his hands behind his head.

With just the two of them in the room Harris didn't

have to weigh his words. "Even after he calmed down I almost choked the guy just for fun."

Damon shook his head. "Let's not do that. Then we'd have to cover up a rich guy's death and Wren would get angry."

"He's off."

Damon tipped the chair forward. "Wren?"

"Don't be a dumbass. Stephen. The rage, the way he went after Gabby, it was pretty sick." Unreasonable, bloated, troublesome. A lot of words fit.

"Weird since they're related."

"We both know blood ties do not guarantee people get along." Harris had unwanted personal experience on that front. He'd seen the same loss of control when his father found out about his mother's secret life.

He'd morphed into a different man, a violent and bitter one, in the space of a few hours. The news hit him and changed everything. He'd prided himself on maintaining the perfect family portrait to the world. The right wife. A child he could mold. Then the bottom fell out. He'd been living a lie. Not only did that upend his world, it made him a laughingstock.

It also made him *the guy who should have known*. There were endless debates, including by the police and prosecutors, about his dad's complicity. Harris knew his father was in the dark. He also knew that more than once his mother had used him, her own son, as cover while she stole items.

Learning those secrets changed everything. He'd funneled the shock into figuring out why she'd done it, which meant trying it himself. His father retreated into a hard shell. He lashed out. He called her names. He threatened to kill her.

That profound loss of perspective never corrected itself. The more his father learned, the more he hated Harris's mom. Harris sensed Stephen had gotten sucked into that same vicious whirlpool of hate. It didn't excuse what he did to Gabby. Nothing could. But it did make Harris worry that Gabby would never move out of her uncle's target.

"It's as if he no longer views her as human." That was the sickest part to Harris. The one that made him fear for her safety and want to convince Stephen, with fists if necessary, to back down. "You'd think he'd hold it together since there isn't any evidence."

"There are statements from some of her supposed friends that say she planned her kidnapping. But there's nothing that suggests she killed Tabitha."

Harris instinctively knew there never would be. Gabby might be flawed and human, but she'd loved and protected her sister the best she could.

That led Harris right back to the problem family member. "What's the uncle's money situation?"

"Now, that's interesting. It is a bit of a question mark because he and the wife are negotiating a divorce settlement. No prenup." Damon moved the files around until he found court documents that were filed by Stephen's wife but never served. "Rich people, man. Go figure."

"Let's dig in." Harris had an incentive. He not only wanted Gabby safe, he wanted to go to her. Tonight, soon . . . now. That meant more work and he was ready to take it on. "You better make more coffee."

CHAPTER 20

Gabby was restless. She wanted to blame the frantic roller-coaster ride she'd been on for the emotional fallout, but she worried there might be a much simpler cause—Harris. He hadn't come back to the guesthouse yet.

She'd spent so much of her adult life alone. She had friends and people she hung out with at different jobs. But the deep, could-say-anything meaty relationships always failed her. Or she failed them. The idea of getting that close repelled her.

The people who were supposed to love her unconditionally had put limits on their feelings for her. She disappointed them. They didn't believe her and demanded she win back their love. She had to prove herself. Only Tabitha had provided a link to the life she once had, and Gabby had cherished that until she lost that, too.

Her entire life had been about loss. Loss of people. Loss of trust. Loss of what she knew and believed in. She developed a hard coating to survive. Accepted what happened and her role in it. Tried to push through, and usually could, but some days the harshness of it all dragged her down. Best her into submission.

With everything she'd been through and handled, the idea of being reliant on someone else in order to get a solid night's sleep struck her as more than a little annoying. It wasn't that she'd somehow surrendered her independence over the course of a few days, but she did enjoy being with him. He made her smile. She'd laughed for the first time in what felt like forever. The sex was amazing but the comfort, the sensation of mattering to someone else, felt even better.

But the bed truly sucked. She kicked off the covers, letting her heels bounce against the mattress, and looked around the dark bedroom. The storm hadn't blown in yet but it was headed for them. The breeze had kicked up and moisture hung in the air. When she'd walked back to the guesthouse earlier a fine mist filled the air. She towel-dried her damp skin and hair.

She loved the moodiness of this sort of weather. Dark clouds. A coolness tucked under the humidity. The sound of rain pounding on a roof. Everything washed away and new again.

She sat up, letting her feet dangle over the side of the bed. Pressed her toes against the hardwood floor. The idea of changing out of her soft PJ shorts combination didn't hold any appeal. But maybe wandering outside, smelling the early start of the storm and walking in the soft wind would clear her head enough to be able to drift off.

One benefit of living on an island was supposed to

be privacy. There were people around but not many. Still, she decided to throw on a sweater and reached for the one over the back of the chair. Harris's scent hit her immediately. She slipped it on and the edge of the cotton dropped down to her upper thighs. The too-long sleeves hid her hands. She wrapped the over-sized garment around her, pretending it still held the warmth of Harris's body, as her hand touched the door handle.

She stepped onto the icy-cold patio stones and hissed. The wind whipped around her and tunneled up her loose shorts. The mist still lingered but it didn't soak her.

The practical side of her brain clicked to life. She should go in and get dressed or go to bed. She skipped both options. With quiet steps she walked around to the side of the guesthouse that faced the water. The journey chilled every part of her, but she didn't go back in. Didn't want to.

Closing her eyes, she inhaled the familiar wel-coming scent of water and freshly mowed grass. The storm likely would erase the last of the fiery residue that had settled over the island. The smoke had long ago cleared but the stank muskiness lingered. Soon that would pass, too.

The wind carried her hair, making it dance as it blew across her face. Standing there she heard the rustling of tree branches and the lapping of the water against the coastline. Tabitha used to talk about stand-ing on the second-floor balcony and letting the cold air wash over her. Her voice would carry this sound of awe.

Gabby understood. It filled her with wonder to be alone while nature churned around her. It humbled her even as it filled her with a strange sense of power.

She put her arms out to the sides and let the wind catch the sweater. The material flapped against her chest and sides, not providing any protection or heat. Tipping her head back, she faced the sky with closed eyes and waited for the first drops of harder rain to fall.

The rustling gave way to an odd crunching. Before she could open her eyes, fingers clamped down on her wrist. The punishing hold had her crying out in pain. A mix of surprise and fear flooded her. She opened her mouth to scream for help and a hand slapped against her lips. A giant weight pressed against her back. She kicked out, trying to nail her attacker in the shin, but when her bare feet met bone a shudder ran through her.

She threw her elbows and tried to reach behind her and punch. The move twisted her shoulder to the point of breaking but she did not stop. She waited for a knife's edge to slice through her or a hard knock to the head to drop her to the ground. That was how her sister died. In a violent mix of stabbing and punching.

She refused to go out that way.

Throwing her weight to the side, she lost her balance. She grabbed for the attacker's hair and touched material . . . a mask?

Through it all, hands held her in a steel grip. An arm snaked around her throat and her breath choked off. Her mind raced back to the guesthouse and Harris's chokehold on Stephen. She searched her memory for a way out, tried to remember if Harris told her how to break the clench.

Her neck ached as she gave into a sputtering cough. Then her body went airborne. Strong arms picked her up and threw her. She tried to grab on to anything, to find some leverage, but she only grabbed air. Nothing else stirred around her.

"Harris!" She screamed as loudly as she could, hoping the house and the wind didn't block the sound.

As she turned, hoping to catch a glimpse of her attacker, he rammed into her from the side. His shoulder connected with her rib cage. The body slam knocked her into the side of the house and she went tumbling. Her fingernails scraped against the stucco as she tried to break her fall.

She landed hard on the soggy ground. It squished around her. Not waiting to be rescued, she crawled around, moving as fast as possible as she tried to remember what might be sitting on the patio that could help her. The world spun around in her head and she tried to think of which way to move.

Concentrate.

Her gaze fell on the stone wall. She lunged for it.

Heavy footsteps followed her. The dark figure dove for her just as she reached the end of the wall. She picked up handfuls of dirt and threw those. Some hit him. Some pelted the ground. He didn't make any noise but he fell back, grabbing at the ski mask he wore.

She screamed. Put her whole body into it. Yelled for Harris and Damon.

But she had to stall. On her knees, she scrambled toward the shrubs, feeling around the dirt for anything she could use as a weapon. A rock dug into her palm and she picked it up. Whipped it at him just as he ducked to the side. She had no idea if she hit him, but he shifted away from her, to the far edge of the patio.

Not ready to give in she picked up more rocks and threw them, letting out another scream as she hurled the handful directly at the attacker. One handful then another. When her fingers wrapped around a garden shovel she picked it up and chucked it into the darkness. Then he was gone.

The attack had taken less than a minute. She'd raced through every second even though the individual beats moved in slow motion in her head.

The adrenaline deserted her. It drained from her body, leaving her weak and unable to stand. Her chest heaved from the force of her harsh breaths. She slumped back onto the ground, trying to remember every detail for later.

She needed her legs to move and energy to swamp her so she could run after the figure but he'd disappeared. She listened for a splash but didn't hear one.

A noise broke through her conscience. Harris yelling. He shouted her name over and over through a thunder of footsteps.

"Gabby! Where are you?"

She glanced up as he and Damon ran around the corner. She tried to say something, to force words out, but all she could do was shake her head. Through the haze she focused on one fact—an attacker could only go so far on an island. But she could narrow it down. She pointed in the direction of where the attacker ran.

"You take care of her." Damon stopped long enough to touch her shoulder then took off.

"Are you okay?" Harris sounded out of breath and shaky as he kneeled on the ground next to her.

"I think so." That was all she could get out.

Strong arms wrapped around her. Immediately heat enveloped her and his scent seeped into her. He rocked her back and forth as his hand brushed up and down her back. She tried to swallow, be brave . . . all that. She promised to get right on that as soon as her teeth stopped chattering.

She heard a noise and then Damon was there, too. He squatted down and stared at her. She saw the gun in his hand. "Did you find him?"

Damon shook his head. "Who was it?"

"I don't know. He was wearing a mask."

"Tall. Young or old?"

"I really don't know. It all happened so fast and blended together." Pieces of what happened bombarded her brain. The guy's grip. How he never made a sound. "But it was a *him*. Strong. Determined. He surprised me when he attacked."

"Shit." Harris ran a hand down her arm then over her leg. "Did he hurt you?"

"He threw me into the building." That thought came back to her as he looked at her dirt-caked fingernails and her butt slipped deeper into the muddy area near the bushes.

The color drained from Harris's face. "What?"

"I'm fine." Her teeth kept knocking together and she didn't think it was from the cold. "Stunned me more than anything."

Rain began to fall harder. No longer a mist, the drops pinged on the roof and uncovered patio chairs. Lightning flashed in the distance.

"We should get inside," Damon said as he stood up.

Harris continued to sit with her. He cradled her on his lap, surrounding her with a bit of protection from the wind. "Can you walk?"

"We need to find everyone and . . ." She didn't actually know what came next but gathering suspects felt right. Everyone needed to be questioned. There was the issue of alibis and whereabouts. Maybe they could find the dark clothes.

"No." Harris offered the sharp response as he lifted them to their feet.

"What?" She leaned against his side. Her brain shouted for her to stand up straight and get it together, but she wanted to burrow in even deeper. Her arms shook as her fingernails dug into his shirt.

"We stay quiet about this," Harris said.

"Uh, yeah." Damon scoffed as he tucked his gun

into the holster under his jacket. "About that . . . no fucking way."

"Listen to me." Harris kept his arm anchored around her shoulders. "This has been dragging on for fourteen months. Now, for some reason, the person who did this or hurt Tabitha or wants to hurt Gabby or did all of it—whatever this person's crimes are—is running scared. He's getting sloppy. Making moves that don't make sense."

"True," Damon said. "It could just be a waiting game now."

"Do you want me to be the target?" The words caught in her throat but she managed to force them out. It might be the right move, and she would do it if necessary, but she wasn't a martyr.

The thought of being the latest Wright-family tragedy, of leaving this world without finding out who killed her sister, made all the muscles in Gabby's lower half turn to jelly. There were times that the unfairness hit her harder than any body slam could. She grabbed on tighter to Harris.

"Of course not." Harris frowned at her as his hand smoothed over her hair. "And you're not going to be alone again."

She knew he meant on the island. Her brain could ferret out the true meaning behind his words. But the thought of staying with him, of taking whatever they'd started here and trying to continue it somewhere else, had hope soaring in her chest. Knowing these were the kind of thoughts that could pummel her until she fell to a heap on the ground, she tried to tamp it down. No matter how hard she tried, that flicker of promise seeped through her defenses.

Damon swore under his breath. Stared at the ground and shifted his weight around as the rain started to come down heavier. Then he looked at Harris again. "So, what's the plan?"

"We go at them one by one. Catch the right one off guard."

The rain fell in sheets now. The sound of rushing water echoed around them. It drenched their clothes. Before they could say anything else, they ran around to the front of the guesthouse and stood under the small overhang.

"Which one?" Damon asked.

"The chokehold." She lifted her head and looked from Harris to Damon.

She hated that the thought moved into her head. She'd been blamed so much and so often that she hated to push that burden onto someone else. But the move had been familiar.

Harris frowned at her. "What are you talking about?"

"The attacker put me in a chokehold." She tried to ignore the anger vibrating through Harris and mirrored in the clench of his jaw.

Damon shook his head. "But he's an old man."

She wondered if Damon had been watching at all. "He's fit and filled with fury."

"I'm going to fucking kill him." Harris pushed her hands away, tried to separate their bodies.

She didn't let go for fear he'd go up to the main house, find Stephen and start punching . . . and maybe not stop. "Harris, no."

"Listen to her." Damon grabbed Harris's arm. "That could be a coincidence. We follow your plan. You two rest and I'll try to figure out where we start."

"We can help." She had to do something. Had to get control back.

Damon's gaze moved over her body. The gaze wasn't sexual. It was assessing. "No offense, but you're a mess."

She glanced down to the soggy clothes and the mud that once caked her bare knees but was starting to streak down her legs. Her hair hung around her face and strands kept blowing into her mouth. The pouring rain made it worse every second.

"How could she be offended by that?" Rage still made Harris's voice rough around the edges, but some of the stiffness in his body eased.

"I'll check everything we've collected in the morning." Damon looked at Harris. "Do you have a weapon with you?"

Harris nodded. "Of course."

Of course. At this point, lie or not, she was happy he wasn't an art appraiser.

"I need a shower." She sighed as she picked a leaf out of her hair.

Harris squeezed her arm. "I'll help with that."

"What if the attacker comes back?" she asked, unable to fight off the shiver that ran through her at the thought.

"He wanted you alone or you snuck up on him by accident." Harris's gaze didn't waver as he stared at her. "Either way, he's not making another move tonight."

"Unless he wants to be shot," Damon added.

Their conviction diffused the new wave of panic before it could take hold inside her. "The guy touches me again and I'll pound him with a shovel."

Harris winked at her. "I do like your style, Gabby Wright."

CHAPTER 21

She stood there, drenched and uncharacteristically shy as she curled her bare toes into the bath mat. Cold, wet, shaken but not broken. Never that.

Harris shut off the water faucet for the bath. He wasn't really a soak-in-the-tub guy. He showered. Did his business and got in and out. It was a practical exercise. But Gabby needed something else tonight and he was going to give it to her.

"You need help taking your clothes off?" God, he hoped she'd say yes.

She didn't need sex right now and he wasn't a fucking animal, but he did want to hold her. Feel her skin against his.

The short PJs set stuck to her skin. His sweater had been soaked and now stretched to twice its size. Pretty soon she'd be able to wear it as a dress. Her hair was plastered to the side of her head and the longer she stood there the more she shook.

He needed her in the warm water, but he had to get her attention first. He lowered his head to try to get her to look at him. "Gabby?"

She finally looked up with a glassy-eyed stare. "What?"
Yeah, not good.

"Baby, get in the water." The endearment came out of nowhere. He pretended it didn't happen.

She nodded. Without talking, she stripped off the sweater. It landed with a weird *splunk* sound when it hit the tile. A wiggle of her hips and she shimmied the wet shorts and underwear down until they pooled at her feet. She stood there in that wet shirt. It clung to every curve. Her nipples pushed against it. He was about to reach for her, to do something, when she lifted that last piece up and over her head.

In just a few seconds, the clothes lay discarded all around her. Big clumps of soggy material. She didn't do anything to hide from him, either because she was dazed or because she felt comfortable. He hoped the latter explained it. He loved the idea of her being calm and naked in front of him.

She leaned over and dipped her hand in the water. Her arm shot back. "Too hot."

He could see the goosebumps on her arms and the way she rubbed her legs together as if trying to get warm. She might think it was too hot, but she needed it. "We're going in."

Her eyes focused. "Both of us?"

"Is that a problem?" He wouldn't go near her if she preferred to be alone. He'd fucking hate it, but he would give her whatever she needed. For a guy who never gave a shit how other people felt, all he cared about was making her happy right now.

She bit her bottom lip as her gaze traveled all over him. "In that?"

It was his turn to look down. His jeans encased his legs and his gray T-shirt fit him like a second skin. "Is it okay if I take my clothes off?"

"I've seen you naked." Some of the color came back to her cheeks. A flicker of amusement showed in her eyes.

He took those as good signs, but he still wanted to be sure she understood he planned to touch her. "I don't want to traumatize you."

She shook her head. "There is nothing scary about the way you look."

If there was a record for getting clothes off, he broke it. The jeans weighed about a thousand pounds and twisted and stuck to him as he tried to peel them off. But before she could say a word he dragged them all down, kicking off the last pants leg, and stood next to her naked.

He tested the water one more time then gestured for her to go first. "Get in."

The sharp inhale of her breath bounced around the room as she submerged one foot then the other. "Are you trying to boil me?"

Women. "Yes, Gabby. I'm into that."

"We're going to soak the bathroom."

"As if I didn't plan for that." He was impressed with how confident he sounded because he wasn't actually sure of the physics of this. He hadn't filled the tub and he kept the jets off, but when they sank down together the water level rose to near-spillage proportions.

As soon as he sat down with her back leaning against his chest he didn't care if they flooded the whole island. An "ah" escaped him as the hot water seeped into his bones. He'd been worried about *her* and wanting to give *her* comfort. He hadn't realized how much he needed it, too.

There with her, body against body, his brain finally turned off. He'd spent days mentally running through scenarios to explain Tabitha's death. He'd searched for ways to tell Gabby about where he was that night but couldn't come up with one that didn't end with her slapping him and leaving.

He'd assessed the suspects and analyzed their moves. He'd seen bank statements and emails—whole lives spilled out in front of him. All of those calculations vanished when he saw her sprawled on the grass in the dark tonight, calling out his name.

He closed his head and shifted until his head hit the small pillow connected to the back of the tub. From this angle, her hair tickled his neck and rubbed against his chin. Looking down the long perfect line of her body he watched her knee peek out of the water then disappear again. The next time her foot broke through the surface, she rested it against the faucet. Her pink-painted toes fascinated him. So feminine. He almost wanted to watch her paint them, to see the concentration on her face as she got them just right.

Her head fell to the side, right next to his bicep. For a second he wondered if she'd dozed off. That worked for him. He'd lift her out and dry her off when their skin started to prune.

"I keep wondering if Tabitha's last moments were like what happened today," she said in a soft, almost distant voice.

Where the hell had that come from? His stomach dropped. He skimmed his fingertips up her arm, hoping to lull her back into a relaxed state. "Don't think about that now."

The water splashed as she dropped her foot into the water. "She had to be terrified. I knew you were nearby and screamed for you, but she didn't have anyone with her. Kramer and I were down by the dock, so far away."

"God, Gabby. I'm sorry." He had so much to apologize for. He didn't even know where to start, but he knew she'd tie this one to how long it took for him to get to her. Too late. She'd rescued herself before he got down the hill.

Her fingers curled around his wrist. "No, that's the thing. I knew you'd rush in if you heard me. That's who you are."

He was a liar. *That* was who he was. A man who said one thing and did another. The fact that she believed in him or saw him as some sort of hero meant everything but it wasn't real.

"This sense of hopelessness washed over me. When my knees hit the ground, this huge surge of energy rushed through me. Suddenly, I was desperate to fight, but it's like I was paralyzed at the same time." Her muscles tensed as she talked. "I fought and kicked but it wasn't enough. I couldn't get enough momentum . . . didn't have enough strength."

One of his arms wrapped around her waist and he dropped his head until his cheek touched hers. Holding her close was as much for him as it was for her.

"She made these questionable choices. Lived her life so privately, so insular." Gabby sighed as she relaxed against him again. "My parents messed up but she . . . I wish so much had been different."

The words didn't fit with most of what she'd said before. Gabby talked about her sister being sweet and dedicated. This was the first time Harris heard Gabby suggest any real frustration with her sister. Sisters fought. Sisters disagreed. To hear Gabby talk, Tabitha was a saint except for the map and the kidnapping, and Gabby even absolved her for that. Both with words and how she'd lived her life.

The slight change in direction filled him with relief. He'd worried Gabby was rewriting history to erase her sister's flaws. A normal reaction, probably. Harris had seen it before, but holding the dead up as paragons actually robbed them of who they were. Worse, it made the living seem even more flawed.

"It's okay to be angry with her, you know." Harris continued to brush a hand up and down Gabby's arm.

She froze. "What are you talking about?"

"I spent years being pissed off at my mom. She made decisions that put something before me, that took her away from me. She risked our family, ruined it, because she had this compulsion. I didn't understand it and tried to figure it out." That last part was hard to admit, but he did it.

Gabby looked up at him. "Your mom made a choice. Tabitha didn't."

"She decided to let you take the blame. She decided to separate herself. She decided to, in some ways, be the victim."

Gabby turned the whole way around in the tub until her legs draped over his knee and she faced him head-on. "That's not true."

"Isn't it?"

"I don't hate her."

He believed her, but that wasn't the point. The way her eye contact bounced in and out, and she fought back with strong words but no real emotion underneath made him think she knew that. This was a big stall. A way for her to gloss over the hard topic and double back to a place where she felt more comfortable.

"You can be ticked off and still love her, Gabby." He fought the urge to touch her until they talked this through. "That's human."

"It's sick."

She'd spent so much time protecting her baby sister that she lost the ability to see Tabitha clearly. There, in the middle of the angst and pain, it was tough to kick to the top and see daylight.

"Tabitha made choices that hurt you." This was the hard part but he pushed through. "And you let her."

"Now it's my fault?"

"I'm talking about how you hold everything. You're so busy explaining her actions that you never talk about how she hurt you."

Gabby stood up in the middle of the tub. Water ran down her legs and soapsuds clung to her stomach. "She was . . . my parents coddled her."

"I've heard these arguments." He slowly got up, giving her time to step away. "Say it, Gabby."

"I don't know—"

"Admit that she hurt you. You can't deal with your emotions if you're hiding them." The words stunned him. Here he was giving the lecture when he should be listening to it.

She began to tremble. "You're talking to me about emotions? You?"

It was a fair argument. He deserved it. He was the last person who should be giving this speech or pushing this talk, but he was the only one there. It fell to him, an imperfect messenger. "Lash out at me all you want."

Her hands balled into fists at her sides. "What do you want from me?"

Everything. That thought hit him and he shoved it back. He had to concentrate on her now. On what she needed.

"It's like poison." He knew that from personal experience.

"What?"

He should reach for a towel and wrap her up in it,

but he had to get this out first. "There's a part of you that's angry with her. A human part. A real, human, decent part. You loved her and miss her, but you can still be frustrated that she left you, and that when she did she left you in this position."

She shook her head. No other part of her moved. "I can't."

"You protected her, but she never protected you."

"She was a child." Her voice cracked on the last word.

"Not at the end. Don't let her off the hook." She'd spent a lifetime doing just that, but he didn't know how to make her see it. So, he kept talking, hoping the sound of his voice might break through.

She was shaking so hard that he ripped the towel from the bar and draped it around her.

Her hands came up and she held the edges together as she huddled under it. "Why are you doing this?"

The pain was right there in her voice. He knew he was pushing her to places she didn't want to go, but he couldn't stop. Deep inside he knew this mattered. He'd spent so much of his life dealing with a form of this. Of trying to justify someone else's choices.

"Because in making her the innocent, lifelong, victimized party you're casting yourself as the bad guy." He knew the drill. He'd lived it.

"Maybe I was the bad guy."

And there it was. Her undying belief that she deserved to be punished for something she'd said as a throwaway line at a teen party. He wanted to shake her parents for letting that happen. They had two children and they protected one. His mother hadn't even done that. "She was a kid. But, hell, so were you."

"She was my baby sister."

That same argument. She kept throwing it out but each time it sounded less persuasive. "And she turned your life upside down." When she didn't argue with him, he kept going. "You didn't kill her and you'd give everything to have her back with you. But you're allowed to be angry about other things."

He reached for another towel and wrapped it around his waist. It did nothing to fight off the chill, but the anger flowing through him on her behalf kept him warm enough.

"If I . . ." Gabby bit her lower lip. Her voice and that look in her eyes—she was pleading with him now. "She's dead, Harris."

"Gabby."

Her eyes filled with tears. "She didn't mean—"

"Gabby."

She shook her head. "I don't get to be angry."

"You do. Here, in this room." He put his hands on her upper arms. "Between us, you do."

She moved and the water sloshed around her feet. "I don't *want* to be angry."

"I didn't either, but I couldn't forgive my mom until I admitted how pissed off I was." By then it was too late to retrace the steps of his life. Everything his mother did influenced every choice he'd made. He wanted to blame her, but at some point he had to own it. That reality hit exactly fourteen months ago.

"It's not fair." The fight went out of her and her shoulders slumped.

"It is, Gabby." He squeezed her arms to let her know he was right there to catch her. "I don't have a sister but I know they screw up and they fight. She was young and naïve when she made the mistake, and by the time she was old enough for you to yell it out she'd changed and you never got that closure."

Gabby inhaled a deep shuddering breath as her body seemed to fold in on itself. Something crashed inside her. He could see it.

"I hated what she did. Hated that I had to protect her. So many times I thought about not doing it." Her voice wobbled and she stopped. After a few swallows she tried again. "That first Thanksgiving my parents didn't let me come home from college. The way my uncle looked at me. My mom crying on the phone."

He pulled her in closer, ignoring the way the water splashed up his calves. "You had and still have every right to be angry."

She rested her forehead on his shoulder. "Then why does it feel so crappy?"

"Because you're human." He slid a hand over her hair and placed a kiss right by her ear. "Perfectly human."

SHE WAS WATERLOGGED and exhausted by the time they left the bathroom fifteen minutes later. Harris had kept verbally poking her, insisting she talk. He was in this big rush to get her to dredge up the past and analyze it.

She'd wanted to be furious with his interference, but she couldn't conjure up the energy. It had taken every ounce of strength to keep from admitting the one thing she'd always refused to admit. The words she hid in the back of her mind and pretended didn't exist. But Harris brought it all to the surface. He gave her opportunity after opportunity. Held her, caressed her, let her know it was okay to say the words she'd been so desperate to keep locked inside. They rattled around inside her then tumbled out.

Dried off but still wearing the towel, she followed him into the living room. He kept his towel wrapped around his waist. A simple knot held it at his side. Seeing it, watching him walk, looking at those amazing shoulders and how they angled down to that trim waist, a new sensation hit her.

The sleepiness slipped away and her muscles snapped back to life. The revving inside her, the tightening and shortness of breath, had nothing to do with the discussion in the tub. No, this bubbling need came from a different place.

She wanted him.

Adrenaline surged inside her. He wanted her to feel, well, so did she. Right now.

"Harris." She waited until he turned around and looked at her—really looked—to drop the towel.

"I . . . damn." His gaze took off on a journey. It

skipped down her body, hesitating on her breasts, before dipping lower.

Well, that was adorable. "Is that a yes?"

"For the record, the answer is *always* yes for you."

She couldn't think of a sexier answer than that. "Then what are you doing over there?"

He glanced at the doorway to the bedroom. The poor thing looked confused. The bed sat a few feet away, but she stood on the opposite end of the room, not moving. She sensed she was going to have to help him because his brain cells were not connecting.

She backed up. "The wall."

"Uh . . . bu . . ." He stammered as his mouth dropped open. "What?"

Okay, that was cute and more than a little flattering. All that control she'd ceded in the bathroom she won back now. His reaction sent a rush of power through her. She believed she could conquer just about anything.

"Go get a condom." She put the backs of her hands against the wall by her head. If the guy didn't get the message now she'd literally start spelling the words.

"Right." He took off. Actually jogged the few feet to the bedroom.

She heard the drawer rattling and then he swore. When he popped out again he was naked and holding the condom. And fully erect. He'd been half hard in the tub during their bath but hadn't made a move. A few words and a dropped towel and the man was ready.

The man was impressive and, for now, he was all hers.

She smiled at him. "There you go."

"Oh, I get it now." He stood in front of her, right between her legs. "I'm going to fuck you against the wall."

Heat burned through her. Every muscle ached to wrap around him and pull him close. "Now would be good."

"It will definitely be good." He slipped his fingers through hers and held her there, pinned to the wall. "So fucking good."

Then his mouth found hers. The kiss shook her as every nerve ending fired. His tongue swept over hers. Their legs tangled together. That weight as his chest pressed against hers. She craved it all and wanted even more.

She slipped a hand out of his and pressed it against the back of his neck. The kiss deepened as their bodies rubbed together.

"Harris, now." She would plead, beg, get on her knees. Whatever it took to get him all over her.

"I want to be inside you." Already hard, he rolled the condom over his length.

She jumped and he caught her. With his hands on the back of her thighs, he pulled her tight against him. His erection pressed against her entrance and up to her stomach. She linked her ankles behind him. The move had her legs open and her body ready.

His mouth dove in for another kiss as his fingers

slipped down her body. That perfect finger rubbed over her, slid into her. She lifted her hips, angled her body to pull him in deeper. When he moved it in and out, her back arched off the wall.

He slipped his finger out of her and then his tip brushed over her, plunging deep inside her. Their lower bodies met and her fingers slid into his hair. She couldn't hold him close enough or tight enough as he moved in and out.

Her head rolled against the wall and her hips moved in time with each thrust. Need pounded her as she shifted so he'd hit just the right spot inside her. It worked and the touch had her gasping. A sexy shiver ran through her. She was warm now. Her skin caught fire from the inside out.

An orgasm hovered just out of reach. She teetered on the brink. Her body cried out for more. Without thinking, she tightened her legs around him, which only brought her closer to the edge. Then he rolled his hips forward and she lost it. Pleasure crashed over her and dragged her under. Her last coherent thought was about Harris.

He had changed everything.

CHAPTER 22

Harris swore at the knock on the guesthouse door the next morning. He knew who stood on the other side because Damon had sent a warning text ten minutes ago. He literally gave Harris a countdown to stop having sex and get dressed. Lucky for Damon, that had already happened.

Harris opened the door. "What?"

"You are the only guy I know who is grumpier *after* sex." Damon pushed his way into the room but stopped when he saw Gabby sitting on the couch, looking at her phone. "Oh, shit."

"Yeah, I'm right here, listening to your male nonsense. I guess locker-room talk really is a thing."

Damon had the grace to wince. "Sorry."

"It's okay. Harris and I are not exactly a secret." She stood up and looked at Damon's hands. "What are you holding?"

He waved the short stack of documents. "More chat room records."

When Damon didn't say anything else, Harris rolled his eyes. "Okay. And?"

Any other morning Harris might appreciate the added drama, not today. He and Gabby had been on this never-ending frenetic ride. Great sex, devastating admissions, danger. It was a whirlwind and most parts of it weren't that great, except the one that was truly exceptional.

He'd been struggling to find his equilibrium and conquer his guilt. The emotion was uncomfortable for him. He rarely felt bad about his work because he picked his target artwork with care. But guilt moved through him nonstop these days. The closer he got to Gabby, the more he cared for her and the heavier his secret became.

He kept finding excuses to put off telling her. At first he'd been determined never to tell her. He thought he'd be able to hide his part in being there that morning with Tabitha and destroying valuable evidence. Just help Gabby out then move on without anyone really knowing anything about him. Then he met her, got to know her and vowed to tell her the truth after they got a lead. After they slept together he shifted his priorities again and decided he'd disclose after they narrowed down the list of suspects. Now he wanted to put it off until they caught the killer, a task that felt impossible most days.

He didn't regret much in his life. He regretted coming to the island that day . . . but part of him couldn't even apologize for that. Without the painting and Tabitha, he wouldn't have met Gabby. It was selfish and sick. He hated to think he benefitted from something so devastating for her.

Damon tucked the paperwork in the inside pocket of his jacket. "We have a morning appointment for a boat ride."

She frowned at him. "What?"

"I haven't had coffee yet." A fact Harris found highly relevant to his willingness to do anything.

"Hurry up. We're late."

DAMON'S CRYPTIC COMMENT didn't make that much more sense a half hour later, but at least Harris now knew what they had to rush off to do. Go boating.

Damon, Gabby and Harris had filed onto Craig's boat. He had more than one. This one, a speedboat, was built to impress. They sat on the cushioned seats behind Craig. He handled the boat with ease, guiding it across the waves and moving them out farther from the land.

The storm clouds had given way to a clear morning. The water shined in a deep crystal blue as they ventured out on the Bay, heading toward the mouth where it dumped into the ocean.

"Why today?" Craig spared them a quick glance as he steered. "For a pleasure ride, I mean. Don't get me wrong. I love being out here, but you two guys don't exactly look like you're on a vacation right now."

Harris glanced at Damon before answering. "We needed a break from the paperwork."

"That does sound pretty boring." Craig nodded as

he adjusted his sunglasses. "Paperwork overload gave me the kick I needed to leave the financial field and get back to something that put me outside."

Damon sat alone across from Gabby and Harris. He stretched his arm across the top of the empty cushions next to him. It was a practiced move that looked relaxed and almost disinterested.

Harris knew better.

"Did you ever take Tabitha out on the boat?" Damon asked.

The question told Harris what he needed to know. In the rush to get to the dock this morning to meet their sailing time, Damon gave them only partial information. He said it would all become clear as they rode along. Now Harris got it. Damon found something in the documents that connected Craig to Tabitha on a more-than-casual-friends level. Since the paperwork in his pocket showed chat room transcripts, Harris knew it all started and ended with Tabitha's true crime obsession.

Craig nodded. "Actually, yes."

"Wait a second." Gabby stopped watching the water and looked at Craig again. "What?"

The engine's roar softened as the boat slowed and Craig turned around to face them. "She liked the feeling of the air on her face." He pointed at the outline of an island to their right in the distance. "She also liked to ride around and check out other houses. I joked that she was nosy, but I think she was trying to figure out if she liked another island better than hers."

Craig and Tabitha had been very familiar with each other. Casual and chatty. That was the one piece Harris hadn't expected. He assumed with her lifestyle Tabitha's relationships were more peripheral and informal. The warmth in Craig's voice suggested otherwise. They had been real friends and not sometime acquaintances.

"But she rarely left the island," Gabby said.

"We circled it. Sometimes she'd let me go out farther, but not too far." Craig's smile didn't reach his eyes and sadness lingered there.

Harris shifted in his seat. The other two seemed fine, but the lumpy cushion made it hard for him to sit still. He thought about switching to Gabby's other side until he realized this likely was a boat-wide problem.

Trying to keep his mind in the game, he threw out a question. "How often did you see her?"

Craig shrugged. "When I dropped supplies off, so pretty regular intervals."

"Intervals?" Damon asked.

The usual smile faded from Craig's face. His personality seemed to be stuck in perpetual friendly mode. He kept his anger hidden and did his job. For Ted and Kramer, Craig stepped up often. Harris didn't operate that way and didn't exactly understand people who did, but Craig struck him as decent and genuine. Or he did until the boat ride started. Damon was onto something and Harris didn't know what.

Craig leaned against the wheel. "Am I being questioned?"

Damon didn't blink. "Yes."

"Wait, what?" Gabby uncrossed her legs and sat forward.

Harris wasn't convinced this was the right way to pull information out of Craig. But he wasn't quite sure what intel Damon possessed. The question was if Harris could sit there long enough to find out. He shifted, running a hand under him. It felt as if he were sitting on something.

With all the moving around, Craig's attention switched to Harris. "Are you okay?"

He was annoyed. He stood up and pushed the cushions around. "This seat is . . ."

Harris saw it then. A ball of black material shoved under the cushion, stuffed half inside. He tugged on it but it didn't move at first. The ripping sound almost made him stop yanking it, but he kept going.

The material gave and he held up a black hat. Not just a hat, a mask. The kind that would cover a guy's face as he slammed a woman into the wall.

He held it up. "Want to explain this?"

Craig squinted as he stared at it. "A tourist probably left it."

"Is that a ski mask?" Gabby grabbed it out of Harris's hands and studied it. Her face went pale as she held it up to Craig. "Is this yours?"

"I don't wear knit caps like that, and certainly not in spring." Craig let out an uncomfortable laugh then turned around with his back to them again.

When she looked at Harris all he could see was the confusion in her eyes. She was damn smart. It didn't take her long to put the pieces together. She clearly already guessed the direction of Harris's thoughts. Craig was on the island the night Gabby was attacked. He knew the family, came back and forth often. And now he had what could be the hat that hid his identity. He had the opportunity but the motive was unclear.

But there was something else. Harris could feel it. "Damon?"

He nodded as he slipped one of the papers out of his pocket. "Do you like chat rooms, Craig?"

Motherfucker. Harris wanted to be wrong, but this was about Tabitha and the hobby she viewed as a job.

Craig didn't say anything but he did cut off the engine. By the time he turned around, Damon had his gun out and up.

"Yeah, not a vacation. I'm working right now." Damon made a tsk-tsking sound. "I'd be careful if I were you."

"You're crimefinder?" Gabby asked Craig.

"Crimesleuthing," Harris said, correcting her. He had the computer username memorized. He could recite passages of Tabitha's chats by now. "Was that your username?"

Gabby stepped around Harris and headed straight for Craig. She practically lunged for him. Harris grabbed her around the waist from behind but that didn't stop her rampage. She shook the black material in her fist at Craig. "You attacked me."

"What? No." Craig shook his head and held up his hands. He took on a pure defensive battle stance now. "I would never do that."

She inched closer to Craig despite Harris's hold. "The guy who came after me the other night wore this or one just like it. That's quite a coincidence."

"What are you talking about? What night?"

Craig's confusion sounded genuine. Harris spent a lot of time lying and heard more than his share in his work. He knew some people could sell the most ridiculous stories. Garbage rolled out of them without any remorse. Harris didn't get that vibe from Craig, but the hat did throw everything off.

Ignoring the hat and the attack on Gabby, Harris doubled back to the chat room information. "Why were you stalking Tabitha on her crime sites?"

Craig didn't bother to deny it. "It wasn't like that."

"Oh, my God." Shock vibrated in Gabby's voice. "You killed her."

"No! Hell, no." Craig's eyes widened and a look of horror crept over his face. "I loved her."

He looked around at all of them. His mouth moved but he didn't say anything else. The waves lapped against the boat, putting it into a gentle rock, as the admission sat there.

Harris's mind scrambled. He rushed to force all the pieces to make sense. "Explain."

"I joined the chat room, but it wasn't to hurt her. It was to get to know her." A gentle pleading moved into

Craig's voice. Stress pulled at his mouth and he used his hands to emphasize every point.

"Nah. I don't buy that." Damon shook his head. "You already knew her. You said yourself you were on the island every day."

"Don't you understand? I was the guy who delivered things. The help." Craig's gaze kept moving until it fell on Gabby. "I wanted . . . I was really attracted to her but she kept her distance. She put up this barrier. Not because of our backgrounds. Not that, but because she held everyone away from her."

Harris couldn't help but look at Gabby. It sounded to him like the sisters suffered from the same affliction when it came to emotional ties. Then his gaze returned to Craig. "You're saying you had a thing for her."

"Not at first." Craig exhaled. "She was sweet and I thought she might be lonely. She talked about the crime stuff, so I made up a username and went online to talk to her. Then I realized everyone on there knew her. She was not a woman hiding on an island in those rooms. She was knowledgeable, the person others went to to discuss ideas and theories. She'd created this world and was a huge star in it, not this lonely person who needed company."

"She was never that," Gabby yelled at him.

"But she was lonely, Gabby. She didn't hide in a closet, but she had learned to use the island as a shield. If she stayed here, she didn't have to face anything.

She could keep living like she had with your parents—protected." He sat down on the bench near Damon.

"Keep going," Harris said.

"I liked talking with her and thought she'd be more comfortable confiding in a stranger, if she needed that, than someone she didn't have to see all the time."

"And then you fell for her?" The disbelief was obvious in Damon's voice.

For a second the pain cleared from Craig's eyes. "She was so enthusiastic and dedicated. In person, so beautiful and a bit mysterious. Young in some ways, but like this bright beam of sunlight. The more I talked with her, the deeper I got sucked in." Craig hesitated as he leaned forward with his elbows on his knees. "I fell for her."

"Why use the chat room? Why not come clean and tell her?" Harris asked, but he was pretty sure he knew the answer.

"How she was in the chat room was different from how she was in person." His words tripped over each other. "That's not what I mean. It's that she was more—"

"Approachable." Harris filled in the blank. "You could pull her out of her shell in the chat room."

It all made sense to Harris. In her element, talking about a subject that meant so much to her, Tabitha could be the person she might have been if the kidnapping fiasco hadn't happened.

Something that looked like hope sparked in Craig's eyes. "Exactly. I thought if I could get her to like me in there, then I could tell her the truth. We talked every single day. For hours each night. Just the two of us. She was the one who suggested the private chat, and in there our conversations went beyond criminal cases."

"Or, to put it another way, one without the pretty spin. You weaseled your way into her life, and when you finally told her the truth she got pissed and you panicked." Damon's summation made it all sound so simple. "Stabbed her."

"God, no." Craig's hands shook. "Don't you get it? I would never have hurt her." He looked at Gabby. "You have to believe me. I loved her. I've been grieving her in silence for more than a year because I couldn't tell anyone."

"Why not?" Gabby asked.

"Because of this. Exactly what's happening now." Craig stood up then sat down again. He was a ball of nervous energy, constantly shifting and moving. Looking ready to pop. "If I mentioned I was talking with her, deceiving her, the police would have blamed me for her murder."

Gabby sighed. "Instead, they blamed me."

"You're not the only one on the radar. I've been questioned numerous times. *Who did I bring to the island? Why did I hate the Wright family? Was this about jealousy?*"

Harris believed him. He hated that he did because tagging Craig now would end all of this. Gabby would finally have that closure and her uncle would have to back off. The entire case tied up in a neat bow, which was exactly the problem. Harris couldn't see Craig throwing Gabby against a wall or burning down the main house. Loving Tabitha wouldn't cause him to do any of that to Gabby.

Harris reached over and took the hat out of Gabby's hands and held it up to Craig again. "Where did this come from?"

"I have no idea. It wasn't on the boat last night." Craig stood up again and paced in the small amount of open space. "I clean it after every use and at the end of every workday."

"You stayed here last night, on the island." It was the first thing Damon had said that wasn't an accusation.

Craig nodded. "Kramer invited me when he saw the storm coming in. I figured it was safer."

Damon had mentally cleared Craig. Harris didn't have to ask for confirmation of that because he could hear it in the change in Damon's voice. Whatever Craig said must have matched with the documents in Damon's pocket.

Sure, this could be an unrequited love thing but Harris didn't see it. Nothing about Craig's demeanor said "killer." Some hid it well. Harris had known more than one sociopath. The art world was filled with them. But they had certain personality traits. A brutal ego and need to hear praise. As far as Harris could see, Craig was hardworking, dedicated and apparently mourning in silence.

This time when Gabby made a move toward Craig, Harris didn't hold her back or worry for her safety.

She no longer vibrated with unspent anger or looked ready to throw Craig overboard.

"Did you ever tell her you loved her?" she asked Craig in a soft voice.

Craig's face crumpled then. The panic gave way to pain. It was written in the series of expressions that crossed his face—from wariness to anguish—and in his body language.

"I planned to when you left after that last visit. I'd practiced what I was going to say. I . . ." Craig stared at a random spot on the Bay. "Honestly, I knew she'd be pissed that I lied to her, so I put off telling her the truth for longer than I should have. There is no good time to go back and clean up that kind of mess."

Harris hoped like hell Craig was wrong on that point.

"Then she never knew you and crimesleuthing guy were the same?" Damon asked.

"No. She thought she was talking with a stranger." Craig was barely holding it together.

He looked on the verge of tears and Harris wanted to spare him that but he wasn't sure how. "Someone could have planted the hat," Harris said, thinking out loud.

It made sense. Why would Craig hide incriminating evidence in the open? There was a vast amount of water right there. He could have thrown it in there or burned it in the fire pit, especially after Damon scheduled time for them all on the boat. No, it looked deliberate. Like someone intended to set Craig up.

"Who was with you last night?" Harris asked, hoping to narrow down the suspect pool even more. It sounded like they'd removed one person but that left too many more.

"After my daily runs I stayed with Kramer and Ted. The plan was to ride out the storm then head back this morning, which I would have done if Damon hadn't called about a quick pleasure ride."

Damon finally put his gun away. "Were you together with those two all the time?"

"Not really. Most of it, I guess." Craig looked at Gabby. "Your uncle was there for part of the evening. But I didn't specifically see anyone go out, if that's what you mean."

"Did anyone say anything?" Damon asked.

Craig frowned. "You mean did they mention hurting Gabby? Of course not."

That would have been too easy. Harris tried another tact. "Have you ever heard any theories on Tabitha's death?"

The skin on Craig's face pulled taut around his mouth. "Rumors and a bunch of garbage about Gabby, none of which I think is true. Honestly, if I knew who killed Tabitha I would kill them myself."

Admirable, understandable even. But the kid had his whole life ahead of him and Harris thought he deserved to at least live that. "Don't."

Gabby took Craig's hand. She didn't say anything. Just stood there, watching him. "I think she would have forgiven you."

"I never got a chance to tell her what I did or how much I loved her." Craig's voice sounded raspy and uneven. "But, God. Gabby, I never would have hurt her. Never."

"I believe you." Gabby hugged him then. Wrapped her arms around his neck and pulled him close.

For a second, Craig didn't do anything. He stood stiff with his arms to his sides then his hands came up and he hugged her. His fingers spread over her back and he buried his face in her neck.

Harris could see Craig's shoulders shake. Hear the sounds he made. He was crying, gulping in deep breaths of air.

The sight had Harris reeling. He felt as if he'd been punched in the gut. He'd spent his entire life vowing not to care for a woman—for anyone—as much as Craig cared for Tabitha. That way led to madness and a clawing sense of disappointment. Looking at Gabby now as she forgave and consoled Craig on her sister's behalf, Harris doubted he could hold on to his personal promise of detachment. He'd already broken it.

When they finally got the boat back to the dock, Harris pulled Damon aside. "Tell me about those transcripts."

"It all fits. There is a note of puppy love in them, though watching Craig out there I'd say it ran deeper than that." Damon shook his head. "But nothing weird or of concern on Craig's part. No trying to ply information out of her. Certainly no fighting. If anything, at the end she was pursuing him as hard as he was pursuing her. He just can't see that right now."

That sense of loss left Harris feeling raw and hollowed out. Here Craig was, driven and smart, and he couldn't reach out to a woman who meant something to him. Not in a way where she could reciprocate. Now she was dead and he'd always wonder what he could have done differently. He'd heal but he'd always carry that what-if guilt.

Craig had lied and no one could predict how much leeway Tabitha would have given for that. Harris wished he knew because he might be able to convince Gabby to listen to him when the time came to tell the truth. And it was coming.

"You think we can eliminate Craig from the list?" Harris asked.

"Yeah." Damon watched Craig and Gabby talk at the other end of the small dock. "The hat being there was a tip-off. It's too clean."

"So, we're back to the same place." Harris almost groaned at the thought.

"Actually, no." Damon held up four fingers. "One down. Three to go."

CHAPTER 23

Gabby no longer drank, which was probably a good thing. Today if she started she might not stop until she downed an entire liquor cabinet. The good news was the days of relying on wine and vodka to numb her frazzled nerve endings and quiet her brain were long gone.

She stood on the guesthouse patio and paged through the chat room transcripts Damon had found. Every word leapt off the page. The affection between Craig and Tabitha struck her. Gabby didn't have to dig through innuendos and subtext to find it. They shared ideas and talked about their struggles. But it was the flirting that made her smile. Craig's gentle coaxing to bring Tabitha out of her shell.

Over time, the tone between them changed from serious crime discussions to something deeper. She could pinpoint the exact week where Craig stopped using a persona and his own voice came through. Gabby had no idea how Tabitha didn't make the connection. Craig all but spelled it out for her. He stopped at using his name, but the information was right there.

They'd been off Craig's boat for over an hour and Damon was back at the main house making phone calls and tracking the movements of all the players still on the island during the months since Tabitha's murder. The police had done that already, but Damon was convinced they'd missed something and vowed to retrace each step.

That left Gabby and Harris alone to work through what they'd learned. She didn't know where to begin. She struggled to take it all in. Her sister had spent time with a man who really cared about her. Gabby never thought something like that would be possible, never imagined Tabitha could experience that sort of happiness. The fact someone stole it away made Gabby violent. She wanted to kick and scream and fight back.

Her stomach flipped over at the thought of how much Tabitha had lost. The cost, the toll, was so much higher than Gabby originally thought. She put a hand over her heart on instinct.

Harris had been sitting in the chair the whole time, watching her with a gaze that skimmed over her like a caress. It grounded her despite the flurry of emotions battling inside her. He didn't say much, which she appreciated. She craved the comfort of silence right now, and he provided that.

A quiet strength radiated off him. Behind the hypnotic deep voice and stunning face lay a man who was much deeper than he pretended. He joked, he deflected when it came to his work to the point that she was convinced he worked undercover for the police, but he'd shared the personal pain about his mother. Gabby sensed his mother's life and her choices went to the very heart of who he was. The son of a woman confined in prison.

In his mind, he may have resolved his feelings about that, but the scars remained. His past made him real and genuine and vulnerable. She guessed he hated all of that, but she didn't. That mix of control and humanity compelled her, reeled her in. Had her wanting more from him—with him.

She, the woman who ran from ties and feared losing one more person, had opened the door. Just a crack, but it was open. In such a short time she had come to think of him as hers. That they were bound together in some way.

She hadn't fallen for someone in such a long time but she remembered this sensation. The free-fall, no net, going-to-crash flailing panic. She wanted to refuse to care about him, to block her heart and abolish the word *love* from her head, but she couldn't do it. Her defenses were down and no matter how hard she tried to lift them again, they would not click into place. Not with him.

She hoped Tabitha had felt a portion of this. That she'd gotten a taste of how exciting, and, yes, scary, it was to fall for someone. To love without a safety net or parents watching over her and guiding her every move.

The man without real emotions—his proclamation, not hers—frowned at her in what looked like genuine concern. "You okay?"

"I will be." For the first time in a long time Gabby believed that. The killer was still out there and someone had attacked her and tried to frame Craig, but life moved forward. She no longer sat and churned and wondered every second what could have been if she hadn't been robbed of her family.

The confusion and pain still lingered. It always would, but it didn't have to define her. She got that now.

"With Craig eliminated, the pool of potential suspects is even smaller." Harris stretched his long legs out in front of him. "Your uncle, Kramer and Ted."

Back to business. It was the right answer, but a part of Gabby wanted to wallow in the happy feeling for a few seconds. "None of them fit."

"One of them has to." Harris leaned his head against the back of the chair and stared up at her. "Look, a stranger didn't sneak onto the island at the start of a storm just to manhandle you. Something else is happening here."

God, she wanted him to be wrong. Life would be so much easier if they were dealing with some unknown person with no connections to the family. Someone who'd wandered in and they could find and then forget. But she no longer believed in that less likely theory of the case.

She sat down on the table next to him, close enough

that her legs rested against the armrest of his chair. "Like what?"

"These things generally break down into pretty simple categories. People kill for money, for revenge, to hide something or because they just like the destruction."

She could eliminate one even though a part of her, that vengeful angry part, wanted to blame him. "My uncle has enough money."

"He's on the verge of divorce."

She swallowed a sigh. "He's a multimillionaire."

When Harris glared at her, she glared back. This was not just a family thing. There was no way to make the leap in her head. She refused to believe Uncle Stephen would hurt Tabitha. He hadn't overindulged her like their parents, but he had talked about the need to keep her safe.

"Fine. I'll give you that one," Harris said, finally conceding.

"I'd think." Right or wrong, she knew her uncle. The man today might be moved to violence. He'd been pushed so far to the edge that it was no longer impossible. Gabby knew if Uncle Stephen had a target, it would be her.

"Maybe Kramer is tired of being the employee."

That didn't work for her either. Then again, neither did Ted because of all of them he spent the least amount of time on the island. As a kid and a teenager, sure. Not as an adult. He only came now to help Kramer.

"Have you seen one bit of evidence to back that up?" she asked because she didn't know of any.

"No, which means this is about something, some piece of information or evidence, Tabitha found. That's why we had the attacks on the library. The person behind all of this thought whatever he needed to find and destroy was in there. The fire, the break-in. It all makes sense."

"It also fits with Tabitha's stolen laptop. It should have been with her or near her when she died, but the police never found it." They rarely included that fact in their decision-making, but Gabby knew it mattered.

Harris broke eye contact to stare into the distance. "Yeah, that."

"And the missing map and kidnapping documents." She hated to add those in but she couldn't avoid them. They were the pieces that didn't fit with anything else, but the ones that wouldn't leave her mind. "That's ancient history but the hiding place being discovered makes it all relevant."

Harris sat up higher in the chair. "If you were Tabitha, where would you hide something on the island?"

"Like what?"

"The map and whatever else you two buried in that wall."

The direction of the conversation made her uneasy, but she answered. "The library."

"No, we're not giving your sister enough credit. She was in the library all the time. If it was something she wanted away from her, to make it hard to find, where would she put it?"

The logic made sense. Gabby couldn't really argue with it. "The hiding place could be anywhere. I don't know."

That was the problem with being detached. She'd kept in touch with her sister over the years, through it all, but she didn't *know* her. That was evident from reading the chat room transcripts.

Harris put a hand on her knee, smoothed his fingers over her. "Think, Gabby."

She conducted a mental inventory of the island. Every building and every space. "She liked gardening and to sit on the second-story balcony. She loved the fire pit and the pool, though not as much as she did as a kid."

Harris shook his head. "What didn't she like?"

"What?"

"If this is something she wanted to hide, something she needed to keep separate from herself, she wouldn't put it where she could see it every day." He turned in his chair, moved in closer. "Where didn't she go?"

That was easy. "The boathouse."

Harris continued to study her. "Why?"

She could almost see his mind working. He was taking all of the information and compiling it. "Tabitha thought the boathouse was creepy. It can be loud in there, and the upstairs was always a mess. She talked about tearing it down and just using the dock."

"Right." He stood up.

"Right?"

He reached down for her. "That's where we're going."

IT TOOK THEM five minutes to get there. Every step of the way, Harris scanned the area. He didn't expect anyone to jump out at them, but nothing would surprise him at this point.

The attacks, the fire—the moves reeked of desperation. The risk of jumping Gabby on a contained island were huge. Damon was right there when the fire started. He could have seen something. It was only by luck—the attacker's luck—he didn't.

Harris finally thought he knew why this was happening now. No one stole the map and the papers relating to the kidnapping. Tabitha hid them, and with her gone the possibility of them being uncovered loomed.

For whatever reason, she'd clearly gotten nervous about the original location of the paperwork and took everything out. Now the documents were somewhere else, but they were not gone. If she'd destroyed them no one would be searching. No, someone was desperate to find that stash, which meant they were in a race to get to it first.

They walked into the bottom floor of the boathouse. The smell of fish and water and wet earth hit him. The mix was concentrated in here because of the walls on three sides. So strong it made him gag.

The steady beat of waves sliding into the open slip and lapping against the back wall mesmerized him.

Like Tabitha, he didn't see the reason for the two-story structure. He would take it apart with his bare hands if he had to.

"Where do we start?" Gabby stood on the side with her hands on her hips. Her gaze traveled over the nets and lines and hooks on the walls. Lots of fishing equipment and a few shelves. The kayaks Harris doubted anyone used.

Off to the side Harris spied what looked like a boat engine that had been taken apart and now sat there. He doubted anyone had worked on it for a long time since it had cobwebs on it. He inspected it anyway, looked around it for footprints. The only trail he saw was the one lone one toward the ladder. He was pretty sure that came from his look around up there when he first got on the island.

The boxes and shelves. The memory hit him as he stood at the bottom of the rungs.

"Upstairs."

Gabby seemed to snap out of the daydream that had her standing there in silence. "What?"

"The place to hide something would be upstairs. There's no water up there and very little reason to venture up these steps." He put a hand on the ladder mounted to the wall.

Gabby moved closer and peeked up into the open space above her. "Tabitha would hate it up there."

Exactly his point. "She only had to go up there once." Harris started climbing then stopped. He looked down at Gabby. "I can do this alone if you want."

She shook her head. "We're in this together."

He liked the sound of that. Too much. He liked everything about her too much. He even liked who he was when he was with her.

This emotion crap was a pain in the ass.

No wonder he ran in the opposite direction. He should have this time, too.

His shoes thudded on the top floor as he stood up. Reaching down, he helped her through the open hole and into the storage space.

She made a face as she looked around. "I don't even know what's up here."

"Let's hope a map and some paperwork."

Gabby touched a shelf then held up her fingers to show off the layer of dust she collected. "It doesn't look like anyone has been on this floor in months."

"Which makes your sister pretty damn smart." Harris studied the floorboards then scanned the ceiling.

He was sure they were in the right place. The space was stifling. With the window closed very little air moved around up here. It smelled stale and old. Everything he touched felt damp from the humidity. He heard a noise and turned to see her dragging a box off the shelf and opening it.

The cardboard creaked as she folded the sides down. "Huh."

"What is it?" He walked over to stand next to her and peered inside.

She lifted out an empty bottle and brushed her finger

over the label. "This is from my great-grandfather's il-
legal brew." She shook her head. "The whole family
had an alcohol issue."

"Why would someone keep that?" He didn't really
get family nostalgia. He liberated paintings and other
artwork in the name of it, so he'd benefitted from
that sense of wanting to be tied to the past. He just
never understood it. The past was something you over-
came.

"Why do people collect anything?" She looked
around again. "There is a huge house sitting on the
other side of the island. This room seems like a waste."

Every word she said made him more convinced.
The room was useless. There was no reason to be up
there, and Tabitha would hate the ladder. So, anyone
who knew her would think she'd skip this as a hiding
place. It only made sense.

For the next half hour, they unloaded every box on
the shelves on the right side and rifled through the con-
tents. They found plenty of papers, just not the *right*
papers. They looked inside things and around things.
The dust kicked up and they coughed. And nothing.

"We're going to suffocate up here." Gabby got up
from her seat on the floor.

She wiped her hands on the back of her jeans, smear-
ing the dust over her ass. Harris almost didn't want to
tell her. He'd rather wipe his hands all over her, too.

"You may have to burn those jeans," he said as he sat
there and watched her move. Those sexy hips swayed

and her neck glistened with sweat as she pulled her hair up and held it there.

She shot him a you're-out-of-your-mind look. "Do you have any idea how long it takes to find jeans that fit?"

"Uh, ten seconds." He didn't find picking clothes off a shelf all that daunting.

She snorted. "You're such a guy."

Okay, but . . . "There's a size on them. You read the size, try them on and you're done."

"Oh, no." She wagged a finger at him. "That's only the start. Sizes differ from designer to designer. Some pockets make your butt look huge."

He knew he was in way over his head on this discussion and threw up the white flag. "Who knew it was such a complicated process?"

"Every woman everywhere."

"Oh." And that was all he had on that topic, so he shut up.

"That's right." She turned around and unlocked the window. With a grunt, she tried to lift it but it didn't budge. "Can you help me with this?"

"What are you trying to do?" As far as he was concerned they could suck it up for another half hour and get out of there, hopefully with what they needed.

"Open the window and let some air in before we either sweat to death or keel over from a lack of fresh air."

He stood next to her and stared out the window to the empty dock below. "That's not dramatic or anything."

"I am the one person on this island who might have sex with you later. You should probably keep that in mind before being a smart-ass."

"A very compelling argument. Let's get this open." He stepped in front of her and shoved on the glass. It didn't move at all. Figuring it had been painted shut he slammed the side of his hand against the right side, trying to knock the old and peeling paint loose.

Nothing happened.

"I thought so." She joined in pulling. "It's stuck on this side."

She pointed to the right side. The molding around the window had either slipped or been put on wrong. The color was slightly off from the original paint and didn't crack like in other spots. It was probably added later, maybe to fix a leak or hole.

"The frame is too far over. It . . . wait." He went over to one of the boxes they'd searched and rummaged through until he found the screwdriver. With the end wedged under the edge of the molding, he shoved. The wood cracked and splintered and a top piece fell off. "What the hell?"

Gabby crouched down and picked up the folded pieces of paper that had been hidden in the fake frame. She held them up to him. "Tabitha's hiding place."

He stuffed the screwdriver in his back pocket. "Sweet damn. Good job, Tabitha."

Gabby stood up and immediately headed for the ladder. "Let's go."

Her demeanor had changed. She shifted from ready

to go to wary. It was as if she couldn't get out of the second story fast enough.

"What's wrong?" he asked as he followed her.

She stopped at the top of the ladder and wiped her hands down her arms. "I don't know. Holding the papers makes me nervous."

"Here, give them to me." He refolded the papers and stuffed them in his front pants pocket. "Now down the ladder."

Her sneakers thudded against each rung. "What if they don't show anything?"

Anxiety welled in him. He wanted to blame her and the sudden change of mood, but a new sensation hit him. Tension wound around him and all of a sudden he wished he'd brought his gun rather than leave it in the guesthouse. "Keep moving."

They made it downstairs and stepped through the side door and into the sunshine . . . and right into Stephen and Ted.

"Hey." Ted offered the informal greeting as he put a hand out and steadied Gabby.

Harris could hear her labored breathing and see the wildness in her eyes. She'd reached some turning point where she wanted this to be done now. He could see it in every line of her body. Her muscles were pulled taut, to the point of snapping.

Harris rushed to fill in the gap. "What are you doing out here?"

"Waiting for Craig to get here," Stephen said. "I

have some contractor meetings. He's bringing some people over. One of us needs to look after the house. Ted and I have been talking about things that need to be done as part of the estate. He has a list and is going to join me."

Some of the energy bouncing around Gabby became more focused. She centered it on her uncle. "And you didn't think to include me in any of this?"

"No." Stephen dismissed her without even a glance and stared at Harris. "Where were you two?"

"Upstairs."

Harris liked the way Gabby kept her answer simple. It was a power play, but it seemed to work. The more terse she got, the more pissed off and fuming her uncle became.

"I thought I heard banging on the window." Stephen performed a quick glance up to the second floor before looking at Harris again. "What did you expect to accomplish?"

Harris debated taking this step. He had two out of three suspects in front of him and Gabby seemed to be unraveling at the idea of carrying this out much longer. A person could only take so much stress and everyone kept piling it on her. Add in the difficulty of holding what might be the only evidence to resolve this thing and the pressure built.

"We needed to retrieve some papers." Harris fought off the urge to tuck the papers deeper into his pocket.

"From my grandfather's boxes?" Stephen asked.

Gabby didn't flinch. "These belonged to Tabitha."

Her voice stayed firm and clear. She was not playing around. She was in it to end it, and he loved that about her.

The point was to lay the groundwork. Harris didn't want Gabby to act as a target, but he would. He'd put his body in front of hers and take whatever hit might come.

"They'll settle some questions once and for all." Harris had no idea if that was true, but he wanted to provide a united front. He even moved closer to Gabby. There was no going back to the house or waiting this out now. "When Craig gets here, we'll have him take us into Baltimore."

"Why?" Stephen asked.

Gabby smiled but there was nothing sweet about that deadly grin. "That's where the lawyers are."

Harris took a step toward the dock and Ted stepped in front of him.

Fucking hell.

Harris didn't want it to be the kid. Stephen, even Kramer, but not this. "Are you going to stop me, Ted?"

He nodded. "Whatever it takes."

CHAPTER 24

Gabby blinked as her mind raced to process what she was seeing. One minute Ted stood there, hanging out with her uncle and saying hello. Now he blocked Harris's path, using his body and the shovel he was holding to do it.

"You?" It was the only word she could think to say.

Ted's expression was blank. Not angry. Not anything. "Just give me the papers and we'll go our separate ways."

Harris didn't move. She could see the screwdriver in his pocket. Her gaze swept over him, but she didn't see any sign of that gun he supposedly had. She debated calling out for Damon but that shovel stopped her. If he swung it he could hit Harris or her uncle. She had no idea what Ted was capable of at this point.

"What's going on here?" Stephen asked, still sounding indignant.

Harris's gaze never left Ted. "I think Ted here is admitting to killing Tabitha."

"What?" Stephen's face fell. It was as if every muscle gave out.

"I'm not saying anything of the sort." Ted tightened his grip on the shovel handle. He looked ready for battle now. "I know about the papers and that Tabitha didn't want them released. She was trying to protect Gabby."

"Me?" The verbal hit came so fast Gabby couldn't prepare or block it. He was blaming her. One more person shoving the responsibility off himself and onto her. The thought stunned her. Pissed her off.

"Everyone knows you were involved in your own kidnapping. Tabitha didn't want anyone to be able to prove it." Ted was in full acting mode now. He looked concerned and talked a big game.

"You . . . you killed Tabitha to protect some stupid papers?" Stephen frowned at her as he stuttered his way through the question.

Screw this. If Ted wanted a battle she'd give him one. She was done with taking shit and being the bad guy. Only one person standing there had something to lose today and for once it was not her. This time she would not run away or back down.

"Not me." Her voice shook from the force of her anger. All those years, all that loss. The fear and unease she'd felt upstairs in the boathouse vanished. Adrenaline-fueled fury raced through her now. "It was you all those years ago, wasn't it? You were one of the kidnappers I couldn't recognize because you didn't talk and I was blindfolded."

Ted shook his head. "Give it up, Gabby. Your uncle and I know the truth."

Stephen opened his mouth and she waited for him to condemn her. This time the words would bounce off her. She refused to feel guilty for one more thing she hadn't done. She'd been barely out of high school when she said something stupid and *other people* acted on it. Not her. Never her. Now she was an adult and she owned her mistakes, and this wasn't one of them.

"What do you mean extra kidnappers?" Stephen looked at her. "I don't get it."

Her mouth dropped open. The shock of having him ask instead of make demands and rule from above had her fighting to find the right words in her head.

The story was long and convoluted, so she tried to cut it short. "I knew the mastermind behind the kidnapping. He was a friend. He gathered people to help him."

Ted nodded as he took a step closer. "And you worked with him to set the entire thing up."

"Stop." Harris moved his body so he stood right in front of her now. "*She* didn't. Wrong sister."

Her desire to get this out battled with her ingrained need to cover for Tabitha. There was so much to tell, so many wounds they'd need to heal. They didn't need to add this piece. "Harris, no."

He didn't turn around. His gaze stayed locked on Ted. "Tell your uncle the truth."

Bile rushed up her throat. That familiar urge to fight back and run hit her. Tabitha was her sister. Her baby sister. "This isn't about—"

"She's gone, Gabby. She doesn't need your protection. I don't think she'd want it. Not at this price."

Ted's gaze moved from her to Harris. The roar of a speedboat engine whizzed by in the distance but didn't approach the island. The warm sun beamed down on them, but no one moved.

"Someone explain . . ." Her uncle's voice trailed off. The confusion was evident in his flat tone. Gone was the controlling, angry guy who'd come after her in the guesthouse. He slumped over looking lost right now.

"She saved the papers, moved the papers, to give you this chance." Harris put his hand on his hip. Two of his fingers inched toward that screwdriver. "Don't waste it."

Ted started shaking his head. "Don't listen to him, Gabby. You don't want to do this. Don't implicate Tabitha to save yourself. You'll never be able to live with that."

"You're a piece of fucking work," Harris said in a harsh tone.

Just a few days ago she would have fallen for the way Ted played on her guilt and her sympathy. Retreated and saved Tabitha at all costs. Not today. Harris was right. Tabitha would never have wanted this ending, not for either of them. It was so hard to turn this ship. She'd been on the same course for so long that she operated on autopilot, but she would make it happen.

"Wait, you mean Tabitha?" Stephen faced Ted then looked over at Gabby. "You're saying she was in on it?"

Harris was the one who answered. "She drew the map for the kidnappers."

"Shut up." Ted turned on Harris. Lifted that shovel slightly, just enough to suggest he'd use it. "You are a liar."

"Gabby?" Harris called out her name. "It's now or never."

Never. The word echoed in her brain. She'd always thought the answer would be never. Then she'd fallen for Harris—full on tripped and fell for him—and things that once seemed impossible no longer were. He believed her from the start. He was the only one who ever did. She engaged in weird behavior, snuck out with the shovel, and still he supported her.

He gave her back something she was sure she'd lost—a chance.

Her heartbeat thundered in her chest. The sound thumped in her ears, making it difficult to hear. Her stomach rolled and her knees grew weak. In every way possible, her body tried to hold the secret in. It was as if every muscle abandoned her and her breathing stopped.

"Tabitha was young and got caught up in something she didn't understand." The second the words came out her body calmed. Her heart still raced, but the need to sit down, fall over and hide vanished. It was enough to keep her talking. "I made a joke, a stupid remark to my friends about a staged kidnapping one night when I was angry with my parents and drinking. Some of the people I was partying with at the time, most of whom I didn't really know and one who I thought was my friend, ran with it."

Harris nodded in Ted's direction. "And you."

"No, I didn't—"

"Stop lying!" She'd never screamed so loud in her life. She poured every ounce of her frustration and anger into it. The words carried on the breeze.

"You're done, Ted," Harris said as his fingers slipped over the end of the screwdriver.

"I was a kid, too. I got caught up in the fun of it, never thinking anyone would get hurt. It was a mistake. That's all." By the end Ted's voice lost its power. The words barely rose above the lapping of the waves.

The admission nearly knocked her to her knees. She knew the truth now. He didn't have to say the words, but to hear them changed everything. To watch him stand there with that shovel, blaming her, when he was the one who'd stopped Tabitha's heart.

Pain shot through Gabby, threatening to double her over. She stood taller instead. "You were friends with Tabitha. You lived on our family's property."

"Don't do this," he begged.

"Why should you get off the hook?" The words tumbled out of her now. "You were in on it. You, not me. You let me suffer and had Tabitha cover for you. What kind of person does that?"

Ted held up a hand as if he were trying to block her words. "It was a mistake."

"Oh, my God." The reality of it all had her moving closer to Harris, pressing her arm against his. She needed contact, his touch. He was on high alert, but everything inside her shattered. She could feel every defense break.

She'd trusted Ted. Thought of him as family.

"None of this was supposed to happen." Ted shrugged, but his hands shook. Whatever was going on inside him didn't match the it's-okay tone to his voice. "Back then it was tough talk. I never thought it would escalate."

Harris took a threatening step forward. "You're a piece of shit."

"I didn't know what to do," Ted pleaded.

He could have stopped it. She wanted to scream that truth but she couldn't get the words out. But she could say one thing.

"You killed Tabitha." He could maneuver and lie and make up whatever he wanted about the past, but that fact happened. "You weren't a kid fourteen months ago. You were an adult and you made a horrible decision that took my sister's life."

"Why, Ted?" Harris asked.

"We were arguing. That's all." Ted glanced at Stephen, who hadn't moved since the conversation took such a vicious turn. Ted looked at Gabby again. "She tripped and fell. Her head bounced off the edge of the desk. There was so much blood and I panicked."

"She knew you were in on the kidnapping all the time." Knew and never said anything. Not even in confidence. Not as a secret between sisters. Tabitha protected Ted.

That thought became clear in Gabby's mind. While she'd stumbled through the last decade, her parents had put Ted through college and supported him. They all cheered when he opened his business and settled into a stable life.

Tabitha never said a word. She let him move on even while Gabby couldn't.

"I got trapped just like she did." One of Ted's arms fell to his side. "She told me she'd destroyed the map, but then . . ." The metal end of the shovel scraped against the ground. "She started doing all this investigating on that crime site. She met people. She fucking fell for someone and thought she should be honest with him about what happened in the past." Ted scoffed. "It was ridiculous."

Harris nodded. "It was Craig. But I think you know that. Is that what all this bar hopping with him is about? Befriend Craig and make sure he doesn't know anything?"

"I figured out that Craig and Tabitha were talking online and Tabitha didn't even know it. Craig moved back to the area and started his business. We started running into each other. At first it was fine but then he started talking about this woman." Ted laughed but there was no amusement in the sound. "Hell, he and Tabitha would quote the same damn conversations to me as each told me about their big loves."

Even through the anger Gabby ached for Tabitha. She'd finally found some real joy with another person and Ted had destroyed it.

"You thought Tabitha would figure out she was dealing with Craig and then tell him the truth." Gabby didn't know if it was irony or just horrifying that Tabitha had finally found love and it led to her death.

"She said she couldn't hold the secret anymore." Ted shook his head. "The guilt never ventured far away for her. Every time she saw you, Gabby, it got worse."

Gabby always thought she was the unlucky Wright sister. Now she wasn't so sure.

Ted pointed at Harris. "I looked all over for those papers. The guesthouse, the pool. That stupid library."

"You killed her." Nothing in Harris's tone said he had one ounce of sympathy for Ted.

Ted shook his head. "It was an accident."

"You stabbed her eleven times." Harris took a step toward Ted then. He held the screwdriver by his side, but Ted didn't seem to notice. "You slashed her chest so deep it was impossible to perform CPR."

Gabby's mind rebelled. She wanted to slam her hands over her ears and wipe her memory clean. She'd never heard every terrifying fact. The police had kept that all a secret. Even the records held back certain aspects in the hope of finding the killer. But now Harris was making her live through it.

Eleven times.

"That came after. It was an attempt to cover up the fact she was already dead." Ted sounded frantic now.

"But she wasn't," Harris shot back. "She was alive and wheezing and you left her there to bleed out on that gray carpet."

The roar came out of nowhere. One minute the waves of blue water provided the only background sound. That and the slight rustle of the tree branches from the wind. Then Stephen let out a howl that sounded as if it had been ripped from his soul.

"I'm going to kill you." He launched his body at Ted.

Ted pivoted just in time. His arms rose and the shovel's edge left the ground. The nightmare of possibly watching one more family member die spurred Gabby to move. Disconnected thoughts ran through her head. Something tickled at the back of her mind but she pushed it away. Her only goal was to get to Ted, shove him in the water if she had to, before he swung that shovel.

Harris took off at the same time. The first whack of the shovel missed him and slammed into the dock. The next time Ted lifted it, Harris rammed right into his stomach and they both took flight. Bodies flashed in front of her and she kept going. Her uncle sat on the dock and she had no idea why he'd landed there. She just knew she had to get to him.

Two more steps and she was there, pulling him down to the deck as a shovel flew over their heads. She covered his body with hers and held on. The metal part of the shovel clattered on the wood deck beside her head. The noise had her looking up.

Harris and Ted rounded on each other. Ted had broken the shovel and held the jagged wooden end, stabbing it toward Harris. Harris had the screwdriver and a look of determination on his face. At the last second, Ted shifted and headed for her. His face was a mask of fury as he lunged. The frayed wood came toward her. Harris knocked into Ted one last time, taking them both down to the dock hard enough to shake the pylons anchoring it.

Ted yelled as the handle fell from his hand. She heard a pinging sound and looked up to see her uncle had batted the handle away from her face with the metal part of the shovel.

He'd protected her. She was so stunned all she could do was stare.

He pointed toward Harris. "Stop your boyfriend before it's too late."

She looked over to see Harris straddling Ted with the sharp end of the screwdriver jammed into his neck. He didn't break skin, but it wouldn't take much.

Shouting sounded all around her. She made out Damon's voice and thought she heard Kramer. None of it got through as she scrambled to get to Harris. Out of breath, she collapsed against his side. "Let him go."

"He's going to lie." Harris shook his head. "He'll say all of this was your fault and people will believe him."

"I won't," her uncle said as he stood up on shaky legs.

"Harris, please." She ran her hand along his arm, feeling the stretch of every muscle. This boiling anger was for her. He was fighting for her and she loved that, but this was the wrong battle. "Don't do this. I need you, but not to do this."

Harris eased his hold on Ted. He started to squirm until Damon aimed the gun at his head. "Please move. Just give me any reason to put a hole in you. A sneeze will work."

The sound of a boat engine grew closer as Harris rolled off Ted and sat down next to her on the dock. His body shook. She guessed the adrenaline still had him in its grasp.

"We got him." She put an arm around his broad shoulders and hugged him.

He finally looked at her then. The stark look in his eyes was too obvious to miss. "I'm sorry."

CHAPTER 25

The police and forensic units walked the yard. Every first responder imaginable roamed over the island. Two hours had passed and there was no sign of the action slowing down. Damon thought the investigation would continue into the night.

News helicopters flew overhead. Every now and then they'd pass close to this side of the island and drown out any other noise. Kramer sat stunned and unmoving as two medics looked him over. Hearing the truth about Ted had driven Kramer to his knees and it took several men to get him back up again. Craig sat a short distance away from Kramer with his head in his hands.

So many lies and so much devastation.

Damon motioned and pointed as he talked with a detective and Stephen. A man Harris didn't recognize except that he worked for Wren walked around. Harris didn't know who was on a legitimate law enforcement payroll and who had gotten here in record time at Wren's insistence. Harris didn't feel anything except for the harsh buzzing in his brain.

"Who are you?"

He closed his eyes at the sound of Gabby's voice behind him. He sat on the porch banister, looking out over the property. She came out the front door. He knew because he heard the bang of the screen door.

This confrontation was inevitable. Hell, he invited it when he went after Ted. He'd said too much, giving away too many details. It was no surprise Gabby picked up on that. Her intelligence was one of the reasons he loved her . . . and that might even be the right word. Watching her handle Ted, stand up when almost anyone else would have broken down, filled Harris with pride.

In such a short period of time he'd fought with her, ached for her, cheered her on and protected her. That was more commitment than he'd ever given any woman. The sick thing was he wanted more. Being with her made him want to stick around. The talking, the sex, just being together. It all fueled him.

He'd fought it for days. Used reason. Told himself he felt admiration and nothing more. Not enough time had passed and he didn't have the ability to care about anyone else. Not on that level. But it was all bullshit. One more story he told himself to get through the day. The truth was he'd been falling for her since he started reading about her in the news. Fourteen months ago she'd screamed and it shot through him. They'd been connected ever since.

And now that her initial shock had worn off it was judgment time.

"You knew about the stab wounds." There was no emotion in her voice.

He refused to turn around to see the hate in her eyes. He looked down at his hands instead. "They're in the report."

"You said she was alive when Ted left. You talked about wheezing and the carpet. The same carpet that's no longer in the room. It was like you were there when she died. Only a person in that room would know those details."

His mind shot back to that day. He'd listened to Tabitha's last words. Watched her die.

He looked up at Gabby then. "Listen—"

"Tell me the truth right now or I will march out to the police and hand you over." Her voice rose but it still didn't reach past the two of them.

All the fight had gone out of him. He didn't intend to deny this any longer anyway. He'd run out of room and out of chances. This was it for them, and he owed her as much of the truth as she could take. "Max Beckmann."

She frowned. "What?"

He spun around, straddling the banister and facing her. "I came to the island to take the Beckmann painting."

"Take?"

While he owned up to the rest of it he had to tell her the truth about this, too. She knew he wasn't a detective. Now she would know what he was. It would be easier for her that way. She could run and not look back. Write him off as a bad experiment.

"Steal." An ache started deep in his gut and moved up to his chest. "I'm my mother's son."

"A thief." She shook her head. "I asked you directly if you were and you lied to my face."

"I've never robbed a bank. That wasn't a lie."

"Convenient how you hold on to the tiny details when it comes to saving your ass."

He took a deep breath and pushed on. "I planned to reappropriate the Beckmann, but the why doesn't matter. The explanation doesn't change what happened that day or anything between us. The point is I walked in on the crime scene. Your sister was on the floor. I realized she was still breathing and tried to perform mouth-to-mouth but it was too late."

Gabby's hands opened and closed at her sides. "But she was alive."

He tried to find the right words but he didn't know what those were. "I tried to save her."

"Shut up."

"I never would have let you be charged." He was begging now. He could hear it in his voice. "I vowed to step forward if that happened. I've been watching . . ."

God, that sounded worse. As if there was a worse in this situation. Every act, every mistake he made, piled up until they choked him.

"Stop talking." She held up a hand as if she could halt his flow of words.

The defenses and explanations rushed up his throat. He beat them all back. "Gabby."

"You were with her when she died." She said the

words nice and slow, as if she was turning them over in her head as she spoke. "She didn't die alone."

He had to get the rest of the details out now. Listening to her, being this close and not touching her, killed him. It sliced him open and left him raw and destroyed.

"I waited as long as I could after I heard your voice. As soon as you were in the hallway I wiped down what I touched, which for the most part was Tabitha, and ran." He took a deep breath to get through that memory. "That's why there wasn't DNA around the body and the rest of the evidence appeared to be corrupted. No one was trying to throw the police off, as the news said. It was me saving my own ass."

She didn't break eye contact with him. It was as if she thought if she looked away he'd run again. "The laptop?"

"I hacked it. Used the camera on it to track her movements. It's how I stake out a place I plan to . . . rob." God, he never said that word. Even now he'd had to spit it out. "I didn't take it but people did do things on my behalf to cover my tracks."

"Unbelievable."

He didn't even fight it. She deserved to know, even if it cost him everything. With the police right here on the grounds, he fully expected to leave in handcuffs. "It was me, Gabby. I fucked up the scene. Not on purpose, but it happened. I was the one who stepped in the blood pool and tracked it onto the lawn. I really did stop and try to save her, but it wasn't enough."

"No one believed me."

"I know." He wanted to get up and go to her but nothing in her body language said she'd welcome that. She was almost frozen except for the slight tremor that moved through her every few minutes.

She shook her head. Her mouth opened and closed a few times before she said anything. "You let me take the blame."

The words slammed into him. All that guilt he'd been trying to hold at bay for days swamped him.

He had so many reasons, most of which had to do with making sure he could keep the life he refused to give up even now that he'd supposedly gone straight. He refused to hide behind that or Wren's protection right now. "I watched from a safe distance to make sure the accusations against you never got past the allegation stage."

Her head shot back as if he'd slapped her. "How is that an answer?"

"I came back because this time I thought you were going to be arrested. That's why I showed up on the island. I had a cover and stuck with it."

"Am I supposed to be impressed that you finally stepped up, even if it was too late and too little?" Before he could answer, she moved on. "And Damon?"

"We both came here to get answers and to protect you." He didn't want to lie to her, so he said the rest. The part that truly made him an asshole. "To make sure nothing connected the murder to me or you."

She stared at him. There was nothing blank about the look on her face now. Pure hatred thrummed off her. He'd been relegated to some sort of mental enemies list. He was just one in a long line of people who'd shit on her. She didn't have to say it because he could read it in the way she stood there and the stark emptiness in her eyes.

"I didn't know you back then, Gabby." He meant it more as an explanation for his hesitation than a justification, but he knew it didn't come out that way.

"So your excuse is that it was okay to rip my life apart because we'd never been introduced? Did your conscience only kick in because once we slept together it felt shitty to watch me go to prison?"

"It wasn't like that. I slept with you because I wanted you." He couldn't keep away from her even though he bargained with his brain to try. But that answer was just as selfish as every other one he'd uttered, so he kept it locked inside.

"Get out."

He stood up and lifted a hand to touch her, but she shrank away from him. "Please listen to me."

"Don't touch me." She held both hands up as if to push him away. "Ever."

"I care about you." The words were so neutral when he felt anything but.

"*Care* about me?" Her cheeks flushed.

"That's the wrong word."

"Get off my island. You have two minutes."

"If you really want that."

"I do."

"Fine." He slipped around her, careful not to touch her. When he stopped on the top porch step to look at her, to try to explain one last time, she was already gone.

TWO HOURS LATER she found Damon walking in the fire pit area. It would have hurt to be there, in a place she'd shared with Harris, if fury didn't hum through her. Rage still beat loud and strong inside of her and she didn't want to turn it down. The sound blocked out the rest of the noise in her head.

Unwilling to cower for one single second, she marched right up to him, not caring who saw or overheard them. "Why are you still here?"

His head shot up at the sound of her voice. "I'm finishing up with the police."

Nothing in his expression gave away what he was feeling. He was a smooth one.

Unlucky for him, she was done with smooth. Attractive, charming and someone pretending to be a good listener were all off her list. Men could keep on walking.

"You're not an investigator." She'd battled one liar today. Why not another?

Damon put his hands on his hips and stared down at her. If her curt tone worried him, he did not show it. "I actually am. This is what I do."

"Prove it."

His eyes narrowed. "What exactly happened with Harris?"

Nothing shook this guy. He didn't even blink. She refused to let it unnerve her. "He's a thief. He came here to steal a painting and almost got caught at the scene. He got lucky. Tabitha didn't."

"Ah." Damon nodded. "He told you the truth about that night. That couldn't have been easy."

"That's what he does. He takes things that aren't his." He'd robbed her of so much. She would have given him the painting if doing so would have spared her the rest.

"No, not anymore. Not really."

Oh, please. "What kind of answer is that?"

It wasn't as if she trusted Damon any more than she trusted Harris. They were different in many ways but a matched set in others. They worked together . . . schemed together.

Damon shrugged. "An honest one."

"Neither one of you knows what it means to be honest." They'd lied to her from the beginning. Damon . . . She didn't care about his choices. But Harris was a different story. He'd lured her in, told her about his past. He made her believe in him and opened up a part of her that had been closed off for so long.

Doubt swamped her now. She was stronger than ever when it came to sticking up for herself. All of this—every rotten, scary moment—had taught her to stop living her life wallowing in guilt. But when it came to emotions, she felt more unsure and vulnerable than ever. The stable ground had been knocked out from under her and she would never forgive Harris for that loss.

"He solved the case, didn't he?" Damon asked. "Fourteen months in without a break, but he made it happen."

That wasn't how she saw it. It had been a joint effort targeted at saving him. Not her. "So the ends justify the means? Is that your life motto?"

Damon shifted his weight as he exhaled. His unreadable expression morphed into something else. She could almost see his mind spin as he decided what to say. Knowing what she knew now about how they operated, she guessed he was trying to determine *how much* he had to tell her to get her to back off. Which carefully chosen pieces he should share.

"He gets paintings back to their rightful owners. Nazis stole art in the thirties and forties and he returns it to them now. Families sell art at unconscionable prices due to financial difficulties or threats, and he evens that score."

"A regular Robin Hood."

"He cuts through the red tape and government regulations. He understands that a lot of these transactions never had paperwork to confirm the details. He investigates and makes it happen without governments having to step in. It's that simple." Damon looked up, stared at the clear blue sky and helicopter buzzing off the coast before lowering his head again. His gaze was intense, almost biting. "Harris thinks he's unlovable and undeserving because that's what he was taught. His upbringing was a clusterfuck and, admittedly, his priorities got skewed."

She refused to let any of that matter. Blocked out these details and the ones Harris had shared because she needed to stay on track. Feeling sorry for people had always screwed her in the past. "We all have a sad story."

"He doesn't know it but he's a good man. Loyal and decent. Someone worth caring about."

Two days ago she might have used the same words. Now, no. "The scam is over. You can stop trying to sell him to me. I know better."

"He's the best person I know, Gabby."

He sounded so genuine. For a guy who'd spoken in straightforward terms from the minute she'd met him, he sounded different now. His tone had an edge of pleading.

Well, Harris had that skill, too. She wasn't falling for the cute-guy-with-an-act thing a second time.

She sighed at him. "Then you need to meet new people."

"Hate him. That's your right."

"Damn straight." And she intended to do just that. It might take her weeks or months or even longer to get her balance again, but she would. Then she would wipe Harris from her mind.

Damon leaned in as if he were sharing a secret. "Remember that he could have kept walking when he got word you were in trouble. He's the one who's been watching you from a distance to make sure the police never arrested you. He, someone who shouldn't give a shit about you, risked his freedom and came back to save you."

No, no, no. "He saved himself."

"I have the letter he wrote right after he found Tabitha's body." Damon pulled a folded piece of paper out of the pocket of his long-sleeved shirt. "It sets out the things that need to be done if you're arrested. You see, he intended to trade his life for yours. Even admit to a crime he didn't commit if that's what it took to keep you free."

Pain jammed up inside her. "He doesn't get a medal for that."

"That's the point, Gabby. He never expected one."

CHAPTER 26

Three fucking weeks.

That was how long it had been since Harris had seen or heard from Gabby. He didn't call her because he didn't have the right. He followed her movements in the news and sometimes begged Wren for details.

Ted's case and all the allegations against him played for a solid three days until a new and equally horrific crime occurred and knocked it out of the headlines. Stephen actually made a public apology to Gabby on television. The two of them engaged in the most awkward hug Harris had ever seen, but at least they were moving forward. Wren kept tabs on everyone and promised to step in if they needed help.

All Harris had to do was survive today.

He'd been called in to provide the findings in his assessment of the Wright-family art collection. Specifically, of the authentication of the Beckmann piece. More than a year ago he'd intended to steal it and return it to the heirs of the original owners. Now he'd been called in on an actual assignment. Stephen Wright wanted to know if it really belonged to someone else. If Harris could trace it, Stephen would return it, no money exchanged and no documents required.

The insurance company he worked for didn't give him a choice on this job. The Wright family was a lucrative prize. They possessed a lot of important pieces and bought more all the time, which meant a lot of potential work. He agreed to do just this one painting. He was fucking out after this.

He'd seen the painting in question in the main house on the island. Studied it in person. Reviewed all the documents pertaining to the provenance, the chain showing ownership, and knew where the holes were.

He'd completed most of the groundwork in person. Today he provided the report. The estate insisted it be done in person and subject to questioning due to the value of the work in question.

That meant he had to think about Gabby. Not that doing so was anything new. Her image danced in his head all the time. He could hear her voice when he sat alone in the darkness. Her laugh, that face . . . the way she talked about her sister. He loved all of it. He ached from missing her.

He hadn't been sure of the L word before, but he was now. The amount of time they'd spent together didn't correlate with the intensity of his feelings. He wasn't convinced the amount of hours spent together mattered. The kicking in his gut, the lack of an appetite, the inability to sleep more than an hour at a time—he had every sickening symptom.

He traced the change in his priorities back to her.

It was as if he'd grown a conscience after being with her. Things he didn't care about and acts he justified previously now haunted him. He no longer just saw Tabitha's face in those times when he couldn't block the race of images passing through his mind. He saw Gabby—full of life and smiling until he'd ruined that, too.

A woman peeked out of the double doors of the boardroom. He was in a typical suite of an expensive office building in downtown Washington, DC. The kind of place where the partners or the owners flashed around cash in the form of renting an overpriced space and throwing up expensive but boring art on the walls. He'd been in and out of places like this almost daily since he switched to his legitimate job.

The smiling face on the twenty-year-old was all he could see in front of him. "They're ready for you now."

She stepped back and opened the door wide. He took that as the sign he should step in first. He walked in and came to a bone-jarring halt. Men in dark suits sat around the table. Three of them, each looking more bored than the one next to him. Stephen Wright sat at one end. Gabby sat across from him.

She didn't look up when he came into the room. She didn't have to. He would have recognized the curve of her neck and bounce of her hair anywhere.

Watching her even for a second paralyzed him. She flipped the pages of his report, scanning each one. The pen between her fingers tapped against the table.

"Mr. Tate." Stephen announced his name then

gestured around the table. "These are the family and estate lawyers."

That sounded like overkill to him. "Okay."

She looked up then. Her gaze locked on his and he lost the ability to say anything. His inclination was to walk back out of the room. He'd barely kept his head in the game since he last saw her. Writing the report, documenting it and making sure it was accurate had taken all of his energy.

"Mr. Tate?" Stephen repeated.

"Call me Harris," he mumbled as he tried to pull his attention away from her and put it back on the room at large.

Something dropped on the table. The loud thudding sound had Harris turning to face Stephen.

He nodded. "You may proceed."

That sounded good but Harris couldn't do it. There was no way he could stand in a room with her and not beg her to understand. Being near her had his brain racing for the right way to phrase the explanation. He had a past he couldn't fix. With Wren's help, he'd cleaned it up, but that would never be good enough for her. She deserved more.

He looked around the table, thinking if he focused on the others he could bully his way through this. But no.

This was why he stayed detached. Getting involved, caring, was a one-way ticket to hell. He'd been miserable every fucking minute since they'd been apart. He'd have to restart the process all over again after this.

God, why did she have to be here? He never thought she'd show up. She didn't care about the island or the money. Until recently, she had been locked in a battle with Stephen over every curtain and every cup. It looked as if that rift might be at the start of a repair.

"You have my report." Even he heard the small shake in his voice as he spoke.

Stephen looked up. "Excuse me?"

"The information is in front of you. I won't insult you by reading it to you." When Harris realized he was shifting his weight and moving around, he stopped.

"We asked you to come here prepared to—"

"Everything you need is right there." That was all he had. His energy expired. He had to get out of there. "You can call my office if you have any questions."

He would give anything to convince her of what happened more than fifteen months ago. He ached to win her back, but this wasn't even about that. She deserved closure and he would beg and plead to give it to her . . . to possibly get one more chance.

He'd picked up the phone so many times to call and never did. Giving her space seemed like the right response even though the days ticked by in agony. The pressure in his chest, the kicking in his gut. He'd never felt that kind of numbing pain before.

The worst? She hated him. Her anger thrummed off her. Tightened every muscle. She didn't deserve to have him hash it out between them with everyone watching. He owed her the chance to punch him, scream at him.

But he couldn't handle sitting there and not talking to her, not trying, so he walked out. Voices called his name but he didn't stick around to debate his position. This likely would end with the loss of his job but he didn't care. He'd find something else to do, or maybe he wouldn't do anything. It would be good for him to travel with all that temptation right in front of him and not take anything.

If he really was going to be a better man, and that was the vow he'd made as he left that island on the boat that day, then he needed to be better when it was hard to do so.

Phones rang as he walked back down the hall of glass-walled offices. Another person called out his name, but he ignored that, too. His goal was simple: get to the elevator bank. He'd almost done it. He stepped into the waiting room and pushed the lobby door to the outside hall. Once there, he let his body relax.

At the elevator bank across from the office doors he pushed the down button. It lit and now he waited. With a hand balanced against the wall. He dropped his head and tried to inhale. He forced his breathing to slow before his heart hammered out of his chest.

"That was quite a display."

Gabby's voice had him dropping his arm and spinning around to face her. "Why are you out here?"

"You look terrible."

This close he could see the dark circles under her eyes. They mirrored his. "I'm sure because I feel like shit."

"Lying will do that to a guy."

The chance waited right there . . . and he took it. Didn't pretty up the words or downplay his behavior. Not this time. Not when he'd been conning her from the beginning.

"I've lied my whole life. To everyone, about everything. Whatever it took. None of that bothered me until you came along." The elevator bell dinged and the doors opened, but he didn't get in.

"Is this your way of telling me I'm special?"

He didn't have anything to lose, so he didn't hold back. The words ripped out of him. "You are."

"See, that's the problem. I can't tell what's real and what's a game with you." She shook her head. "I want to believe you but—"

"I fell in love with you." He held his arms out to the sides then let them fall again. "God, Gabby. Can you really not see that?"

"Love?"

"Yes, love." Pain raced through him, leaving his muscles shaking. "There it is. Me, the guy who didn't care about anyone except this specific group of guys I've known for fifteen years. The guy who didn't get involved and could always walk away. I fell hard. For you."

"I'm supposed to believe you care about anyone?"

He didn't deserve to have this go easy, but to finally tell the truth and have her shoot it back to him with sarcasm . . . He rubbed the aching spot on his chest. "I'm trying to explain."

"Are you saying . . . Wait, what are you saying?"

"I believe in these friends. I depend on them. I would give my life for them. Just them."

"For them and no one else." She visibly swallowed. "I get it."

He could tell from the flatness in her eyes she didn't. "From the minute I met you, maybe even before, I included you in that select group of people who mattered to me."

"Why?"

"Really, Gabby?" It was tempting to read off a list of her qualities, but he didn't know if mere words would convince her. "You *are* special. You are a survivor. Loyal, smart, amazing, beautiful."

She shook her head. "I don't—"

"Believe me?" He stepped toward her and put a hand on the side of her face. Cupped her soft cheek in his palm. "Then believe this. You changed everything for me."

The words were simple but he meant them. She'd walked into his life and flipped it upside down. He now wondered every day what she would think or say about certain things. They'd spent time together and he craved more.

He also needed to survive this conversation, so he pushed the elevator button again. "I love you and I will continue to love you." When she frowned, he rushed to say one more thing. "Trust me, I didn't see it coming either, but it's true."

The bell dinged again and this time he stepped inside. He walked to the back and leaned against the wall. He wasn't sure how he'd stand up without the support.

Right as the doors closed, she turned sideways and slipped inside. She slammed the heel of her hand against the emergency stop. The elevator hung there, not moving. "That's what you do? You say something like that and then run?"

His brain misfired. "I thought . . ."

He had no idea what was happening right now. Fire sparked in her eyes and her body vibrated with anger. She looked ready to hit him. He deserved it. He didn't debate that, but he wasn't sure what had set her off. One second she looked disinterested and the next she turned into this ball of energy aimed right for his head.

"You do not tell a woman you love her and then slink away."

He knew his mouth had dropped open because he could feel it. "Okay."

"I have spent three terrible weeks trying to hate you." The pain slipped into her voice.

He didn't understand what he was hearing. "And?"

"You're here. In my head. I can hear your voice." She walked toward him and didn't stop until she stood between his legs. "I don't like it."

"Okay." A repetitive answer but he really didn't have anything else.

He feared moving or talking or ticking her off.

Part of his brain skipped ahead. He had questions and needed clarification because it sounded like she wanted him to love her. But that couldn't be right.

"Say something," she demanded.

"You're so hot I can barely breathe around you." At least that was honest. Probably not the right timing, but he hoped he was close to what she wanted.

She rolled her eyes. "Okay, fine. That's good to know, and very sweet." She rested her hands against his chest. "And?"

"I will say whatever you want me to say." *Literally anything.*

"No. Not this time. I can't make this easy for you." She shook her head but her hands didn't move. "I need the truth. Only the truth."

He could give her that. He wanted that more than anything.

His hand slipped over hers. He caressed her skin as warmth flowed through him for the first time in weeks. "I love you and I'm sorry I wasn't honest from the beginning. I hate that I've given you any reason to doubt me, but I'll win your trust if you give me a chance."

"Good start."

He half thought he was dreaming. "You're forgiving me?"

She snorted. "Not yet."

That made sense to him. It was the first thing that had in the last few minutes. "Okay."

"You're going to have to grovel and beg and do everything I say."

"Done."

"Really?"

"Yes." He didn't hate any of that. He'd do it willingly, starting today. But still . . . "But why are you doing this? Why let me off the hook and give me a chance at all?"

"Because I couldn't fall asleep without you." She sighed. "I don't need people. I don't get the whole caring thing because it's never worked out for me."

"I understand that."

"Do you get that I want to need you? That's new for me." Her fingers brushed against the underside of his chin. "But I also want you to need me back." She leaned forward and pressed a quick kiss on his lips before pulling back. "Because I love you."

The air punched out of his chest. "Gabby."

"My uncle had to tell me. He accused me of being mopey and annoying."

Stephen? "It sounds like you guys are getting along."

"That's an overstatement. Mostly he's feeling so guilty he's pathetic about it." She shrugged. "I'm trying to figure out a way to forget most of what he's said to me for a decade. Admittedly, it's a work in progress."

"If you're giving him a chance, I guess it's easier to give me one."

"We—the two of us together—have so much work to do and so many things to talk about, but I want to try. I want to give us a chance to make this work. For us to be open and honest about everything." She smiled up at him. "That's why I made it a requirement that you show up at the meeting today. I figured I could spring this on you here."

Hope soared inside him. "That was you?"

She wiggled her eyebrows at him. "I'm resourceful."

She was so many things and he loved all of them. "Definitely."

A man's voice broke into the silence. It blasted through the speakers and filled the room. "We have help on the way to fix the elevator."

The security team. Harris actually found that to be a fitting end to the meeting he just walked out of.

"Take your time," he yelled as he wrapped his arms around her waist and pulled her close. "You want to start with a date? Maybe dinner."

She frowned at him. "We're going to sleep together after, right?"

"Oh, yeah. I wasn't clear on that?" His hands slipped up her back. "This dinner and all the dinners after that will take place at the house we live in. Together."

"Now, that's more like it." She pulled back just a bit and stared him down. "We're going to buy this house, not steal it. Not right away because those things take time, but my point is your stealing days are over. You'll be getting your thrills at home from now on."

A shot of anxiety moved through him but it faded just as fast. "Technically, I have not agreed to that stipulation. We should negotiate."

She snorted. "Wrong. You're done stealing things. We are not playing a game of verbal gymnastics."

"Of what?"

"I'm serious. No stealing."

For her, he would do it. He'd sure as hell try. They'd need to work on it and he might need some help, but he'd find a way. But that didn't mean he didn't want to poke her. "Wait, so you mean not even from Nazis?"

"Nope."

"But they're Nazis."

"I'm not running the risk of you going to jail." Her fingers slipped into his hair. "You have had more than one wake-up call and we're going to heed them."

"That's fine so long as I'm waking up next to you." That sounded so good he almost repeated it.

"We should go to your place or a hotel or wherever we live temporarily and get started."

"No wonder I love you."

ACKNOWLEDGMENTS

A huge thank you to my agent Laura Bradford for believing in this series, and by that I mean *selling* it. My mortgage company also thanks you.

Is there something bigger than a thank you? Because that's what I owe May Chen. She's a fabulous editor who makes me laugh, offers great ideas and endless support, and doesn't yell when my books are a few weeks late (I'm writing that here so she feels guilty when she's tempted to yell in the future).

Also, huge thanks to everyone at Team Avon for polishing, editing, marketing, and packaging this book and the entire Games People Play series. I love writing these books and you make it possible for me to do so.

My biggest thanks, as always, go to my readers and to all the reviewers and booksellers who help sell my books. Consider this a heartfelt group hug.

*Next month, don't miss these exciting
new love stories only from
Avon Books*

The Trouble with True Love by Laura Lee Guhrke
For Clara Deverill, standing in for the real Lady
Truelove means dispensing advice on problems she has
never managed to overcome. But then Clara overhears a
rake waxing eloquent on the art of "honorable" jilting.
The cad may look like an Adonis, but he's about to find
himself on the wrong side of Lady Truelove.

Indecent Exposure by Tessa Bailey
Jack Garrett isn't a police officer yet, but there's already an
emergency. His new firearms instructor—the one who just
dropped every jaw in the academy gym—is the same sexy
Irish stranger Jack locked lips with last night. The Olympic
gold medalist and expert markswoman is now officially
off-limits, but Jack's never cared much for rules . . .

Tempest by Beverly Jenkins
What kind of mail-order bride greets her intended with a
bullet? One like Regan Carmichael—an independent spirit
at home in denims and dresses. Shooting Dr. Colton Lee in
the shoulder is an honest error, but soon Regan wonders if
her plan to marry a stranger is a mistake. Yet she's soon
drawn to the unmistakable desire in his gaze.

Moonlight Sins by Jennifer Armentrout
Julia Hughes always played it safe until she learned a
painful lesson. Now she's starting over with a job in the
Louisiana bayou, working for the infamous de Vincent
brothers. Hired to care for their troubled sister, Julia can't
afford any distractions, but the ever-present temptation of
the handsome Lucian isn't something anyone can ignore.

REL 0118